Praise for *Phoebe's Light*

"Fisher weaves together a pleasing romance that sets a high standard for future series installments."

Publishers Weekly

"Fisher's superb command of her historical setting is particularly commendable as she launches her Nantucket Legacy series, and many readers will find themselves fascinated by how the Quakers were treated when they first arrived in the New World."

Booklist

"Based on actual historical events and people, Suzanne Woods Fisher has taken her research to the next level and brings to life the forgotten beginning of Quakers on Nantucket Island."

RT Book Reviews

"A book that will sweep you up and take you away."

Interviews & Reviews

"In this brand-new series, bestselling author Suzanne Woods Fisher brings her signature twists and turns to bear on a fascinating new faith community: the Quakers of colonial-era Nantucket Island."

Fresh Fiction

Books by Suzanne Woods Fisher

Amish Peace: Simple Wisdom for a Complicated World
Amish Proverbs: Words of Wisdom from the Simple Life
Amish Values for Your Family: What We Can Learn from the Simple Life
A Lancaster County Christmas
Christmas at Rose Hill Farm
The Heart of the Amish

LANCASTER COUNTY SECRETS
The Choice
The Waiting
The Search

SEASONS OF STONEY RIDGE
The Keeper
The Haven
The Lesson

THE INN AT EAGLE HILL
The Letters
The Calling
The Revealing

THE BISHOP'S FAMILY
The Imposter
The Quieting
The Devoted

AMISH BEGINNINGS
Anna's Crossing
The Newcomer
The Return

NANTUCKET LEGACY
Phoebe's Light
Minding the Light
The Light Before Day

Nantucket Legacy
Book Three

The Light Before Day

Suzanne Woods Fisher

Revell
a division of Baker Publishing Group
Grand Rapids, Michigan

Published by Revell
a division of Baker Publishing Group
PO Box 6287, Grand Rapids, MI 49516-6287
www.revellbooks.com

Printed in the United States of America

Library of Congress Cataloging-in-Publication Data
Names: Fisher, Suzanne Woods, author.
Title: The light before day / Suzanne Woods Fisher.
Description: Grand Rapids, MI : Revell, [2018] | Series: Nantucket legacy ; 3
Identifiers: LCCN 2018013681 | ISBN 9780800721640 (pbk. : alk. paper)
Subjects: LCSH: Young women—Fiction. | Quakers—Fiction. | GSAFD: Christian—fiction. | Love stories.
Classification: LCC PS3606.I78 L54 2018 | DDC 813/.6—dc23
LC record available at https://lccn.loc.gov/2018013681

ISBN 978-0-8007-3544-9 (casebound)

Scripture used in this book, whether quoted or paraphrased by the characters, is taken from the King James Version of the Bible.

18 19 20 21 22 23 24   7 6 5 4 3 2 1

To my mother, Barbara Benedict Woods (1927–2018),
who first sparked my interest in Nantucket with memories
of her visit to the island as a girl in the 1930s.

Her treasured antique lightship basket
is shown on the cover of this book.

Cast of Characters

17th century

Mary Coffin Starbuck: daughter of one of the first proprietors of Nantucket Island, highly revered, considered to be like Deborah the Judge of the Old Testament

Nathaniel Starbuck: son of proprietor Edward Starbuck, husband to Mary

Peter Foulger: surveyor, missionary to the Wampanoag Indians of Nantucket Island, joined the proprietors

19th century

Hitty Macy—daughter of Reynolds Macy, twin sister to Henry

Henry Macy—son of Reynolds Macy, twin brother to Hitty

Jeremiah Macy—father of Reynolds Macy, grandfather to Henry and Hitty

Reynolds Macy—sea captain, father of Hitty and Henry

Daphne Coffin Macy—wife of Captain Reynolds Macy, stepmother to Henry and Hitty

Anna Gardner—teacher, social reformer, abolitionist

Benjamin Foulger—law clerk to Boston-based attorney Oliver Combs

Marie-Claire Chase—secretary to Benjamin Foulger

Isaac Barnard—experimental inventor

Maria Mitchell—astronomer

Tristram Macy—cousin to Reynolds Macy, uncle to Hitty and Henry

Glossary of Nantucket in the 18th and 19th century

come aboard: a greeting or welcoming for visitors

coof: a Scottish term for an off-islander, generally meant for one who lived on Cape Cod

First Day: Quaker word for Sunday—the Friends did not use the days of the weeks, nor the months, as they had pagan origins; instead, they numbered days and months

greasy luck: originally used to wish a whaleman a good voyage and to return with many casks full of whale oil; on the island, to wish friends well in any venture

headwind: difficulties to overcome

mad as huckleberry chowder: equated with craziness

Old Town Turkey: Martha's Vineyard

on deck: meaning "up and around"

rantum scoot: a day's expedition with no particular destination; from "random" (unplanned) and "scoot" (to move quickly or freely) *skimming the slicks:* a fishing expression that indicates securing the full limit of return from any effort (comes from the smooth, oily patches seen over a school of surface-feeding fish)

"Twist not my words": "Don't misunderstand me"

watching the Pass: observing people on the street

wild as a Tuckernuck steer: beef cattle, raised on Tuckernuck Island, troublesome if brought to a populated area like Nantucket town

"*Wind, weather, or whales permitting*"*:* "If there are no obstacles"

weather breeder: a warning that things are too still, too good, too calm, and trouble is ahead

Part One
1840–1842

1

"By the deep twelve!" The seaman called out soundings high above Hitty Macy as the schooner eased toward Nantucket Island, a thick mist shrouding the ship's path. Hitty yanked her brother Henry's coat sleeve and hurried to the starboard bow as the Grey Lady—their beloved home—in all her beauty emerged in front of them. The island wore the fog draped over her shoulders like a Quaker lace fichu.

The twins leaned against the railing of the schooner as it sailed through Nantucket Sound, barely mindful of the bracing salt air that stung their faces, or the people who milled around them on the deck. They were still dumbfounded by the news they'd just received from their late grandmother's attorney in Boston: Lillian Swain Coffin had made Hitty and Henry sole heirs of her vast estate. And it was truly vast.

Hitty gathered her bonnet strings with one hand to keep them from whipping against her face. "Why us, Henry? She didn't even like us!" They'd been going round and round on the inheritance since the schooner left Boston Harbor.

Henry shrugged. "Grandmother Lillian didn't like anyone. She kept changing her will to disown relatives. Mayhap she died before she could cross out our names to add someone new."

Hitty felt as if someone had taken her insides and shaken them up. She and her brother might soon become full owners of the Grand House that their grandmother had built on an exclusive cove, and her investments of stocks and bonds, cash and cattle, as well as deeds to multiple properties. Why, even a small island! For most of their lives, Grandmother Lillian had scarcely acknowledged Hitty and Henry, never without disdain or criticism, yet she bequeathed to them her entire fortune.

And they didn't *want* it.

Henry turned around, his back against the railing, and crossed his arms against his chest. "We didn't sign anything yet, Hitty. We don't have to accept a single pence."

She pivoted, heartened to hear that he was waffling in his thoughts about it. The crusty old lawyer had told them they must accept the inheritance together or refuse it together. He was a stickler for details, that Oliver Combs. "What did Oliver mean when he said there were conditions to the will? And why couldn't he have just told us what they were? Why wait to send a law clerk to Nantucket?"

"Transferring titles can't just happen overnight, Hitty. Paperwork takes time. Oliver said that the law clerk would finalize all the estate holdings. It could take a long, long time, he said. And forget not," Henry swept the deck with a distracted gaze, "Oliver's an old man. He must be sixty. He doesn't want to spend months on a fog-drenched island copying over documents. A law clerk can handle it."

"Still, those mysterious conditions he alluded to. What were they called?"

"Codicils."

Hitty made a sour face. "It sounds like a rare and foul-tasting fish."

A laugh burst out of Henry, and Hitty's spirits lifted a little. How she had missed her twin brother! Henry had returned just days ago from coopering on his father's whaling ship, the *Endeavour*. He'd shipped out three years ago in a great hurry, without confiding to her the reason for it, though Hitty knew his haste had something to do with Anna Gardner, his childhood sweetheart.

Ironically, Henry had sailed back into Nantucket Harbor on the very day of his grandmother's funeral, only to be promptly summoned to Oliver Combs's office in Boston. Her brother barely had time to catch his breath, much less be welcomed home with any fuss or fanfare.

"Henry, this . . . fortune, this sudden wealth . . . I fear it will change our lives. And I don't want my life to change." That wasn't entirely true. There were a few things she'd like to change, but they didn't have anything to do with money. She would like for Isaac Barnard to declare his love and propose marriage to her, for one. She frowned, mulling over how barely conscious Isaac seemed of her. But that deficiency, she believed, was part and parcel of being a genius . . . and Isaac was indeed a genius. She had a unique insight into brilliant people because of her enduring friendship with Maria Mitchell, also a genius, also not terribly sociable.

At times Hitty wondered why the Lord God had placed so many overly intelligent people into her life, and why she felt such a fondness for them, as they could be immensely frustrating. She considered her brother Henry, in his own way, to be one of those types.

Hitty assessed the changes she noticed in Henry, how much broader and bigger his shoulders had grown, how the creases were etched into the corners of his eyes. A result of squinting from the sun, she thought, like all seamen. Twenty-four now, and a very handsome man, she realized with surprise, as he turned to face the wind, elbows on the railing, his legs braced in the mariner's wide stance. He'd left Nantucket as a grown boy and returned as a grown man.

She wondered what all was running through Henry's mind. He'd always been slow to speak, careful with his words. Although twins, they were opposites in that way. In nearly every way. He was tall and thin, bookish and brainy; she was petite and curvy, and she kept her distance from books. Why waste precious time reading about people who never were, doing things they never did, or about people who were long dead, when her own imagination more than sufficed? Life was to be lived, not read about.

Aunt Daphne had tried to turn Hitty into a reader, like Henry. It was so easy for him, and so difficult for Hitty. The more words jammed onto a book's page thrilled Henry and horrified Hitty. Each letter took a malevolent turn, upside down and inside out. It was a double helping of the Starbuck curse upon Hitty, her grandmother had said of her more than a few times. Nathaniel Starbuck, one of the first to settle on Nantucket Island and a direct relative to Hitty, was known to be illiterate.

When Hitty had turned eight years old, Grandmother Lillian hired an expensive tutor to work with her, an odd man who claimed 100 percent success in his ability to teach anyone to read. That was before he had met Hitty. The reading sessions were pure torture, every bit as much to the tutor as to her.

One rainy day after a particularly frustrating reading session, Hitty found an old book on her aunt's bedside table and, purely out of spite, cut out as many pages as she could—snipping them into tiny bits—before Aunt Daphne walked into the room, saw what she was doing, and burst into tears. The tutoring sessions ended.

Grandmother Lillian declared that Hitty's stubborn ignorance would send her to the poorhouse, but she was wrong. She was wrong about so many things. Hitty loved her life. She was the headmistress of the Cent School, a private education for children who weren't school age yet. Ideal for Hitty, as the little ones weren't expected to read. Instead, the children played, talked, drew stories, started friendships, and nourished their imaginations.

Hitty much preferred the ways of children. So many questions arose when one spent her days with them. Last week, four-year-old Josiah Swain peered deeply into her eyes, then asked her, *Since she had brown eyes, did that mean everything she saw was brown?* And then there was the little girl who wondered how Hitty had felt on the last day she was a child.

The Congregational church bells chimed and the sound floated over the water, snapping Hitty back to the present. The schooner's sails were getting reefed as they drew close to Nantucket Harbor. She tugged on Henry's shirtsleeve, wanting to settle this conversation before they made land. "What about thee, brother? Does thee want this money, along with Grandmother Lillian's conditions?" Whatever they might be.

What trick, she wondered, could Grandmother Lillian have had up her sleeve? No doubt it had to do with the Society of Friends, of keeping it intact and firmly grounded. The young had grown weary of the nitpicky behavior of the elders. For goodness' sake, so many were read out of meeting that Hitty was astonished anyone was still left to attend.

Grandmother Lillian was the chief instigator of disciplinary action. Every single week up to her untimely death, she had a list of grievances—one man's hair was cut too long, a woman's dress was the wrong shade of blue, a Friend had been spotted coming out of a tavern. And then the most outrageous of all—Maria Mitchell had coughed excessively in Meeting.

She had been ill with a cold! Maria was furious with Grandmother Lillian and gave serious consideration to quitting Meeting altogether. (Hitty talked her back into it.)

Henry's silence concerned her. Was he, indeed, waffling? He was a born waffler. "Has thee given thought to how this inheritance might affect thy friendship with Anna Gardner? Thee knows how stridently she opposes excess." How stridently she opposed *everything*. Anna held many strong beliefs. "She has not settled on any other man in thy absence. I believe she has been waiting for thee to return home."

As Hitty said the name of Henry's sweetheart, a frown came over his face. "Candidly, Sister, I have thought of little else. But what to do, that I do not know."

Well, Hitty knew exactly what to do. Refuse the inheritance. If Henry did not agree, she would just have to convince him.

So much had changed on Nantucket Island. Henry could see evidence of change even before the anchor was dropped. For one thing, the anchor dropped much farther out in the harbor than it had three years ago, when he'd sailed off on the *Endeavour*. The hidden sandbar continued to build up, creating a dangerously shallow harbor. And then there were the new buildings that cradled the harbor—tall church steeples that scraped the sky. If steeples had been built in his absence, that meant the Society of Friends was no longer the dominant religion.

By all outward appearances, Nantucket was not the island he remembered.

Or maybe it was him. Maybe he was the one who had changed. Three years spent chasing whales felt like three years lost. He'd only agreed to sign on as cooper because he didn't know what else to do with his life, and his father insisted he give seafaring a reasonable try. He did. He hated it.

It was strange how life went. As a boy, Henry wanted nothing more than to crew on a whaling ship, like his father and his grandfather Jeremiah. But that was when Nantucket was the wealthiest seaport in the world, whales were plentiful, seamen of any and all rank were considered heroes by beautiful maidens.

It was a different story today.

Fewer and fewer ships came to Nantucket because of the sandbar, New Bedford had begun to emerge as the center of whaling, and the whale population had grown scarce. Ships had to seek new whaling grounds in the Pacific to fill their hold—which meant painfully long durations.

Henry found the reality of the seafaring life fell far below his expectations. Only a fraction of the crew's time at sea was spent pursuing whales. The rest was filled with utter boredom. Henry's mind needed more to fill it—books and spirited lectures and intellectually stimulating people. Sailors, he had found, had little on their minds.

And then there was Anna Gardner.

Anna. Henry hoped to see her waiting at the wharf alongside his father and Daphne as the dory brought them in, but alas, she was not. Hitty told him that Anna now taught at the African School, and no doubt that was why she hadn't met the schooner. It didn't surprise him to hear Anna was teaching. She had a passion for learning, for fairness, for equality for all. It was a Gardner trait. When Anna was only six years old, her parents had risked hiding a fugitive slave, Arthur Cooper, in their attic. That experience, coupled with her parents' broad-mindedness, left a permanent mark on her. She was fierce in her feelings, his Anna, if she was indeed still his.

Moments later they were on Straight Wharf, heading home. His father, Reynolds Macy, carried their bags under his arms. Hitty walked alongside him, chattering at full speed. Henry and Daphne trailed behind them, talking quietly to each other.

"Just like it's always been," Daphne said, tucking her hand around his elbow.

Daphne was as near a mother to him as a woman could be. She was actually his late mother's sister, married to his father. Some Friends snickered that she was a poor replacement for Jane Coffin Macy, but Daphne had never tried to replace his mother. Daphne was Daphne. He and Hitty adored her, as did their father.

"It's so good to have thee home." Gently, Daphne squeezed his elbow. "But I suspect there is much weighing on thy mind."

Indeed, there was a great deal on Henry's mind. Including the news his father had just greeted him with on the wharf—announcing that he and Daphne would be heading out to sea as soon as the ship could be outfitted. "Why does Papa want to captain the *Endeavour*? Why now? At his age? And why in the world are you going along on the journey?"

"He's wanted to take to the sea again for many years. When he received Abraham's letter that he wanted to retire, and that the *Endeavour* was in surprisingly good condition after this voyage, it seemed the time was right. As for me, Henry, I am eager for an adventure."

"I know there is more to the story than wanting an adventure. Please, Daphne, I want the truth."

Daphne dropped her chin to her chest. She did not speak for a long moment, as if gathering her words. In a voice so quiet that Henry had to lean in to hear her, she said, "We are penniless, Henry."

Henry's mouth fell open. "Penniless?"

"The *Endeavour* is the only asset we have, but for the Centre Street cottage."

"How is that possible?" His father was a savvy man, though he was also known as a generous one. Some would say generous to a fault.

"I suppose it all began with Tristram's treachery."

"Uncle Tristram," Henry said flatly. His uncle, business partner to his father, had disappeared, absconding with everything his father had earned on a six-year whaling voyage. His father had sold his Orange Street house—on the prestigious captain's street—just to provide his crew with their lay.

"Thy father has paid off every debt. There's also been thy grandfather's debts to settle."

"Jeremiah?"

"He's made some unfortunate investments in his later

years. And then . . . thy father has also been the sole benefactor of the *Endeavour*'s voyages."

Most ships had many investors—syndicates, they were called—to provision a ship. The *Endeavour* had an all-black crew, led by a black captain, Abraham, a former slave. No syndicates would back the enterprise. "But Abraham has been a successful captain." Mayhap not as successful as other sea captains on new whaling schooners, but the *Endeavour* was a small ship and an old one.

"Aye, and thy father has rewarded him amply." She smiled. "Reynolds Macy has done more for others than anyone could possibly know. So many anonymous gifts to help others. It is the way he is made—to be a blessing."

"Daphne, why did Papa never tell me about his finances? I know you lived modestly, but so do most Quakers."

"He never wanted thee to know."

"But . . . my education. Prep school, then Harvard College." He'd taken his time graduating too, because there were so many classes he found interesting. "He never balked at the cost."

"He is so proud of thee, Henry, for getting an education. He left for the sea as a boy and never had a chance for proper schooling. 'Tis a regret of his, and he wanted to be sure his own son was well educated. I know that he would never want thee, nor Hitty, to know that his finances are in a dire condition. When Abraham told him he wanted to retire, it seemed like an ideal opportunity for thy father. One last voyage, to prepare for his own retirement. A greasy voyage, he hopes." She grinned. "Greasy enough, that is, to feather our nest into old age."

"And you really want to go along?"

"Oh, I do! I would like to see more of the world, and I truly do not want to be separated from thy father. Not for a single day."

They walked up Main Street without talking, veering around horses and drays, vendors selling from their carts. "Daphne, were we to accept Grandmother Lillian's fortune, I could help you and Papa."

Daphne's eyes went wide. "Nay! Do not accept it on our account! We will find a way to carry on. We have no fear of the future."

"But you are her daughter, and she left you with nothing." Reynolds Macy had Indian blood in his veins, a trait Lillian Swain Coffin could not tolerate in a son-in-law.

"I was not surprised by that. I had no expectation."

"Think on this, Daphne. If Hitty and I accepted her fortune, we could provide for you and Papa. Amply provide."

"We would never accept that, Henry. But I thank thee for offering." She squeezed his elbow. "So thee has not decided? To accept . . . or refuse it?"

How well she knew him. Decisions were difficult for Henry, small or big. Anna Gardner once told him that he was the only man she knew who could sit on a fence and watch himself walk by. "Daphne . . . if Grandmother Lillian *had* left her fortune to you . . . would you have accepted it?"

She did not hesitate. "I would not."

"Because . . . ?"

"Any gift from my mother comes with a very steep cost."

The corners of Henry's lips lifted. "Even from the grave?"

Daphne stopped, and he turned to face her. "Even then." She reached out to take his hands. "But I dare not tell thee what to do. I would only suggest that thee give seasoning to the decision, pray long and hard, to let the Light show thee what is best." She looked down at their joined hands. "But I worry thee has left the faith."

He squeezed her hands and released them. It was true that he had stopped using the Quaker way of speech, stopped wearing the somber, grim clothing of the Friends. He would be disowned soon if he did not make adjustments. "I'm not sure that I have left the Friends. I'm not sure that I haven't. I suppose you might think me lost, Daphne, but I think not lost. I am only trying to discern my destiny."

She watched him for a long while, thinking something through before she spoke again. He knew what was coming would be significant. That was Daphne's way.

"Henry, when thee was a boy, thee helped me find a way to save Abraham from the bounty hunter who tried to return him to his slave master."

He grinned. "I well remember that night. Digging for a buried treasure." He took off his hat and spun the brim in his hands. "I wonder if it's still there. I hope it is. I hope it stays hidden. A Nantucket secret."

"Thee has kept our secret all these years."

"Of course. Of course I have."

"I learned of the treasure through a family heirloom that thy mother gave to me before she passed. 'Tis a journal, Henry, of a well-lived life. It's brought me much wisdom over the years." She gave him a gentle smile. "I think the time has come to pass it to thee."

"Me? Why not keep it for yourself? Take it with you on the sea voyage." He leaned in to whisper, "You'll have a surfeit of time for reading, that I can guarantee."

Slowly, she shook her head. "The journal is meant to be

passed along to the next generation." She reached into her drawstring purse and pulled out a worn-out sheepskin journal. She held it to him with both hands, as if it were made of spun sugar. "I carry this with me wherever I go. Henry, 'tis Mary Coffin Starbuck's journal. Thy ancestor, and mine."

Henry's eyes went wide. "Great Mary? 'Tis her journal? I thought this was the stuff of legends! And you've kept it secret all this time?"

Mary Coffin Starbuck was one of the first settlers to Nantucket, considered by all to be a wise and influential woman, mayhap the most significant individual who had ever lived on the island. He almost felt nervous to touch it, as if he should first wash up from the sea journey. But Daphne continued to hold it out to him, waiting for him to accept this gift. He took it from her outstretched hands and was surprised at how light it was. The cover was cracking, the pages were yellowed with age. It was so very . . . old.

"The journal has a way of ending up in the right hands. Thee will see why, when thee reads it. I believe thee will find Great Mary to be a Weighty Friend to thee." Lowering her voice, she added, "But I must ask thee to keep it a secret."

"You can trust me on that." Then he looked up. "Hold on. Even from Hitty?"

"Especially from Hitty." Daphne sighed. "Years ago, as a child, Hitty took a pair of scissors to this journal." She squeezed her eyes shut as if the memory hurt her still. "I cannot give it to her for safekeeping. Even now, she would not care for a cherished book the way thee will."

And he would. He would cherish this journal. He put an arm around her shoulders. "Daphne, have I ever told you that you"—his voice sounded perilously shaky, even to his own ears—"that you are the greatest gift that Papa, Hitty, and I . . . were ever given?"

Daphne tipped her chin down so that her bonnet shaded her face, and he realized she was trying not to cry. "And to me, Henry Macy. Thee is a gift to me as well." She wiped her cheeks, one after the other, and lifted her face. "Henry, thy father would not have done anything differently. Not a thing. We may not be wealthy, yet we are rich indeed."

As they crossed Main Street to head toward Centre Street, Henry felt the fog lift—a fog that was so much a part of him that he hadn't known it rested so heavily on his shoulders. His head felt cleared of cobwebs. For the first time in his life, he knew what to do next. He was going to persuade his sister that they should accept their grandmother's fortune.

Mary Coffin Starbuck

28 March 1683

Stephen Hussey came into the store this afternoon. He settled into Father's rocking chair by the fire and drank gallons of my mullein tea, talking to every person who came in. He carried his ear trumpet with him, which struck me as ironic for he has little need of it. Despite being a Quaker, he is not fond of listening, only of talking. Stephen Hussey never had a thought that he couldn't turn into a sermon.

Today, though, he remained oddly quiet until the store was brimming over with customers. Then he rose to his feet and announced in his loud, shrill voice, "I have a riddle for thee, Mary Starbuck!"

The store grew quiet, all eyes turned to Stephen, as everyone enjoyed a good riddle, and he enjoyed a good audience.

"What's gray and old and likes to be everywhere at once?"

"Nantucket fog," I said, hoping he would now go home.

"Nay. The answer is . . . Mary Coffin Starbuck!" He laughed and laughed, thoroughly amused with himself, until tears ran down his cheeks.

That man! He sorely tries my patience. He is the foremost reason I will never, ever become a Quaker.

I am too irritated to write more.

2

Henry stood below the steps of the African School, looking it over from top to bottom. It was a simple wooden building used for just about everything needed by the New Guinea community: school and church, weddings and funerals. He was only ten when it had been constructed in 1825, yet the dilapidated building looked much older. Any wooden building on Nantucket showed effects of moist and salty sea air, but this seemed different. As if it had never been expected to last.

The door opened and children poured out, whooping and running down the wooden steps like they'd been sprung from gaol. Varied shades of brown skin, all. Only a few Wampanoags, Henry noticed. Mostly, they were black children.

He had come to the school at quitting time in hopes of meeting Anna alone. He took a deep breath, shook off his nerves, and climbed the school steps. The door had been left open, and he paused, leaning on the doorjamb. There she was. There was Anna.

Her face was half turned toward the window, and the streaming afternoon light limned her profile, making the curve of her cheek look like it was sculpted from marble. Her attention was focused on correcting a paper on her desk. A coffee-colored teenaged girl stood beside the desk, hands clasped tightly behind her back. Something significant seemed to be going on. The girl's hands kept moving, squeezing and releasing her fingers. She was nervous, waiting for some kind of response from Anna. Henry could empathize.

Three years ago, Anna had made it clear she thought the time had come for them to marry. Shocked, Henry had made a number of mistakes, one right after the other, starting when he had asked, "But why?"

"That's what comes next" was her reply.

"So thee wants to marry me because that's what comes next?" From the upset look that came over her lovely face, he realized he had just made another mistake.

"When thee loves someone, marriage comes next." He remembered how she had held out her hands, palms up. "I love thee, Henry. Does thee not love me?"

Startled by her declaration, he stumbled for an answer and finally blurted out, "I don't know. I think so."

His hesitant response was thoroughly disappointing to Anna. Her eyes glistened and pink streaked her cheeks. "Thee *thinks* so?" She took a deep, exasperated breath, as if she was trying very hard to remain calm, and pressed her fingers to her temples. "What makes thee *think* so? What does it feel like to be with me?"

"Feel like?" he echoed. He struggled again, trying to find a way to put words to a feeling—a feeling he hadn't even realized he'd had—and especially to not heighten Anna's upset. "Um . . . like a warm ray of sun after a foggy morning."

Wrong again. A steely look had come into her eyes. "That's nice, Henry. It's nice, but not essential."

"Essential?"

She let out a sigh of defeat and said, "I think thee could sit on a fence and watch thyself walk by. Thee is a born ditherer." And then she said something that turned everything upside down. "Henry, please don't come calling until thee has found thyself."

The next morning, his father seemed to sense that a drastic step needed to be taken in his son's life. He told Henry that when a ship was stuck in the doldrums, it was time to pull in the sails and put out the oars. It was a family motto: "When there is no wind, row." He encouraged Henry to crew on the *Endeavour*. Henry signed on.

The reason Henry left on the whaling voyage was because Anna's assessment of him—and his father's too—was absolutely correct. His life, after graduating college, was stuck in the doldrums. He did not have any passion to speak of, nothing like Anna. She was passionate about every injustice on the island, determined to make a difference. Her zeal fascinated him, mainly because he couldn't quite understand it. She had a vivid sense of destiny. No one lived up to her expectations, no one could. Yet her zest and determination and passion—they were everything Henry wasn't.

He corrected himself. *That's not entirely true. I do have purpose.* He'd learned that much about himself. But it wasn't the kind of purpose that most Nantucketers valued—he didn't have a hunger for wealth, as did his peers. Nor did he have a burden to right every wrong, like Anna did. What he did love, with a purpose and passion, was . . . to think, to mull. Ponder and consider. Read and write.

That was probably the single thing he had enjoyed as crew on a whaling ship—with an abundance of spare time, he read every book he could get his hands on. Each time the ship made port, he would find a bookstore and seek out books published in English.

Through words, he thought he was finding himself. But would that ever be enough for Anna? He considered that question until the girl standing beside Anna let out a loud sneeze and he snapped back to the present. He'd been so lost in his memories that he'd momentarily forgotten where he was and why he was there. A common occurrence in Henry's life.

"Eunice," Anna said, setting the pencil down, "thee did a fine job on this essay. Thee is ready for the test."

"You really think so, Miss Gardner? If I pass, you really think they will let me in?"

"We can hope for that outcome. And if ever a student deserved this chance, it would be thee." As Anna raised her head, she noticed Henry standing by the door. At first she seemed confused, then as their eyes met, she let out a little gasp.

Remember that, Henry Macy. She gasped!

"Eunice," Anna said, her eyes on Henry, "I will see to details about the test and let thee know what I find out."

Eunice whirled around to see what had captured Anna's attention. She spotted Henry, then turned back again to Anna. She gathered her books and shawl and hurried down the center of the room, nodding shyly at Henry as she passed him at the door.

"She is a prize pupil?" he asked, taking a step inside the schoolhouse.

"Indeed she is. The most able student I have ever taught." Anna rose and walked toward him, her steps echoing in the empty schoolhouse. "Thee did not seek me out after thy grandmother's funeral."

"It was a confusing day. I had arrived just as the funeral was under way, and afterward, my family needed me, then the next day, Hitty and I had some pressing business to attend to in Boston." Pressing business. What a feeble-sounding excuse.

"Three years ago thee did not tell me thee was leaving the island. Thy sister had to tell me."

"That day, it, too, was confusing."

"Thee did not write to me. Not even one letter."

Henry lifted a finger in the air. "I did, actually. Many. I just never . . . sent them."

"Thee is still confused?"

"Nay." Not quite so confused, anyway. He took a step toward her, then another. "You look well, Anna."

"I've been teaching at the African School for three years now."

"It suits you."

"It does." She interlaced her hands and held them against her midriff. "Hitty said thee has no plans to sign on again."

Hitty already told her that? "My sister has been here?"

"Yesterday afternoon. She wanted me to know thee had returned from Boston."

And yet Anna had not bothered to seek him out. He realized it would not be fair to hold that against her. She had a classroom full of students to teach. He had nothing on his calendar.

"So what *are* thy plans?"

Henry shifted his weight from one foot to another. This

was an uncomfortable topic between them. The last time he'd seen Anna, they hadn't parted on good terms, after she had asked him a very similar question.

"Henry, twist not my words. I am not asking to pressure thee. Samuel Jenks is looking for an editor for the *Gazette*. I thought of thee."

"But . . . Sam Jenks is the editor."

"He is. But he wants to leave the island for some new venture. He has big shoes to fill. Certainly he could be doing more for the underprivileged, but he has spurred on the construction of public schools."

"Like this one."

She sighed, eyes gazing around the little room. How well he remembered that sigh and all it conveyed—exasperation, annoyance, impatience. "Like this one. Still segregated."

"You have plans to do something about it, don't you? Is that not what you were talking about with the girl named Eunice?"

Startled by his comment, she swept past him to shut the door. She turned to face him. "Her name is Eunice Ross, and she is a gifted student. Somehow I am going to find a way to have her take the exam to qualify for the public high school. I can promise she will outshine any student. If she qualifies, as I'm sure she will do, we are going to petition to allow her to attend high school."

As she spoke, she was almost glowing. She was so beautiful, so filled with fire. How he had missed her.

Somewhere outside, church bells chimed the hour. He hadn't grown accustomed to their particular sound on the island. Four bells. *Four!* The meeting with the law clerk! Hitty had reminded him three times to be at the office above the hat store at four o'clock sharp. "I must go. I . . . will come again."

As he reached a hand out to grab the door's handle, Anna said, "Henry? If thee kept those letters thee wrote to me . . . I would like to read them."

He froze. How he responded to her request would make all the difference in how they moved forward from here. He knew Anna well enough to know that simmering just below the surface was another question: Has anything changed between us?

Or was he still the same spineless creature who had walked away from the love of his life . . . simply because he didn't have enough sense to seize the moment? He took in a deep breath and turned around to face her. "I'll see if I can find them."

She smiled.

Henry was late on the tide again. Hitty sat in a chair, facing the law clerk sent from Boston by Oliver Combs, waiting for her brother to arrive. She didn't want to begin without Henry, but she also felt extremely awkward. Her silk skirt crinkled and rustled as she shifted nervously in the chair. The loft office above William Geary's hat store was not large, and the room was stuffy, and this man made her acutely uncomfortable. He hardly smiled, all business. She had met him briefly in Boston at Oliver Combs's office and couldn't help but notice his good looks.

Hitty's hand fluttered up to the lace at her throat, and she could feel herself blush whenever he glanced up at her. She knew his type—overly handsome, overly educated, overly charming. No doubt he had grown up overly blessed by inherited wealth too.

Her stomach twisted. *She* could now be considered one of those overly-blessed-with-inherited-wealth types. She'd grown up with an aversion to opulence. Early in her father's whaling career, something terrible had happened between him and his business partner, Tristram Macy, a man she had loved and known as an uncle. Tristram stole everything from her father, then vanished without a trace. Nay, her father was not wealthy like he could've been—should've been, had his partner been an honest man—but Reynolds Macy was a content man. Mayhap that was upside-down thinking, but she had grown up seeing firsthand that happiness and wealth were not always tied together. Often it was quite the opposite, as in the case of her grandmother Lillian. A more unhappy woman did not exist.

The door opened and in burst Henry. "Sorry, sorry. I lost track of time." He reached out to shake the law clerk's hand. "Good to see you again, Benjamin." Henry sat down in the chair next to Hitty but avoided looking at her, for he knew she would be scolding. "So, Oliver said there are things to discuss."

Benjamin Foulger lifted an extremely thick sheaf of papers. "I have a few details from thy grandmother's will to clarify." He glanced at the pile. "More than a few."

Hitty and Henry exchanged a glance.

"About the will," Henry started.

"We don't want the money," Hitty finished.

"Aye, but we do," Henry said, still avoiding her eyes.

"What?!" Hitty slammed back in the chair, as if hit with a gale-force wind. "I thought thee was waffling!"

"I often waffle," Henry said, "but I believe I am done waffling."

Done waffling? When did *that* happen? An idea broke through Hitty's despair, and she sat forward on the chair. "Could I not give my brother my share of the inheritancc?"

"Nay," Benjamin said. "Thee must both accept it. All or none. That was one of the conditions."

Henry stretched his legs out and crossed one ankle over the other, as comfortable as a man could be. "So . . . just what are these conditions?"

Benjamin picked up an envelope. "Lillian Coffin left a letter for thee to read." He passed the envelope to Hitty.

Hitty opened the letter and looked at her grandmother's spidery handwriting. A shiver went down her spine. Quickly, she passed it to Henry to read aloud.

Dear Mehitabel and Henry,

There is a saying I have observed to be true on this island: The first generation makes the money. The second generation manages it. The third generation squanders it.

I have decided to consider thee as the second generation. (Logically, my daughter Daphne should be considered the second generation, but she made choices with her life that I cannot condone. Therefore, I have skipped over her.)

I have grave doubts over whether thee can manage my estate and am confident thee will squander it. Thus, I am placing conditions on the inheritance.

Assets will be parceled out in two sections. The first part will contain my house, a small island filled with sheep, and a portfolio of stocks. The second part, not re-

ceivable until the day that marks my eightieth birthday, will include the remainder of the estate. The following requirements must be met at that point, subject to the scrutiny of my able and trusted attorney, Oliver Combs.

Every pound and pence must remain on Nantucket Island throughout thy lifetime.

Thee must remain in good standing among the Friends.

Thee must both marry a Nantucket Friend in good standing, one with an ancestral alliance, in which thee "Sees the Look."

If thee does not satisfy the conditions of this will, or if thee rejects the inheritance, the entire estate will be bequeathed to Tristram Macy, without any conditions.

Sincerely,
Lillian Swain Coffin

Hitty was shocked silent, which did not happen often. She glanced at Henry to gauge his reaction. Henry's head remained bowed over the letter as if he was deep in thought. Or praying. The room was quiet, so quiet that she could hear the buzzing of a fly against a window. She leaned forward to see if Henry had fallen asleep, and if he had, she would kick him. *Hard*.

Benjamin Foulger gave a polite little cough. "Might I ask, what does it mean to 'see the look'?"

When Henry didn't answer, Hitty did. "Grandmother Lillian kept a very detailed census of family lineage. She disapproved of most everyone, but slightly less so of those who had a genetic tie to the early founders. When someone shared a specific family resemblance—the Coffin aristocratic nose, or the Swain forehead, that kind of feature—it's called 'Seeing the Look.'"

"I see," Benjamin said, though she doubted he did. "And who is Tristram Macy?"

Henry snapped his head up at that. "He's a worthless, no-good, cheating scoundrel. If you met him on the street, you'd think he was a fine, upstanding Quaker." He scowled. "The worst kind."

"He's our father's cousin," Hitty said. "They were business partners . . . until Uncle Tristram disappeared with everything our father worked to build."

Confused, Benjamin asked, "So . . . why would thy grandmother want to bequeath anything to him?"

"She doesn't," Henry said firmly. "But this is her way of ensuring that we will do what she wants. This is the way our grandmother operates."

"Was," Hitty said. "It was the way she treated people. She has passed."

"And yet . . . her grasp remains." Henry held out his hand for the quill. "All right. We will take on this challenge."

"What?!" Hitty couldn't believe Henry didn't need time to ponder these conditions. What had happened to her slow-to-decide, overly reflective brother? This was most unlike him. "Hold on! Put down that quill. I do not intend to marry a Nantucket Friend! Isaac is a Methodist."

"Isaac?" Benjamin asked, eyebrows lifted.

"Isaac Barnard," Henry volunteered.

Benjamin looked at Hitty. "Thee is engaged?"

Henry snorted. "Not even remotely."

"This Isaac, he's a Nantucketer?"

"Aye. Fancies himself an inventor. More like a tinkerer. So far he's patented a life jacket that sank upon use, a fire alarm that rusted in the sea air, and a vaporizer to produce steam that caught fire and melted into slag."

Hitty scowled at her brother. Why had she told him so much about Isaac? She'd regretted it immensely. "Isaac Barnard is trying to protect people."

"Failures, all."

Hitty dug the heel of her shoe onto Henry's boot until he squirmed, but that did not stop his blathering on. "Isaac is a widower, with a child of his own. He's much too old for Hitty, don't you think?" Henry added, as if he was discussing a new dress she was wearing.

"I'm not at all qualified to comment on matters of the heart," Benjamin said, nor did he sound like he had any interest in them. All business, that man. "However, I do want to clarify the way the inheritance will be parceled out."

"In two portions," Hitty said, eager to change the subject.

"Aye, two parcels. Thy grandmother's estate is quite extensive, filled with more assets than currency. The first parcel is rather small, at least in light of the entire estate. It will be the second parcel in which the bulk of the estate will be transferred. There's a great deal of paperwork involved in the holdings. Even in this first parcel, time will be required to transfer titles. Especially if thee chooses to liquidate assets."

"Avast!" Henry tilted his head. "We can liquidate the assets? Cash out?"

"Of course. Buyers must be found, and that can take time. But there's no condition in the will that prohibits thee from liquidating assets. As long as the money remains on the island."

A thoughtful look came over Henry. "All right." He turned to Hitty, his hands lifted in surrender. "We'll take this on." He reached out to pick up the quill, then signed the papers and passed them to her to sign.

"My life is ruined," Hitty said. But so was Henry's. Why was he acting so buoyant, so jubilant? What did he know that she didn't?

With a heavy heart, she added her name under his. She looked up to find Benjamin Foulger gazing at her with an odd look on his face, as if he had just noticed her for the first time.

Henry jumped to his feet. "We thank thee, Benjamin, for thy time."

Hitty scowled at her brother. She noticed. He had switched back to using the informal Quaker pronoun. *That* was fast.

Benjamin lifted his hand. "Hold on a moment. There are a few things to discuss, such as thy grandmother's house. Thee should make plans to reside in it immediately. Today is not too soon."

"Oh no," Hitty moaned. She hated the Grand House. Hated it! It was cold and dark and large and heartless. "Must we *live* in it?"

"For the time being, it would be best. The household staff . . . they are waiting for direction." Benjamin put a cork back into the inkpot. "I will be bringing a secretary to Nantucket to remain on island. She is quite competent, and will assist in the paperwork."

"I thought thee was staying here." Hitty glanced at a cot tucked in the corner of the small office. She noticed details like that—curious little things that revealed a person's life. Nosiness, Henry called it.

"I must go back and forth to Boston, but my secretary will remain on island. She'll be able to carry out much of the detail work." He clasped his hands together and leaned forward on his desk. "I suppose that's all for now. But . . . before thee takes leave, allow me to give thee one word of advice."

Henry sat back down.

"Tell no one, other than family, about the inheritance."

"Why?" Hitty said.

"Rumors run like wildfire. If word gets out, thee will find all kinds of peculiar relatives at thy door, begging for handouts. Money can bring out the worst in others."

So true. Henry was already using thees and thous like he was a Friend in good standing, which he wasn't. "I don't know how it can be kept quiet. Nearly everyone on the island is related to each other."

"Frankly, all of our relatives are peculiar," Henry added.

Benjamin swallowed a smile. "Even more of a reason to be discreet."

"But the Grand House," Hitty said. "If we have to live in it, others will know she bequeathed it to us. We must be truthful." *Quakers might be hypocrites, but we are not liars.*

Benjamin ran a hand through his hair. Rather a thick head of hair, Hitty noticed. "Well, then, admit that thee inherited the house. But I caution thee strongly not to volunteer any more information about thy grandmother's will. Not a word to anyone. Trust me on this. 'Tis in thy best interest."

"Sister?" Henry said in a warning voice. "Can thee be discreet?"

How insulting! Hitty could be discreet when she really wanted to. And when it came to this inheritance, she *wanted* to. It was an embarrassment. Everyone knew how Grandmother Lillian regarded them as peasant stock because their father's mother was part Indian. Frankly, she doubted anyone would even believe that she and Henry were mentioned in the will. She stiffened her back and lifted her chin, and Benjamin Foulger's eyes danced, amused. "Have no worry. My lips are sealed."

As they walked toward home, Hitty noticed that Henry seemed positively lighthearted, a newfound bounce in his step. He walked right into the center of Main Street—it was teeming with people and horses and drays—stood in a mud puddle, and turned in a circle. "Still no cobbles, eh?"

"Henry, what does it matter? Our lives are over. Grandmother Lillian has clipped our wings." She covered her face with her hands. "I will become an eccentric old maid, wealthy and lonely and odd. I'll end up talking to my parrot, like our batty cousin Lucinda."

"Hitty, look at me."

She dropped her hands.

"Think for a moment. Grandmother Lillian has thrown down the gauntlet, daring us to challenge her."

"But I don't want the money! Now more than ever."

"Hush!" He put a finger to his lips. "I don't either. But we can't let Tristram Macy have her fortune, not after what he did to Papa. 'Tis an extraordinary problem. A Gordian knot."

"A what?"

"A Gordian knot. A difficult situation. But like Alexander the Great, we will cut through it." He made a slicing motion with his hand. "We will find a solution that satisfies everyone."

"Impossible."

"Nay, Sister. Not impossible. Where is that imagination thee is so fond of?" His face lit up. "So the money must stay on Nantucket, and the two of us, we don't want it for ourselves." He turned in a circle. "But we do love this island. Think on it, Hitty. We could use Grandmother's money to build the island, to make it last for generations."

"What is thee getting at?"

"What if we provided funds to improve Nantucket?" He kicked at the puddle, splashing water into other ruts. "Cobble this street, for example."

"Cobble Main Street? Does thee have any idea how much money that would require?"

"Nay, nor do I care. Does thee not see, Hitty? We'd have the last word on Grandmother. The money stays on island, 'tis used to benefit the island, and we do not squander a penny."

"But, did thee not hear the other condition? We must marry Quaker Nantucketers within . . . let's see, when would be Grandmother Lillian's eightieth birthday?"

Henry had already done the math. "Not for six more years. Six years."

"Hear me, Henry. 'Tis not about how many years, but who. Friends in good standing." She lifted her hands. "Isaac is not a Friend but a Methodist. Anna may be a Friend . . . but she's teetering on disownment."

Henry's eyebrows lifted. He folded his arms against his chest. "We are facing a difficult headwind, Sister. I do not deny it. But one problem at a time." He punched his right fist into his left palm, making a sound like a rifle shot. Once, then twice.

All Hitty could think was, *Where has my meek, waffling brother gone?*

As Henry packed up his belongings into his satchel, he came across the journal Daphne had given to him. Great Mary's journal. He had glanced at a page when Daphne had first given it to him, but there had been no time to study it. Reading through this journal would require patience and good lighting, for the ink was fading and the pages were brittle. Daphne said that Mary Coffin Starbuck would become a Weighty Friend to him. He wondered. He promised Daphne he would read it through, despite low expectations. How could a woman who had lived over one hundred years ago have wisdom to pass along to this modern age?

As he gently turned the pages, he was startled to discover that large sections of the book were cut out in a childish, haphazard way. What was left jumped from one year to another. Huge portions were missing.

Oh my. No wonder Daphne hadn't passed the journal to Hitty.

Mary Coffin Starbuck

22 June 1683

And so I am a grandmother! My baby has had a baby.

It hardly seems possible, for I still feel such a young girl within. Now and then I catch a glimpse of my reflection in a still pond and I wonder, "Who is that woman with the gray in her hair? Surely, 'tis not me!" And yet, 'tis me! (Stephen Hussey was right about that.)

I wonder if all of life will move so swiftly. I fear it will.

5 December 1683

Nathaniel asked me what has been troubling me since the baby's birth, and I was astounded by his observance. For he is right. I have been troubled of late, and I think it began when I became a grandmother. I had felt so certain about something for most of my life, yet it no longer seems a wise course.

Christopher Swain has been on a campaign to bring clergy to the island. Itinerant preachers have come to the island now and then. I am always interested in listening to their sermons, to ask them questions and learn of their mission. I credit Peter Foulger with teaching me to have a broad mind, to be willing to listen and learn no matter any age. ('Tis certainly not something I learned from my father, may God rest his soul.) I welcomed these clergymen to come and visit. As long as they did not plan to stay.

If they did have plans to stay, I reminded others of what life was like on the mainland with paid clergy among us. Had they forgotten? Intrusion into private matters, enforced conformity masquerading as unity. "Do you not recall the time when my father was banished to gaol for a night only because he helped a man after a public whipping? And do you remember that the man's only crime was to become an Anabaptist?"

If their memories have grown woolly, then I bring up the one forgotten thing that has never failed to shock Nantucketers' senses: fines and taxes.

"Who remembers when Elizabeth Macy was fined for missing a Sunday church meeting? She had given birth to twins two days prior, but that was not sufficient reason for Reverend Rodgers."

The notion of permanent clergy has always been promptly dismissed and the itinerant preachers are encouraged to make haste to depart the island. Pennies and pence are dear to us.

But generations are starting to accrue on Nantucket Island, and we have no religious scaffolding to offer them. We have been preoccupied with claiming our land, protecting and preserving it for the next generations as a legacy . . . but we have neglected to provide any spiritual legacy.

If Peter Foulger would lead a congregation on island, I would attend weekly, if only to hear his sermons. But he has refused my offer to help start a church. He says his church is with the Indians—and they have many small churches. But we, the settlers, have none. We have mixed notions on this island, he says, and one clergyman would not suffice. Peter is right, of course. I cannot imagine the conflicts that would arise if a clergy tried to get us all into the same pew.

I know not the answer to this vexing concern, but like a nettle's stings, it does not leave me be.

3

The Centre Street cottage seemed shockingly quiet and empty with Papa and Daphne gone to sea. Hitty knew Henry felt rather bereft about their sudden departure, but he hadn't been around home the last year or so when her father spoke of little else. He wanted to captain his own ship, one last time.

One morning over breakfast, mayhap six or seven months ago, Daphne had announced that she planned to go with Papa, like it or not. He smiled slow and sure in that way of his, and said, "I like it." And the years seemed to slip off him. He turned into a young man, eager and excited, planned routes after long talks with returning captains, spent long days at outfitters. His plan was to unload the *Endeavour*, sign a crew, outfit the ship, and set right out again before the weather changed.

So now the ship was gone.

Hitty looked around the small keeping room. The children would be arriving for school shortly and she should make ready for them. The Cent School had been started by her mother, Jane, and Aunt Daphne while Papa was at sea. After Hitty's mother died, Daphne continued the Cent School, and later married her papa. Now Hitty ran the Cent School. A variety of young children attended, though they all had one thing in common: they were not the Nantucket rich. Those children had nannies or governesses. The children at the Cent School had working mothers and away-at-sea fathers. School tuition continued to cost one cent per day, thanks largely to the fact that Hitty's father did not object to the keeping room of the Centre Street cottage being transformed into a small school each morning.

Hitty removed the breakfast dishes from the table and set them on the counter. Daphne had wanted to clean up, but there was no time. The tide waits for no man, her father chided, eager to be off.

She set out some toys for the children who arrived early—Isaac Barnard was usually the first to arrive with his daughter, Elizabeth, nicknamed Bitsy—not as a term of endearment but because she bit. Often! Hitty wondered what her mother must have been like, as Bitsy was a child of fierce emotion, so unlike her father. The first day Isaac had enrolled her in the Cent School, Bitsy marched over to stand on the hearth and announced to all that she did not want to be there. Hitty instantly adored her. Such spunk!

Then came a familiar tap at the door. *Isaac!* Earlier even than usual. Hitty hurried to the mirror to check her hair. She frowned, tucking loose curls under her lace cap. Whoever thought curly hair was desirable certainly did not have it themselves. She flung open the door and found Isaac standing there, a glaring four-year-old Bitsy by his side. Flustered, Hitty had trouble drawing a breath. This happened every morning.

She stepped back to let Bitsy in, as the child insisted on

claiming her rightful chair for the day. She pulled her father by the hand and stood by a chair as he untied the bonnet bow under her small chin and helped her set the bonnet at her place. This, too, happened each morning. Hitty watched the routine, bemused.

Why, Isaac was *not* old. Henry had unsettled Hitty with his disparaging remarks about Isaac's age. While it was true his hair was lightly peppered with gray, and he had crinkle lines at the corner of his eyes—to Hitty, those lines only made it seem as if he was starting a smile even when he wasn't—she didn't think he was over forty. She'd always felt her own age group was a good bit more immature than her. Not Maria, not Anna, but most everyone else. All the young men.

Isaac Barnard was different. Unlike the young men Hitty knew, Isaac had much on his mind. Unfortunately, Hitty did not seem to be on Isaac's mind.

Lately, what filled his wonderfully intelligent mind was finding a way to adapt some kind of lens for a lighthouse he had read about in Europe. He had tried to explain it to Hitty twice, and she still wasn't sure she understood. Something about a flat lens made of a number of concentric rings, to reduce spherical aberration—whatever that was.

Hitty was too embarrassed to ask him a third time. She thought she could ask Maria what spherical aberration was. Maria knew everything.

Isaac gave Bitsy a goodbye and turned to leave.

Hitty scrambled to find a way to engage him in conversation. "Isaac, might I have a word?"

He glanced at the grandfather clock in the corner of the room. "I am on a mission to fetch more glass."

"Glass?"

"Glass. To crush. I am close to a breakthrough on the Fresnel lens . . . but I need more glass. Hurricane lanterns, jars, whatever glass can be found in town."

"Before thee goes glass shopping, I wanted thee to know that my brother and I will be moving into Lillian Coffin's house this week. My late grandmother's house."

Startled, he turned his head to look at her. She saw the stubble on his jaw and knew he'd been up much of the night. At such close range, the effect of his dark eyes on her was bracing. She felt acutely conscious of his physical proximity and wondered if he felt it too. He was rather inscrutable.

"Thee remembers that my grandmother passed away." It was a rhetorical question, as the Cent School had been closed for a mourning period, but Isaac was a man who lived in the present.

"Lillian Coffin. But that was awhile back, was it not?"

"A week ago. So . . . recently, I found out that my brother Henry and I . . . we . . . our grandmother . . . well, she gave us her house to live in." Her cheeks warmed as his gaze lingered. "I thought thee should know."

He bowed his head slightly, absorbing the news. "So, then . . ." Isaac began, coughed, then started again. "You are giving notice?"

"Nay." Yes. *Yes, Isaac. Take notice of me!*

He lifted his head. "You are not quitting on me?" He coughed. "On us?"

Never. "I thought thee should know."

He seemed baffled. "If you have suddenly become an heiress of a fine estate, why would you continue to operate a Cent School?" He lifted a hand toward the small keeping room. "Here?"

Oh. She hadn't looked at it that way. Now that he put it like that, she could see how it might seem odd to live in the Grand House by night and work by day in a tiny cottage for a pittance. She was determined not to change who she was or how she lived. Other than residing in the Grand House, of course. But she couldn't explain all that to Isaac without explaining more. She had made a promise to Henry to be discreet about the inheritance and she intended to keep her promise.

Isaac waited for her response, a puzzled look on his attractive face.

"I have no plans to quit."

He seemed relieved. She noticed. "Then why did you tell me?"

Why *did* she? "Um, well, because I will be walking past thy house each morning. I thought I could fetch Bitsy and save thee a trip."

Isaac turned to his daughter, who sat at the table scribbling on paper with a piece of charcoal like a queen issuing a declaration. Bitsy was a quirky child, with chubby little legs and a permanently cross look on her small face—thick, unmanageable hair, dark eyes like her father. Bossy, stubborn, dramatic. Hitty found her thoroughly endearing.

After Isaac left, Hitty reviewed the interaction she'd had with him. All things considered, she did think Isaac seemed pleased she wasn't quitting the Cent School. He did not reveal his feelings easily, but she thought she detected a slight crinkle in the corners of those brown eyes when she said she would pick up Bitsy each morning. She was sure of it.

Isaac was a brilliant man, complex and preoccupied, as were all geniuses. Maria Mitchell, for example, Hitty's oldest and dearest friend. Complicated certainly described Maria—brooding, compulsive, more than a little unaware of life carrying on around her. But oh, the destinies of those two with their fine minds! Hitty could hardly wait to begin a new day and see what Maria had found in the night sky with her scope, or what latest invention Isaac had been tinkering on.

She glanced at the clock. There were still thirty minutes to go before the other children arrived. She grabbed Bitsy by the hand and hurried across the street to the Pacific Bank, promising the child a treat if she would come along without a fuss. Bribery worked quite well with Bitsy.

Maria's father was the cashier of the Pacific Bank and the family lived above the bank in an apartment. As Hitty passed the grand steps of the Methodist church, she thought of how many times she and Maria had run back and forth across Centre Street to visit each other over the years. They'd been fast friends all their lives, bonded through being socially ostracized. Maria was unpopular because she was prickly and temperamental—the opposite of Hitty, but she, too, had few friends. The Macy family had weathered quite a few scandals and Nantucketers had very long memories.

Hitty remembered the first school days as their friendship took shape. Maria sat alone for lunch, as she refused to join in with other girls and partake in idle chat. Even then, Hitty had thought, that big brain of Maria's was filled with splendid and important thoughts—reaching far beyond the walls of school. And Maria, unlike Hitty, had no care for what other girls thought of her. Hitty found such indifference to the opinions of others to be admirable. She gathered up her courage one day and offered Maria a banana—a rare treat on Nantucket Island, recently brought from the Caribbean on a ship. Maria took the banana, peeled it, ate it thoughtfully, then turned to Hitty and said, "I suppose we can be friends."

And that became a defining moment for Hitty. For all Maria's stiff and odd ways, she grew very dependent on Hitty. Maria needed her. Being needed became a comfortable place for Hitty and it was probably why she felt at ease with Isaac Barnard, who was considered stiff and odd in his own ways.

She found her friend in the cupola-like observatory on the rooftop, fiddling with the inner gears of a chronometer, a clock built for seagoing vessels that was used to determine longitude. "Maria! Does thee know what a Fresnel lens is? Can thee tell me how it works?"

"Of course. Why?" Maria straightened her back and stretched. It was then she noticed Bitsy, who'd been studying her as if she was a curiosity. Maria stared back. "Don't touch anything," she said, pointing at Bitsy.

"I need to understand it."

"Is that what Isaac's been up to? 'Tis already invented. By a French physicist. Augustin-Jean Fresnel."

"Maria, does thee think Isaac is not aware of that fact if he knows the name of it?"

"Point taken."

"Maria, please tell me how the Fresnel lens works. In plain English." Not the umpteen-syllable words she used that only confused Hitty.

Maria set down the fragile balance wheel she'd had in her hand. She gathered her words carefully. "Imagine a staircase, with each step being a curved glass. Those steps act as light waves, sending out several beams of light from the flame within the staircase. The light emerges as a perfect beam that can be seen far over the surface of the ocean."

Hitty thought carefully through the concept. "So those steps . . . that's what Isaac meant when he called them concentric rings."

"Exactly. Those rings actually bend the light, reducing spherical aberration. 'Tis quite a novel concept. But tell Isaac he should try to invent something that hasn't been invented yet."

Before Maria could say anything more, for she was quick to criticize Isaac, Hitty clasped Bitsy's hand and went to the door. "I thank thee for thy illumination on the subject."

Maria burst out with a loud guffaw. "Hitty, thee always makes me laugh!"

Hitty was halfway down Centre Street when she realized the pun she had made.

Henry stood on Straight Wharf, waving goodbye as the *Endeavour*'s sails were hoisted and bellied out with wind. Running through his mind was the conversation he'd had with his father as they walked down the dock. "Is thee not even a little worried about us?"

His father raised a quizzical eyebrow, surprised by the question. "Should I be?"

"What if we were to squander our inheritance? Become foolish and lazy?"

His father tilted his head. "The very fact that thee is aware of the great responsibility thee has been entrusted with—that *very* fact—is why I have confidence in thee. In Hitty too." He put a hand on Henry's shoulder and gently squeezed. "Son, thee has been given a great opportunity for doing good. I know thee will use it wisely." He thrust out his hand to shake Henry's, added a "Be well" and a "Look after thy sister," and then, more quietly, "Mind thy grandfather, he's getting on in years," and released him to help Daphne into the dory that would take them to the ship.

Henry wondered what his father would have said, had he known of the conditions that tangled the great gift. He had warned Hitty not to say a word about the conditions, even to Daphne and Papa, and for once she seemed to be cooperating. He knew that his father would have felt ashamed that Tristram Macy's name was used as a carrot, dangling the money in front of them. But Henry also hadn't confided to Hitty that Papa was penniless.

So what would Captain Reynolds Macy have said, had he known? Henry knew. His father would insist that they forgo the inheritance. Bad money follows bad money, he would say. Like a curse. Let it go. Wash thy hands of it before thee is stained from it.

Henry shuddered. He hoped he had done the right thing by accepting it.

The *Endeavour* would be gone from the horizon soon. Henry choked up, dangerously close to tears. Hitty was not here; she had said her goodbyes at the cottage, partly because she needed to prepare for the day's school, mostly because she knew if she started to cry, she'd be unable to stop. She was fearful that Daphne and their father would never return to Nantucket. Jeremiah, his father's father, who refused to be called anything but his given name, stood stoically beside Henry, eyes fixed on the masts of the ship. He wondered if his grandfather was thinking the same thought as Hitty, that he would not see his son again.

Use it wisely. What a mantle. How in the world could Henry be expected to use sudden, massive wealth wisely? He had no wisdom in him, none at all. Hitty had even less.

Mary Coffin Starbuck

10 January 1685

Eleazer Foulger came into the store today to settle his debt, which had grown rather steep in the last year. He seemed untroubled by the credit we have extended to him. My son Nathaniel has wanted me to discourage the extending of credit to him, to all the Foulgers, but I cannot do that. We are old friends, Eleazer and I. And Peter, his father, is so dear to me.

The Foulger family is such a curious one. They are unusually intelligent, gifted at learning, extraordinarily insightful, clever with inventions. (Recently Peter built a transportable chair for his wife, Mary, as she has "widened" over the years. She takes it with her when she goes visiting.) There is hardly a question a Foulger cannot answer, or find an answer to. But they have one area that plagues them: finances. Peter juggles many jobs, but has always struggled to provide for his family. 'Tis the same with Eleazer and his siblings. I think it is that they are so generous with others. When Peter met Mary, she was an indentured servant. He paid off her debt, and always claimed it was the best appropriation of money he'd ever spent. Money is a means for them, 'tis not the end goal. They simply do not care about money, and give most of it away.

When I told my son that very thing, he shook his head in wonder.

10 April 1685

Captain John Gardner came into the store. Although I am a Coffin, John will frequent the store. He knows that I did not take sides on the half-share conflict that threatened to split apart the island, but even with my father's passing, he will hardly speak to any other Coffin but me.

That conflict created a rupture that has yet to mend. The first proprietors insisted they should have full authority over the island. The half-shares objected to their lack of voice in town government and inability to own land.

While I am a Coffin, and my father led the charge for proprietors to retain their dominance, I leaned more on the Starbuck side of this dispute. Nantucket needs newcomers. We need more skills, more craftsmen, more families to settle the island.

I have found a seasoned principle to apply to most problems. At the heart of any decision should lie this question: What is best for the future of Nantucket? What will make it a better place for all to live? To thrive?

11 April 1685

My nephew, Jethro Coffin, has come to live on the island. For the time being, he is staying at Mother's house and is good company for her. He is my brother Peter's son, and a pleasant young man. Older than my boys, and a fine example to them.

He happened to come into the store today when Captain John Gardner's daughter, Mary, was picking up a box of nails. Jethro offered to carry the box to the cart for her.

When he returned to the store, I pointed out, with what I thought was a smile in my voice, that I had just brought that very same box in from the back room. "Yet you did not offer to carry it for me, Nephew."

Jethro blushed a mighty shade of red.

Oh dear, I thought, and Oh my. A Coffin and a Gardner. Oh dear, dear, dear.

4

Rumors did spread like a wildfire. It was a strange thing, Henry was quickly discovering, to be known as an heir, even if others were ignorant of the extent of the inheritance. Relatives he barely knew came out of the woodwork to befriend him, all with a dire need. Dire, at any rate, in their mind.

Two distant cousins came calling for the first time to Centre Street, oblivious to the fact that Hitty and Henry were in the middle of packing to move to the Grand House. The cousins sat at the table in the keeping room, sipping tea as if time had stood still. Hitty grew exasperated and left them to Henry. She continued to wrap up kitchen belongings around the cousins, placing them noisily into packing barrels, making no effort to be quiet. They took no notice.

The older of the two cousins, a middle-aged man both short and stout, poured himself another cup of tea. "We have come to request funds for a serious personal matter."

"A loan?" Henry said.

"A gift."

Walking behind the cousins, Hitty shook her head and mouthed the word, "Nay."

Henry tried to ignore her. "What sort of serious personal matter? Is someone ill?"

"In a manner of speaking. My wife needs a rest."

"Oh, I am sorry to hear she's infirmed."

"Really?" Hitty asked in a dubious tone. "I just saw thy wife at the market, not one week ago. What illness has she succumbed to? Cholera? Tuberculosis? Is she in need of an asylum?"

The cousin shook his head. "Nay. Twist not my words. I did not say she was ill. She needs . . . a rest. A change of scenery."

Henry shared an uncertain look with Hitty. "Such as?"

"I thought it might be nice to take her abroad."

Hitty let out a snort.

"Europe is in between wars. 'Tis an ideal time for a visit."

"I see," Henry said, though he didn't. He turned to the other cousin—the one whose name he kept forgetting. "And thee?"

"Gout," he said, lifting his big boot. "It flares up in the winter. 'Tis best for me to go to a warmer clime, come autumn."

Hitty poked her head out of the backroom. "Florida, mayhap?"

He lifted a finger in the air. "The very place. 'Tis just the right clime to cure my gout."

Hitty swept through the room with a crate in her arms, scowling at Henry. He picked up on her silent message and slapped his hands on his knees. "Well, cousins, I am sorry to inform thee that my sister and I, we are unable to provide funds for thee, for we have no currency to speak of. None at all." And that was the truth. Before they could ask anything more, he rose to his feet. "I thank thee both for the visit." Henry went to the door and opened it wide. The two cousins looked at each other in surprise, started to sputter, but Henry waved his arm toward the open door. "If only we had time to linger . . . but alas, 'tis moving day." He angled his head slightly. "Unless, of course, thee would like to help us?"

The two bolted to their feet, muttered that they must cast off without delay. Hitty grimaced horribly behind their backs, and Henry had to stifle a laugh so they would not hear as they hustled to the door.

The most mind-boggling visit came from cousin Kezia Coffin, who insisted she had been dearly devoted to her great aunt Lillian (despite being off island for the last twenty years) and felt she was entitled to items from the Grand House. "Especially so," Kezia said, "when one considers that Aunt Lillian and I shared a common love for porcelains."

"Porcelains?"

"Chinese porcelains. Blue and white. She had always wanted me to have her collection."

Hitty gasped. "Thee would sell every piece in thy Boston shop and pocket the change!"

Kezia cast her a dark look from the corner of her eyes.

"Ah, well, there's the rub," Henry said. "We have a strict condition about Grandmother Lillian's belongings."

Kezia leaned forward, eyes sparking with intrigue. "Do tell."

Hitty coughed loudly, intentionally. Do not tell her, Hitty's cough said. Say not a word. "Cousin Kezia," Henry said in a sorrowful tone, "that is another strict condition. We must keep all details private."

Offended, Kezia called them an unrepeatable name, and

stomped out of the cottage. Hitty and Henry looked at each other, mortified by Kezia's profanity.

"We must tell Benjamin Foulger about this," Hitty said.

"About what?"

Henry whirled around to find Benjamin at the door, left open for the June sunshine. With a curious look on his face, the law clerk fixed on them.

"Come aboard," Henry said, waving him in. "Word is out that we are moving to the Grand House. We are getting inundated by distant relatives who suddenly feel a warm kinship."

"And the moment their requests are denied," Hitty said, "we are just as suddenly given a very cold shoulder."

"I suspected as much," Benjamin said. "That's why I've brought along someone to help."

Henry hadn't noticed there was someone standing behind Benjamin. A young girl, she looked to be fifteen or sixteen years old, brunette, petite, with eyes cast downward in a bashful way. He stretched out his hand, remembering his manners. "My name is Henry. Henry Macy."

"Marie-Claire Chase." She glanced up at him briefly as she spoke and he noticed her eyes. Large and brown and winsome, like a doe.

Henry stepped back quickly and cleared his throat. "This is my twin sister, Hitty Macy."

Hitty smiled at the young woman and received a shy smile in return.

Benjamin, as usual, was all business. "Marie-Claire will be acting as my secretary to help sort out the details of thy grandmother's estate. Thee can send any and all distant relatives her way."

"Is that fair, Benjamin?" Henry asked. "Our relatives are quite persistent, and Marie-Claire might not be experienced with such bold persons. She seems rather . . ." What was the word?

"Young," Hitty supplied, rushing to add, "not that there's anything wrong with being young. It's just that our relatives are quite obnoxious."

"Have no concern about Marie-Claire," Benjamin said. "She's not to be underestimated. I have found her to be extremely competent, equal to any task. Thee will discover soon enough."

Marie-Claire's cheeks turned a charming shade of bright red. Henry noticed such details.

Hitty clapped her hands together. "Well, I, for one, welcome all the help we can get."

"Judging from the reaction of those relatives who just left," Benjamin said, "it reassures me that the wisest course of action is to keep the details of the inheritance within the family. I think it is the best way to shield thyself as thee grows accustomed to new positions in society."

"We don't want to grow accustomed to it," Hitty said. "We want to remain very unaccustomed to it."

"Indeed," Henry said. "Very unaccustomed."

A stunned look came over Benjamin, followed by amusement. "Surely thee jests."

"Nay, we do not."

Henry glanced in Marie-Claire's direction. His expression must have revealed some concern, for Benjamin pulled Marie-Claire forward by the elbow. "Marie-Claire is entirely trustworthy."

Henry assessed the girl carefully. She looked like a frightened rabbit, but a trustworthy one. "All right then. Hitty and I have decided that we are going to liquidate and give it all away. Every pound and pence, every shilling, every dollar, every bit of silver." He lifted his hand in a wave. "Anonymously, of course."

Benjamin looked from Henry to Hitty, then back to Henry. "Is thee both of sound mind?"

A laugh burst out of Henry. "I think so. It must sound crazy—"

"Indeed it does," Benjamin said. "Irrational. Illogical." He frowned. "Is someone putting pressure on thee?"

"Nay, nay," Henry said. "Hear us out, Benjamin. We will honor the conditions of the will, each one, but we plan to give the money away. All of it. Portion one and portion two, both. That is our plan."

"But . . . why? I realize it's not my place to question thee, but I am acting on behalf of Oliver Combs, and I am confident he would have objections. He will want to speak to thee himself, no doubt." Benjamin shook his head. "Most anyone would receive such an inheritance with open hands. Grateful ones."

Henry looked at Hitty and gave her a nod to answer for them. "Our grandmother," Hitty started, then stopped, and gathered her thoughts. "This wealth of hers . . . it did not bring her happiness."

Benjamin shrugged. "Money might not guarantee happiness, but it does help."

"Not true happiness," Hitty said. "It has nothing to do with true happiness."

His brow furrowed. "So thee considers it cursed? An inanimate object can be cursed?"

"Nay, not cursed," Hitty said, though she didn't sound convinced. "We just don't feel that it will bring us much happiness, either. So instead, we are going to try to use it to benefit others."

Well said, Henry thought, yet Benjamin still did not understand. He seemed rather frustrated with them. "Trust us on this, Benjamin. We have given it much thought and discussion. 'Tis not an impulsive decision."

Benjamin's eyebrows lifted. "And the conditions will be met? The wealth will all stay on Nantucket Island?"

"Indeed," Hitty said. "All of it."

"What a lovely idea. Thee intends to make Nantucket a better place to live." Marie-Claire spoke so softly that Henry barely heard her.

Henry looked curiously at her. "Pardon me?"

Her eyes went wide and she glanced at Benjamin before repeating herself. She cleared her throat. "I said, so thee will make Nantucket a better place to live."

Hadn't he just read that very thing in Mary Coffin Starbuck's journal? That very thing! Henry clapped his hands. "That's it. That's it exactly!"

"I think 'tis a wise thing to do," Marie-Claire said, in that dulcimer voice.

Use it wisely. Henry's father's voice echoed in his mind. It was an interesting pursuit, this idea of finding wisdom.

"And what about the other part?" Benjamin asked. "The second portion. The part about marrying Nantucket Friends, held in good standing. That will get accomplished in due time as well?"

"We plan to worry about that part later," Henry said, and Hitty rolled her eyes.

"Far be it from me to dissuade thy philanthropic intentions," Benjamin said, "but the clock started to tick the moment thee signed those papers. Six years might seem a long way off, but it will be here in the blink of an eye. If thee neglects to comply with the conditions spelled out in the will, each one, all the remaining assets will be given to Tristram Macy . . . even if it would have been spent making Nantucket a . . . how did thee phrase it, Marie-Claire? A better place to live."

"We will find a way," Henry said, sounding far more confident than he felt.

"Hold on," Hitty said, her voice shaky. "Does thee know where Uncle Tristram is? Thee is in contact with him?"

"Apparently, thy grandmother kept abreast of his whereabouts."

Henry avoided looking at his sister, for he knew the thoughts running through her mind. How could their grandmother have stayed in contact with a man who caused such pain to their family? Tristram Macy was a wolf in sheep's clothing. A fine, upstanding Quaker wolf.

Tristram had a way of ingratiating himself with others, charming but crafty. Henry remembered that his grandmother had been exceedingly fond of Tristram, mightily pressuring her daughter Daphne to marry him though she did not love him.

What Hitty was not privy to, but Henry knew from Daphne's confidences, was that Tristram had been responsible for the death of their mother, Jane. He had regularly supplied her with laudanum during their father's long absence at sea—not an uncommon occurrence on Nantucket. But he'd given her a tainted dose, albeit unintentionally, and it proved fatal.

Rather than face what he had done, Tristram turned tail and vanished from the island. But apparently, even he could not vanish from Grandmother Lillian's reach.

Benjamin picked up his leather satchel and turned to his secretary. "Well, Marie-Claire, with this update, I think thee arrived not a moment too soon."

Marie-Claire blushed furiously at the compliment and Henry wondered to himself, *Hmm. Is there something going on between those two?* But the girl was so young, and Benjamin didn't seem the type to take advantage. Just the opposite; he seemed like a youthful Oliver Combs. Buttoned up, gentlemanly, a stickler for details. He could see why Oliver took him on as his apprentice.

Why should he worry? Henry thought. Why should he care? Benjamin Foulger's private life was none of his business.

Mary Coffin Starbuck

14 April 1686

Stephen Hussey came into the store today with a complaint (when does he not have something to grumble about?). The Starbuck sheep are overtaking others in numbers, he said, and wonders if we are doing something tricky, like Jacob did to his uncle Laban in the book of Genesis. I was shocked by his insinuation. "Our sheep are growing in numbers because my husband is a fine farmer and cares well for his animals!" Unlike you, I barely held back from saying. Stephen Hussey is a poor caretaker and his animals (and wife) suffer for it.

Two more came into the store and I was eager to send Stephen on his way.

"Stephen, if you have something you need in the store, I can help you. If not, I suggest you take this conversation up with my husband."

"Ha! Everyone knows that thee is the one who wears the trousers in thy family, Mary Starbuck."

The vile man!

I know not to let Stephen Hussey rankle me, but it upsets me when Nathaniel is misunderstood or disrespected. My husband is a quiet man by nature and does not have a need to push himself forward, as most all men do. He can graciously accede to the importance of others without detracting from his own sense of self.

Stephen Hussey . . . the vile man!

5 July 1687

Today we received word that Nantucket property taxes are due by month's end, to be paid to the colony of New York. The payment is either one lamb or two shillings.

My brother James is loading a sloop full of lambs, bleating noisily for their mothers. I can hear their woeful cries floating up from the harbour, all the way into the store.

What will New York do when a full ship of unhappy lambs arrives?

5

A thick, cold fog descended on Nantucket. Not an unusual occurrence in the summer, but tonight it gave Hitty a very unsettled feeling. Or maybe the unsettled feeling came with the Grand House. It was so large, so expansive, so filled with treasures that could not be touched. She felt as if she had moved into a museum. A museum filled with servants. Aye, servants.

Henry had given Hitty the task of gently firing all the staff. She tried. She couldn't do it.

She didn't really know what to do with herself. Each time she started to do something the way she would have done at the Centre Street cottage, a servant whisked in and took the task away from her. She ended up hiding in her bedroom for the rest of the day.

Where had her brother gone? Just as the boy with the horse and dray had arrived to move their belongings to the Grand House, a bell sounded to indicate a ship in distress, so Henry dropped everything to rush to the wharf and join other men in a lifesaving attempt. Hitty went on ahead to the Grand House. That was hours ago, and she had paced around the entire house, four times, anxiously waiting for some kind of word about the distressed ship. Finally, long after the summer sun had set, she heard a rapping at the front door. She hurried to the foyer as the butler, a solemn elderly black man named Philemon, held the door open and peered at Henry and her grandfather Jeremiah.

"Henry! Jeremiah!" she said. "What's happened?"

"We should've gone to the kitchen," Henry said, his teeth chattering, "but we couldn't remember which door went to it."

Henry and Jeremiah warmed by the fire in the parlor and told Hitty about the foundering ship. "'Twas a bark from New Brunswick," Henry said. "The vessel ran aground in the south shore. The captain had no idea he was in shallow water until the ship was in onshore waves."

"Was anyone hurt?" Or worse?

"Nay, nay." Jeremiah rubbed his hands in front of the flames. "Though it could have been disastrous." He coughed once, then twice, deep and raspy.

Hitty jerked her head up at the sound of that thick cough. Jeremiah's skin color looked bad, pale and grayish. "Jeremiah, I'll get some tea."

He shook his head. "A bit of brandy, now that I would not object to."

Hitty poured a small amount of brandy into a tumbler.

"A little more," Jeremiah said, watching her.

Good, he would be fine. She smiled, handing it to him. He took a sip and leaned back in the chair, legs outstretched, content.

"Tell me more about the shipwreck," she said.

"I'll let Henry do the talking."

Henry pulled off his heavy sweater, still damp with seawater, and dropped it on the hearth. How her grandmother would throw a fit! A damp sweater on her precious hearth. The very thought of it lifted Hitty's spirits.

"No one on shore was quite sure how to proceed. We all stood on the beach, barely able to see the ship's tilting mast in the fog, but desperate shouts floated in and around us."

Hitty shivered at the eerie vision. "Could not dories have gone out for them?"

"Not among the shoals, and not in this fog. Too dangerous. But then one man volunteered the most extraordinary solution." Henry took the poker and turned the coals to spur on the flames.

"Oh Henry, don't stop now," she said. "Do go on." Listening to her brother unravel a story was an exercise in patience.

"We threw a sling to the vessel with a line attached and were able to bring twenty-one crew to shore. It was like pulling laundry in off a clothesline. The rope-and-pulley system of saving lives." Henry picked up the fire bellows and pumped it once, then twice. "Guess whose idea it was?"

"The rope-and-pulley? One of the lifesavers, I would think."

"Isaac Barnard."

Hitty had been watching the flames sputter and flare, but at the mention of Isaac, she snapped her head up. Isaac!

Jeremiah lifted his tumbler to let Hitty know he wanted a refill. She hurried to pour another glass for him, not wanting Henry to slow down the story.

"I had not thought Isaac Barnard to be a man of practical knowledge," Jeremiah said. "He seems the bookish type."

Henry frowned. "I'm the bookish type."

"Exactly." Jeremiah set down his glass and closed his eyes, hands folding over his stomach.

Hitty urged Henry to finish the story with a wave of her hand. Isaac was a hero!

"He seemed to have experience at lifesaving," Henry said. "He knew just what to do, ordering men around as if he were captaining a ship. It was . . . quite impressive. No one questioned his authority. They followed his orders like low-ranking sailors. And not a life was lost. Not one."

The clock in the hall struck midnight.

"Jeremiah, stay here for the night," Henry said, and his grandfather replied with a nod, yawning. "Hitty, why hasn't thee gone to bed long ago?"

Should she say why? "I feared it was the *Endeavour* that had run aground. That the tide was bringing it back in, broken and mangled. Everyone on it drowned."

Jeremiah opened his eyes. "There y' go again, girl. Creating catastrophe with no evidence to support it."

"He's right," Henry said. "Papa knows these waters better than anyone."

Hitty *did* have evidence to worry, and she'd had plenty of time to think it through this evening. "But Papa hasn't sailed the *Endeavour* in years. The sandbar is building. And the shoals are as dangerous as ever."

"The *Endeavour* sailed at morningtide, Hitty," her grandfather said. "She's miles and miles away by now. Y've got to stop yer worrying." He sneezed once, then twice, before he rose to his feet. "Point me to a bedroom."

Hitty opened the parlor door and there stood Philemon, waiting patiently. Past midnight!

"I'll show him to a room, Miss Hitty." He escorted Jeremiah upstairs.

Henry whispered, "I thought you were going to pay the servants and let them go."

"I was. But I can't." Hitty bit on her lower lip. "Henry, they count on these jobs. Philemon, the butler, why, he has seventeen grandchildren. His oldest granddaughter is Eunice Ross, the girl Anna speaks so highly of."

Henry sighed. "I'm too tired to think about anything now. I'm going to scrounge something to eat in the kitchen, then head to bed. I've got an early morning meeting." He stopped short to look back at her. "Which bedroom?"

By now Philemon had come back down the stairs. "I'll take you to it, Master Henry."

"Just Henry, please. I'm no man's master. First, though, which door leads to the kitchen? I've forgotten."

Philemon started down the hall toward the kitchen and Henry followed behind. He spun around to grin at Hitty and mouthed the words, "I could get used to this!"

Don't, Hitty thought.

Jeremiah woke in the morning with a headache and sore throat. He'd felt a little under the weather yesterday but couldn't resist the excitement of the shipwreck. He'd had to hurry down to the waterfront to join the others. Today, he was paying for it. A cold had come on, hard and fast, and his granddaughter insisted he stay put, in bed, in the Grand House. Lillian's house.

He knew he was an old man. He wasn't sure exactly how old because he'd never paid much attention to details like that, but most of his friends had passed. Those who hadn't died yet looked shockingly decrepit to him. He didn't feel so very old, at least not on the inside. There were times when he knew he'd been around a long, long time, and that was the very reason he didn't like sitting still. Memories descended on him like a flock of birds.

His thoughts often wandered back to his mother, Libby Macy, a practical woman who did the best she could with her sea-loving husband and two sons. Jeremiah had signed on to a ship as soon as his mother gave him her permission. He said goodbye to her, and also to his childhood sweetheart, Lillian Swain. To both he gave repeated reassurances that he would return a wealthy man, and an earnest promise to settle down.

When his ship returned to Nantucket for the first time, he was not so very wealthy as he had hoped, and he discovered his mother had passed away from winter grippe during his long absence. It had never occurred to him, not once, that he would never see her again. She'd been his anchor, his rock. Missing those years with her was a great regret of his.

His older brother Matthew had married Phoebe Starbuck, and they lived in Phoebe's childhood home on Centre Street. Jeremiah had made a promise to Lillian to stay put, so he set up a cooperage in the Easy Street cottage, which his mother had left to him. Barrel-making was always needed on Nantucket, and soon he began to flourish. He had not lost his love for the sea, though. She called to him constantly.

So did Lillian Swain.

Life was going along as planned, until a beautiful young maiden, Angelica Foulger, a half-Indian princess, came into his cooperage one day to order a special gift for her brother, Silo. One conversation with Angelica led to another, and another, and Jeremiah's heart was soon captivated.

He did not feel for Lillian what he felt for Angelica. It was tricky, explaining his change of heart to her. "We've outgrown each other," he said in his blunt way. "We're different people. 'Tis better for both of us to be released from childhood promises."

Lillian was disappointed, which was to be expected. What he hadn't expected was her cold and constant fury. She promptly married a Coffin, an unsuspecting, mild-mannered man who happened to be fabulously wealthy. Blessed with a sharp and shrewd acumen, she made him wealthier still. And she gave him two lovely daughters, Jane and Daphne.

Jeremiah and Angelica married, had a child together. He loved them both deeply. He loved the sea more.

Jeremiah hadn't been much of a father to Ren, he knew that. His own father had died when he was young, and he simply didn't know how to be one. He treated Ren, as a child, like a cabin boy. Later, as crew.

Ren took over the captaining of the *Endeavour* as a young man, newly married, went to sea for six long years, and returned a stranger to his children, Hitty and Henry. When he heard those two little ones refer to their father as "Captain," Jeremiah feared his son was repeating his own life. Distant, detached from those he loved.

Somehow, his son knew what he didn't—that this father-child relationship was unique and required nourishment. It touched Jeremiah deeply to see his son work hard to build a relationship with his children. He felt a sweeping regret that he had not tried harder with Ren, but there was still time to be a grandfather to Henry and Hitty. Lord knows those two needed a sage in their lives.

Jeremiah had always had a tender spot for Hitty, for she

loved wholeheartedly and forgave others easily. But she made it easy for others to take advantage of her. With Ren off island, he aimed to make sure she was watched over.

Henry was not as easy for Jeremiah to relate to. He'd never understood the boy. Bookish, long and lean, a thinker in a family of doers. Where did all that pondering come from? Certainly not from the Macy side; they were people of action. The first to jump in on everything. Now that he thought of it, Thomas Macy, Jeremiah's great-great-grandfather, had settled on Nantucket nearly a year ahead of the other first proprietors.

Someone needed to keep an eye on Henry and Hitty as they adjusted to Lillian's bequeathed fortune. Something didn't seem quite right to him, though he couldn't put his finger on it. Just a general uneasiness.

Jeremiah remembered a time when whales were spotted, and his son Ren, the ship's captain, had swung the *Endeavour* around to head off the whales, some of them forty feet long and weighing forty tons. Then the boats were launched and rowers and harpooners chased after those placid, peaceful beasts, who were completely unaware of the dangers into which they were heading.

Henry and Hitty, he worried, were the placid, peaceful beasts. Drifting amiably on, unaware that an enemy was pursuing them. He couldn't quite figure out who the enemy was—mayhap Lillian? mayhap these unknown relatives who emerged to ask for handouts?—but Jeremiah had lived long enough to pay attention to gut feelings. Not always, but more often than not, his instincts were correct.

Rain had begun to fall, but Hitty hardly noticed. She was eager to leave the Grand House, which made her quite edgy and irritable, and hurry back to the Centre Street cottage to start the day at the Cent School. The Grand House, so cold and echoey and sterile with its oh-so-perfect belongings, put her in a bad mood. It almost felt as if her grandmother still filled it, with her sharp tongue and judgmental ways. She had not often been invited to it—summoned, was how the family worded it—but she could practically hear her grandmother's sharp chiding at every turn. "Mehitabel, put down that bread roll. Thee has eaten more than thy share." "Mehitabel, has thee grown even rounder since the last time I saw thee?" "Mehitabel, I do believe a darker shade of clothing would help thee appear less . . . portly."

Portly. What an unpleasant word. It even sounded fat. Hitty was not fat, but she was not thin, not like Nantucket maids were supposed to be. Not svelte like her grandmother, nor petite like her mother. She was butterball-round as a child, much like her aunt Daphne had been, and everyone told her she would have a growth spurt, just like Daphne. But she never did. A corset could only do so much.

But then again, a corset did do much. It poked Hitty, jabbed her, squeezed her so tightly she could hardly breathe, stiffened her spine until she felt like an unbendable tree. A corset, she'd always thought, was a perfect metaphor of her grandmother. Stiff and unpleasant and unbending.

A loud coughing sound floated through the transom from a room down the hall. Her grandfather had been coughing all night long and gave Hitty cause for concern. She tried to make an onion poultice for him, but Philemon was already downstairs (did the man ever sleep?) and told her he would see to it. She peeked in on her grandfather and was satisfied he was sleeping, so she told Philemon not to let Jeremiah leave the house until she returned midday. Then she put on her bonnet, tied its strings, and set off to Isaac's house.

Fetching Bitsy each morning, she felt, could provide a wonderful opportunity to get to know Isaac better, to understand him. He did not volunteer much about himself. Her spirits lifted with each step down the porch steps onto the quahog shell walkway.

She reached the bottom step, lifted her head and saw Benjamin Foulger, standing at the open gate. "Thee is up early," she said as he approached her.

"I am on my way to speak to Henry. He sent word he wanted to see me as soon as possible. Any idea why?"

"He has a notion to put cobbles on Main Street."

Benjamin laughed. He had dimples, two deep brackets at the corners of his lean cheeks. She hadn't noticed before, but then, there had been nothing to laugh at in the reading of her grandmother's will. "If he's not awake, have the butler throw cold water on him."

Benjamin laughed again. It was a charming laugh, low and rumbling. "Hitty, thee is an uncommon woman."

Was that a good thing? She felt her cheeks grow warm at what she hoped was a compliment but couldn't be quite sure, so she dipped her head goodbye as she passed him.

She found the door to Isaac's house cracked open. She knocked gently, but when no one answered, she tiptoed in. She'd never been inside Isaac's home but was not at all surprised by what she saw in the front room. Very little furniture and an abundance of books, piles and piles of them. Rolled-up drawings filled the corners of the room. She called out Isaac's name, unsure where anyone was or if anyone was home, and heard an odd sound down the hall. She walked toward the noise and peered around the doorjamb. There she found Isaac, his head turned to its side on the kitchen table, sound asleep, snoring, a pencil still in his hand. Scattered around the table were paper drawings.

"Isaac?" she said again in a gentle voice.

Isaac startled, blinked rapidly, then rubbed his eyes as he sat up. "Mehitabel!" He looked around the room as if he had no idea where he was. "What brings thee here? Don't tell me I've slept past the start of school!"

"Nay, nay. I have come to take Bitsy to school. Remember? I'm sorry to startle thee. The door was left open and no one answered my knock."

He matted down his hair and adjusted his spectacles on the bridge of his nose. His hair had the appearance of a freshly hatched chick, a sight which Hitty found rather endearing. "I must have forgotten to close it after I brought Bitsy back from Sister Hannah's. 'Twas a late night."

"I heard. Thee was heroic, my brother said."

Isaac blushed like a boy. "Many men helped to save the crew."

"My brother gave thee much credit."

He blushed more and said softly, "Henry is far too charitable."

She laughed. "Nay, he is not! He is maddeningly objective." Her eyes caught on a shelf against the kitchen wall. Curious, she went to examine it. The shelf was lined with seashells, bird feathers, eggshells, and the skeleton of some small rodent. She turned to Isaac with a question in her eyes.

Isaac's cheeks went pink again. "Those . . . they're just

things Bitsy and I have found on our beach walks. We thought they were . . . interesting."

She had just discovered something else about Isaac she would not have expected. He was a noticer. They were just bits of flotsam and jetsam that most would overlook, but he saw they were beautiful and brought them home. She felt pleased with herself for offering to fetch Bitsy each morning. It was a wonderful excuse to spy on Isaac and his way of going at things.

She noticed a sketch lying on the kitchen table and picked it up. "A ship? Thee wants to be a shipbuilder?"

He reached out to take the paper from her. "Last night, as I returned from the shipwreck, I had an idea. A notion of building a lightship."

The poor dear. He was so exhausted that he was confusing his words. "Thee means a lighthouse."

"Nay, nay. Hear me. I meant a lightship. A lighthouse only warns a ship of a point of land. Nantucket has dangerous shoals, shallow sandbars. Imagine how helpful it could be to have a lightship fitted with a Fresnel lens, situated out in the waters to warn ships. Think of the lives that might be saved." Isaac ran a hand over the stubble on his chin. "Bitsy is still asleep. 'Tis quite early, is it not?"

"Oh?" Hitty feigned innocence. "Isaac, thee needs a good strong cup of tea." It struck her ironic that she had been served tea by a servant not twenty minutes ago in the breakfast room of the Grand House. That unsettled feeling returned. She didn't belong in that house. In that lifestyle.

Isaac's attention had returned to his lightship. "I think this is the answer to keep ships from running aground."

"Then, thee should do it!" Hitty tried to sound cheerful and confident, though she felt neither. "Why not pursue it?"

He dropped the paper on the table with a tired sigh. “Money, Mehitabel. Even a lifesaving venture will come down to a lack of funds.” He glanced at the stairs. “I’ll go waken my sleeping daughter.” At the bottom of the stairs, he turned back. “Did thee say something about tea? That does sound rather nice.” The corners of his mouth lifted, in that bashful way he had that made her feel all swirly and twirly inside.

Hitty started the fire in the hearth, then filled the kettle with water and set its handle on the trammel to boil. She bent down to search through the cupboards for a tea tin. If only circumstances were different, if only Isaac had some success with his inventions, Hitty was sure their relationship would have progressed further by now. Suddenly she heard her brother’s voice shout in her head: *There is no relationship with Isaac!*

But there was! she insisted in her mind. Isaac was shy and reserved, mayhap a little distant, but the more time they spent together, the more comfortable he would be, Hitty reassured herself. Or at the very least, he might take notice of her.

Money. She straightened up with a start. *Why, I have money. Lots and lots of it!*

That evening over supper, Henry listened to Hitty’s plan to donate money to Isaac to build a lightship with a Fresnel lens. A lightship? A lightship. The notion did hold intrigue. He wasn’t sure Isaac could actually see to the building of something, for most of what he did seemed to be on the idea side. Then again, Henry realized, Anna Gardner had often made the same observation about himself. “Thee starts things and never finishes them," she had said to him this very afternoon.

It had been such a lovely afternoon after the morning rain that, emboldened and inspired, he had stopped by 40 Orange Street to take a turn with Anna. Her parents welcomed him coolly and he did not hold it against them. Three years ago, he had wounded their daughter's heart by his abrupt departure. But Anna's heart had mended, that he could tell.

All Anna could talk about was Eunice Ross, the black girl who took the high school admittance test. "It was just like I thought, Henry," Anna said. "Just like I told thee! Eunice had the highest score of all the children. Every single one, boy or girl. Whether they had gone to Admiral Coffin's school, like thee did, or the Young Ladies, like I did. Not a single white child tested anywhere close to Eunice."

"Hitty mentioned that Eunice is the granddaughter of Philemon Ross."

"How does thee know Philemon?"

"He's my grandmother's butler. At least until Hitty gathers enough courage to give notice to the servants."

"Why? Why would thee fire the servants?"

"We don't need the help. 'Tis only Hitty and I, and possibly our grandfather Jeremiah, in that big drafty house. Hitty is pressing Jeremiah hard to move in to the Grand House and keep her company, and I hope he will. But even still, we're accustomed to Centre Street, to doing for ourselves. I tried to make my own tea this morning and was chased out of the kitchen by Cook." He shuddered. "'Tis an odd thing, to have people wait on me, hand and foot."

"'Tis not odd for most Nantucketers."

Not for Anna. The Gardners were a well-to-do family.

"Well, if thee intends to fire the staff, I would hope thee would find employment before letting them go. They rely on that income to feed their families, Henry."

"Of course," he said, but the look on her face told him she didn't believe he had thought that far. Something about Anna made him feel like a scolded schoolboy, always falling short. But to be fair, the entire experience of servants was new to him. He remembered a time when Patience, Abraham's Wampanoag wife, had worked in his home, but she was like a second mother to them. Around the time when his father married Daphne, Patience and Abraham were also married. Abraham became captain of the *Endeavour* and Patience stayed at home to raise their children.

They started down toward the wharf until Anna sniffed the air and made a face. "Rendering whale oil. Ugh. Let's go upwind." She turned on her heels and headed down a side street, and he had to pick up his pace to fall into step beside her. Had she always walked so quickly, or had he forgotten? It seemed a metaphor, somehow. He suddenly wished he could feel more relaxed around Anna. More natural, not always on his guard to say just the right thing in just the right way. That feeling was not new. He sometimes felt as if she was standing back, judging him, and it made him all the more awkward and reluctant. He'd nearly forgotten that ridiculous cycle—she wanted him to be more "fired up," and he, inexplicably, turned cool and distant. Annoyingly passive, even to himself.

"Henry," she said, "what does thee plan to do with thy grandmother's house? If thee doesn't like living there, mayhap thee could sell it."

"Anna, could we talk about something else?" He was weary of even thinking of the inheritance. It felt like an enormous burden, an ill-fitting yoke that rested uncomfortably on his shoulders.

She stopped, and her face softened. "I'm sorry, Henry. Thee has had much to deal with since thee returned to the island." She wrapped her hand around his elbow.

There! There was the Anna who made his heart sing.

"I would enjoy hearing about the exotic places thee saw while at sea. Fiji, Hawaii, oh . . . what about the Spice Islands? Ah, I would love to go there one day. I imagine it all smelling of cinnamon! Not the stink of whale blubber."

This was now the second time Anna made reference to the scent of Nantucket. Most islanders called it perfume, not stink. Had Anna's perception changed? Or, more likely, his own nose had become so familiar with the smell of whale oil that he didn't even notice anymore. "Alas, the *Endeavour* does not have the strength to go around the wild seas of Cape Horn, into the Pacific." Hadn't he explained that to her dozens of times? "We went north, to Greenland. Most of what I saw was barren wilderness." Henry had enjoyed the vastness, like a blank canvas that God was still tinkering with. He thought of saying as much to Anna, but caught himself. She could be a little touchy over the topic of religion.

They walked along in companionable silence, until they came to a point in the land where they could stop and look out at the sea. It was a calm afternoon, with the sun shining down on the silvery water. He took in a deep, contented breath.

"Henry," Anna said softly. As he turned to her, she reached out and took his two hands. "I am serious about reading those letters that thee wrote me. I have a hope that we might find our way back to each other."

Uh-oh. "At the moment, I am unsure of where my belongings are. Surely, thee can understand how chaotic a move from one house to another can be." She smiled, slightly, and he sensed she was disappointed. "I will keep hunting."

"I know thee wasn't ready for marriage three years back. I know I insisted on it, and I am sorry." He started to speak, but she shook her head. "Hear me, Henry. I should not have asked more of thee. I feel as if I pushed thee to run off on that sea voyage. I regret that . . . and I want thee to know that while thee was away, I have waited for thee. There has been no one else."

He squeezed her hands, his heart felt warm.

"I have a hope we can begin again, my darling."

Darling. She called him her darling.

"There is something thee must know. My name is soon to be written in the Book of Objections. For absenteeism. I have not gone to Meeting in many months. There is no point. The same people stand up and speak each week, saying the exact same thing."

Hitty had warned him about this change in Anna's outlook. "Anna, would thee reconsider? For my sake?"

"For thy sake?" She cocked her head. "As I recall, thee had many complaints about the Society of Friends. I thought . . . thee would be pleased. Thee told me once that thee felt distant from God."

Pleased? Nay, he was not. But to try to explain this nettlesome inheritance to Anna would only make her dig in her heels and refuse to attend Meeting, strictly on principle.

After three years at sea and some perilous moments when he was not sure if he would live or die, he was not so distant from God as he once had been.

Mary Coffin Starbuck

5 January 1689

On the mainland, trouble with the Indians has escalated into open warfare. There are reports of attacks on entire villages, many colonists have been killed, or taken away by Indians, and houses burned to the ground.

My brother Peter's house was one of those burned down by the Indians. Thankfully, he was here at the time, along with his entire family, to attend my niece's wedding. But it haunts me to think what might have happened if he had been home.

16 April 1690

Christopher Swain burst into the store, looking for someone to help him bind and whip Peleg, a Wampanoag who had bought seed from Christopher and had yet to pay him for it.

The amount of debt the Wampanoags carry on the island is indeed staggering. They do not value currency like we do. The Indians do not understand our ways, nor do we understand theirs.

But Peleg does understand returning a favor for a favor. Rather than whip Peleg—which does no one any good—I suggested that Christopher have Peleg plow five acres of Swain land. That satisfied Christopher, for he is not a man who likes turning over dirt. And Peleg was also satisfied (as well as relieved and grateful).

Our island has been spared of the kinds of conflicts that are ravaging the mainland. Peter Foulger and Edward Starbuck laid a foundation of living peacefully together. The Wampanoags call our island "Canopache" or "Place of Peace." My hope is that it will always be such.

6

Summer's morning sun shone brightly as Hitty made her way to Isaac's house to fetch Bitsy for the Cent School. Isaac was waiting outside his front door. "Bitsy will be out in a moment."

He had something on his mind. Hitty waited patiently, eagerly. Could this be the day in which he would declare his affections for her? Ask to take a sunset walk on the beach together? Invite her to share his life?

"Yesterday I received a legal-looking letter from someone named Benjamin Foulger."

Oh.

"It stated that a benefactor has provided funds for a lightship." He kept his eyes on the tips of his shoes. "Mehitabel, do the funds belong to you? From your inheritance?" He glanced up at her, then down again. "I can't think of anyone else who knew of this venture."

She swallowed. She had kept her word to Henry and not told another soul about the inheritance. But Isaac had guessed; she hadn't *told* him. "Aye, 'tis from the inheritance. I spoke to Henry about the Fresnel lens and the lightship and saving lives after those awful shipwrecks . . . and he agreed that it was a worthy project." She was watching him carefully, but he did not look up to meet her eyes. "I'd hoped thee would be pleased."

"I am." Isaac looked up, right into her eyes. "Twist not my words. I am most grateful for this opportunity. I only hope you know that, the other day, I was not asking you . . ."

"Isaac." She took a step closer to him. "This lightship, 'tis a fine and noble venture. 'Twill save many lives. We are the ones who are grateful to thee."

"You've helped bring it closer to fruition, Mehitabel." He blushed like a schoolboy. "Your brother, he calls you Hitty."

"Everyone does."

"Mehitabel is Hebrew in origin. It means 'God rejoices.'" He looked down at his boot tops. "It suits you. Being as how you're always so—" He didn't finish because Bitsy opened the door and let out a delighted shriek before rushing to Hitty for an embrace, and then the moment was gone. Hitty could feel Isaac's eyes upon them. *Being as how I'm always so . . . what? So what, Isaac?* But she couldn't determine, could never seem to fathom, what he was thinking.

On First Day, Hitty tried not to show surprise when Henry joined her to walk to the old meetinghouse. It shouldn't have come as the surprise that it did, for she had heard him rummaging through his wardrobe to emerge with the Friends' plain long overcoat and flat-brimmed hat, and she'd already noticed how he'd quickly reverted back to the informal use of "thee." It was the Quaker way, to avoid the more formal "you" along with other titles; all were equal in the Lord's eyes. Hitty wondered of Henry's sincerity but dared not tweak him. She was glad he was with her on this morning.

As she and Henry parted ways down the aisle of the meetinghouse, he to the men's side and she to the women's, she was pleased to see Marie-Claire. As she scooted down a pew to sit beside her, Hitty felt someone's eyes on her.

She glanced up and met Benjamin Foulger's bold gaze. He was sitting across the aisle, and looked so different from the other somber Quaker men that she hardly recognized him. Different from the others, she thought, not for his attire, but for how shockingly attractive he was. Something in her eyes must have given her away because he smiled at her, and she had the distinct feeling that he knew exactly what she was thinking. Hitty quickly turned away without smiling back. She chided herself. She should not be so aware of Benjamin Foulger.

Quiet descended over the congregation, a time of waiting, of silent expectation. Normally, Hitty looked forward to this peaceful time, a thick, enveloping silence, for it calmed her spirit as she prepared her heart to receive Light. She tried to focus, but her thoughts wandered like a jackrabbit. Then Benjamin stood up, prompted by the Spirit to speak, and suddenly her mind was entirely focused. On him.

"I am a newcomer to this island, and have heard much dismay regarding the Society of Friends on Nantucket—that it is a place of factions and disharmony. I did not know what to expect."

Hitty listened keenly, sitting up a little straighter, watching Benjamin glance around at the congregation. Where was he going with this?

"Yet this last week, as the ship *Eliza* was foundering in the shallows, I saw the Spirit of God at work in the rescue. There was a united effort to save that crew, and to salvage the ship. 'Twas a moment I shall never forget. I believe such unity is a hallmark of vibrant faith." With that, he sat down.

Benjamin Foulger seemed to take meeting seriously. Not that it mattered, she reminded herself. It didn't.

Hitty noticed that Marie-Claire tipped her head down as Benjamin spoke, and her cheeks flushed pink. It was sweet, Hitty thought, to see her pride in her employer. She had gotten acquainted with Marie-Claire when she had stopped by the Grand House with paperwork, and found the young girl to be quite mature. Far older than her years, as if she'd experienced much in her life. Hitty had tried to inquire of her family, but Marie-Claire cautiously deflected personal questions. Hitty admired such deflection. Too often, especially if she felt nervous, she blurted out far too many private details and instantly regretted it.

After meeting, Hitty turned to Marie-Claire with another question, one of many that had bounced around in her mind during the service. "Where is thee lodging?" She knew Benjamin had a cot brought into his office above William Geary's hat store on Main Street, for she had seen it, along with his shaving brush next to a water basin, but she knew not where Marie-Claire had room and board.

"For now, I am at a boardinghouse near the wharf. I'm seeking a room in a house."

Near the wharf? Nay, nay, nay. That would not do for a maid. Hitty clasped her hands together. She had the perfect answer. "Thee must stay at the Grand House. With me! Me and Henry, and my grandfather Jeremiah—who might seem a bit curmudgeony, but don't be fooled. He has a tender heart. Please, please say yes. 'Tis so big." And so lonely and empty. "There are plenty of bedrooms."

Marie-Claire's eyes went wide. "Oh, I could never impose on thee. I'm sure I will find something."

"It can be difficult to find lodging on this island. 'Tis one thing to be a sailor, 'tis another altogether to be a maid seeking shelter."

She nodded. "I have found that to be true." She bit her lower lip. "Would thee speak first to Henry? And I will seek out Benjamin's opinion."

"I will. I'll go now." She gave Marie-Claire's hands a squeeze. "And thee must start packing." She scanned the front of the meetinghouse to find Henry. She found him outside, talking to Anna Gardner with a particular look on his face.

Oh, she remembered that look. She called it his Anna face.

Henry was amenable to having a tenant in the Grand House, so long as the tenant realized the house would be sold soon. It was far too big and drafty, with a leaky roof. Grandmother Lillian had not maintained the house well in her later years. Repairs to it, such as a new roof, were prohibitively costly, and that wasn't how Henry wanted to use the inheritance.

"Sell this old dinosaur? Oh, that would be wonderful!" Hitty said, her face lit with joy, then its brightness slipped away. "Can we? Or would it cancel the will?"

"Quite honestly, I don't know. I don't remember anything about the Grand House, other than it was given to us to use. I'll check with Benjamin." He buttered a piece of bread. "Who is the tenant?"

"Marie-Claire Chase."

Henry's butter knife froze in the air. "The girl?"

"She's not a child, Henry. She's fifteen."

"Aye, 'tis young. Where is her family?"

"I don't know. She doesn't like personal questions."

Smirking, he finished buttering his bread. "I've never known thee to not get information out of someone."

"I'm working on finding out more. I do like her. She is rather refreshing. Different than most Nantucket girls. Unspoiled." Hitty added a teaspoon of sugar to her tea with a silver spoon—*silver!*—and stirred. "And she really does need a place to live. Benjamin Foulger has her trotting all over this island on Grandmother's behalf."

"Sister, thee often sounds as if Grandmother is still with us."

Hitty shuddered. "I feel her presence everywhere."

"Doesn't Marie-Claire have lodging? It seems like Benjamin Foulger could have seen to that. *Should* have. He's the one who brought her over here to work for him."

"She said she's staying at a boardinghouse—near Water Street." She shuddered again. "She's looking for a room in a house to lodge in. That's what made me think of offering her a place to stay here. This house is so big, Henry, and thee is hardly home."

She was lonely. He realized it just now. He relished time alone, Hitty loathed it. Most Nantucketers considered Hitty to be warm and friendly—which she was—and Henry to be aloof and cold. He was neither.

If Marie-Claire were to be a tenant here, Henry decided he would make an effort to get acquainted with her, as he understood and empathized with her acute shyness. He'd suffered bouts of it as a boy, and it had helped that Hitty was so friendly with others, for she had a knack of pulling him along into her warm circle, effortlessly. It took great effort for Henry to be friendly. Hitty gave her whole heart to others, assuming the best of them until proven otherwise. He wanted others to first prove themselves, then he would offer his heart. Once offered, he would not take it back. He loved with a fierce loyalty.

Hitty frowned. "Where has thee been, anyway?"

Henry sat taller in his chair. "Sister, I'm glad thee asked. I have something to tell thee. I am using some of Grandmother's funds to start a newspaper."

"To start one?" Hitty put down her teacup with a clatter. "Why? What about the *Gazette*? Anna told me she wants thee to write for Samuel Jenks."

"Nantucket has but one newspaper, and it should have a new voice."

"Anna told me she thinks Samuel Jenks has done a fine job with public schooling, but she feels thee could lend thy voice to the cause of integration."

"Hear me, Hitty! I said I was starting a newspaper. I have rented an office in the loft of a candle factory near the wharf, right on Candle Street. I've ordered a printing press from Philadelphia. It should arrive within the month."

Her mouth dropped wide open. "Thee has been doing all this, without talking to me first?"

"Oh. I hadn't thought of that. I suppose I should have, or could have. It took me awhile to think it through—thee knows how I am about pondering, and how fragile a new idea can be. I suppose that I didn't want to be discouraged."

"Henry! I would not have discouraged thee. Just the opposite! 'Tis a wonderful idea! Nantucket is changing and it does need more voices. Thee loves to write and read and think and . . . well, I think it's an excellent use of Grandmother's inheritance. Excellent! I wish thee greasy luck."

"And I will take it." He grinned. "Wind, weather, or whales permitting."

"So," she said in a tone like she'd found him out, "*that* was why thee went to First Day meeting. Thee is trying to get back in good graces with influential Friends."

Henry took a sip of tea, eyes cast down. She was right on that account. He hadn't been to a First Day meeting in many years and had dropped the informal language as he climbed the rigging to sail away on the *Endeavour*. It felt like he'd slipped off a tightly fitting overcoat, and it was not so easy to put back on. "I plan to call it the *Illumine*."

She tilted her head. "Wasn't that the name of the ship Uncle Tristram commissioned? The one that bankrupted Papa?"

He was surprised she'd remembered that piece of information. They were only six years old when their father returned to Nantucket to learn that his business partner had ordered a new ship to be built, leveraging the lay from the *Endeavour* to pay for it. It was the first hint of Tristram's misuse of funds. "Yes and no. It was indeed that ship's name—but as thee might recall, it was sold back to the shipbuilder. Mama had named it, and I'd always had the feeling that the name was appropriate. To illuminate something means that light is shed on the topic—and that's what happened with the ship. Light was shed on Tristram's treachery. That's how I see it. I think Mama gave him a gift with that name. I'd like to use it, if thee is agreeable."

"Of course. I think most Nantucketers would see it as a nod to whale oil."

He grinned. "That too." That was another reason he liked the sound of it—he was fond of double entendres.

"What made thee think to start a newspaper?"

"Anna sparked the notion when she suggested that I write for Samuel Jenks, but when I spoke to him about the position, it had already been filled. By his wife's nephew. Has thee ever noticed that his entire staff is related to him? Nay? Well, I noticed. And the more I thought of it, the more I realized that very thing is a great danger to Nantucket."

"What very thing?"

"Everyone is related to everyone else. People are set firmly in their ways of thinking, of living. The world is changing, and we must change with it."

After Henry had been home for a few weeks, he landed on a surprising realization: Nantucket was gripped in a kind of paralysis. It came to him one morning, during tea with his grandfather. Jeremiah had pointed out how polarized the island was becoming, especially contentious over the topic of school integration. Even the Society of Friends—the heart and soul of Nantucket—had splintered into three separate factions, fractured by heated theological differences.

But it was Jeremiah who posed the idea of starting a rival newspaper to the *Gazette*, which had been the only newspaper on the island for over twenty years.

At first, Henry had dismissed it. "Samuel Jenks is an able editor. He's a fine, forward-thinking man."

His grandfather tamped the burning tobacco in his scrimshaw pipe, lit it, and took a big draw. "I agree, I agree. But I think there is room for another paper. To foster balance, to spur on conversation." He put his pipe to his mouth again and took another draw. "Sam uses his paper to push his own ideas. Most of them, I agree with. But not all. 'Twould be a good thing for this island to have a fresh voice."

"I don't know," Henry had said. "I haven't really decided what I should do, now that I'm back to stay."

His grandfather took the pipe from his mouth and leaned forward, elbows on his knees, blue eyes piercing Henry's. "Boy, if there is no wind, row."

Ah, yes, a family motto aimed squarely at Henry.

Yet the more he considered the notion of starting a newspaper, the more it grew on him. Not only did he like it, he did a little investigating about it. He ran numbers on it, sought out where to purchase a printing press, even scouted a few possible locations for the office. He woke up each morning with his mind brimming full of ideas. This was a new experience for him; he felt something stir within him, a feeling he'd never had before: *passion*. It felt good. Was this how Anna faced each day? It was a marvelous way to wake up.

Hitty tapped her spoon on her teacup saucer to remind him she was still there. "Might I ask, how did Anna take the news?"

"I haven't told her yet." He set down his teacup. "Thee must not tell her, Hitty. This is my venture. I will tell Anna in due time. Are we clear on that?" It was important to highlight that kind of thing to Hitty, to spell out clear expectations.

She crossed her heart. "Have no worry, Brother. That is one conversation I do not want to be in the middle of."

Neither did Henry.

Mary Coffin Starbuck

29 June 1690

Eleazer Foulger came over this morning to tell me his father, Peter, passed in the night, quite unexpectedly. I had to sit down when I heard the news.

I am bereft, even more so than after my own father died nine years ago. Peter was my spiritual father, better than clergy, and my dear, dear friend. I turned to him often for advice, for counsel, for insight to solve a problem. So many did. The Wampanoags called him the "white chief's old-young man," meaning he was wise for his age.

How will I carry on without Peter? I think I will miss him every single day for the rest of my life.

1 July 1690

Peter was buried today in the Founders' Burial Ground, not far away from my special oak tree.

There are no words.

7

Hitty was bone tired but couldn't sleep. The bed was lumpy and the room musty. She tried not to let the Grand House bother her, for she knew it was short-term, only until a buyer could be found.

She heard the sound of hard rain pounding the roof. If the storm moved on quickly, the ground would be soft and pliable and tomorrow would be a perfect morning to garden, as there was no Cent School in session on Seventh Day. Marie-Claire had purchased a dozen geraniums in town that were waiting to be planted. She had suggested adding flowers out front, to give the house a bit of warmth. Less stern and austere was what she meant. It certainly needed something to appeal to buyers, for so far there was a scarcity of interest.

Hitty wondered what kind of home Benjamin Foulger grew up in, and what he thought of the Grand House.

What's wrong with me? she wondered. She turned over and punched her pillow. *Why am I even wasting time thinking about Benjamin Foulger?*

Because thee likes him, a little voice replied.

Nay. I do not, she argued back. *He's not the kind of man I favor.*

Thee means, thee is not his *kind.*

So true. Benjamin was startlingly handsome, polished, and educated. He came from a great and distinguished ancestry. The Foulgers could be traced back to Peter Foulger, immigrant from England, one of the first settlers to Nantucket, and grandfather to the illustrious Benjamin Franklin.

Hitty, on the other hand, despite having a familial linkage to the first proprietors of Nantucket, descended from a line that brought generational scandal. They were the poor relations to the great Macy, Coffin, and Starbuck names. Her uncle Tristram brought shame, her grandmother brought disapproval. And then . . . there was Hitty herself. She didn't fit. Round and curvy, generously proportioned, at a time when women were stick thin, bound tight in a horrible corset. No matter how tight the corset strings, Hitty could never look like those prized Nantucket maidens. She yawned once, then twice. If only Rubenesque-shaped women were esteemed. She yawned again, growing drowsy, and fell asleep listening to the drumming rain.

The storm had blown over by daybreak, so after breakfast Hitty found some garden gloves and went out front to plant the geraniums. She walked along the front of the house, noticing how many dandelions were in the lawn. She bent down to pull one, yanking hard on the weed. When it finally came out, long root and all, she fell backward to land squarely on her backside. The stays in her corset dug into her ribs. How she hated corsets! That's when she noticed Benjamin Foulger standing on the quahog shell walk, trying hard to keep a straight face.

She stared up at him, aware of his amusement, holding the dandelion in her gloved hand, feeling every bit the fool. "I'm trying to plant some flowers. Marie-Claire thought it might help take away the austere look of the house. She drew a sketch of what she had in mind, and I must say, she's right."

He gave her a warm smile. "Thy presence is all that's needed to soften the house."

Her mind went blank. Why did this man turn her into a silly, blushing schoolgirl each time he so much as smiled at her?

He reached out to her. "Need a hand?" He pulled her to her feet and she brushed the dirt off her dress. "I have a question, Hitty. Something I've often wondered. How does thee know the difference between a flower and a wildflower?"

"Whatever thee does not plant . . . is a wildflower."

"Aha!" Benjamin laughed. A rich, warm sound that made her pulse quicken.

"'Tis early for a social call." Why in the world did she say that? Something went awry with the connection between her brain and mouth whenever he was nearby.

"I'm sailing to Boston at high tide. There are a few things I wanted Marie-Claire to deal with while I'm off island."

Off island. He had started to adopt Nantucket vernacular. She noticed. "More paperwork?" she said. "This will is unending."

"Actually, thy grandmother's estate, that's what's unending. It's rather . . . vast. This is only the beginning. These papers are for steer on Tuckernuck Island. She kept a herd there."

Hitty yanked off her gloves and dropped them in the basket

she used to hold gardening tools. "Marie-Claire is upstairs, having tea with my grandfather." Jeremiah's cough had yet to improve after the night of the shipwreck, and Hitty would not let him leave the Grand House until he fully recovered. She went up the porch steps and turned to Benjamin. "Come in. I'll let her know thee is here."

She felt his gaze on her as she opened the door. She caught sight of her reflection in the brass detailing on the door. *Could I possibly look more disheveled?* Her face had streaks of dirt, most of her hair had sprung loose in the humidity, with damp ringlets hanging on her forehead.

Luckily, Benjamin seemed more interested in the architectural details of the house as he walked inside, glancing around at the walls and moldings. He seemed especially taken by the fireplace in the parlor, with its carved marble mantel. "This is quite a fine house."

She heard a note of surprise in his tone. She watched him peer at a Ming China blue-and-white vase, noticing how his overcoat stretched taut over his back, outlining his shoulders. When he suddenly turned around, she felt herself blush, as if he could guess she'd been studying him.

"I'll go get Marie-Claire." She made a dash up the stairs.

Jeremiah had the *Gazette* newspaper spread out on his lap, but it wasn't holding his interest this morning. It never did.

He looked up to realize that Marie-Claire was sketching on a pad with a piece of whittled charcoal. "Of me?" he asked. "Let me see."

Reluctantly, she passed the sketchpad to him. Her drawing was a likeness of him with surprising detail, down to the river of veins on the back of his hands. "Ah, what a handsome devil I am."

She grinned. "I can only imagine how many maidens' hearts thee broke when thee was but a lad."

"Indeed I did," he said. Two. And they belonged to the two most beautiful women on the island. He handed the sketchpad back to Marie-Claire. "Y've got a talent there." He enjoyed this young lady. She was very unspoilt, unlike most Nantucket girls who were raised with servants wiping their noses with silk handkerchiefs.

Marie-Claire refilled his teacup. "'Tis a beautiful day."

"Good to hear." Jeremiah threw off the covers. "I need some fresh air. Real air."

"Going outside?" Hitty said. "I don't think it's a good idea. Not with thy cough still persisting."

Jeremiah hadn't realized Hitty stood at the open door. He rolled his eyes and yanked the covers back over himself with a scowl. He turned his attention back to the newspaper as she told Marie-Claire that slick lawyer clerk was downstairs. He was eager for Henry to get the printers rolling on that newspaper of his and get it out, into people's hands. That grandson of his could be as slow as molasses in January when it came to action. The *Gazette* was only good for kindling. This island, it needed something more to stir people's stumps.

Henry had never noticed the power of money because he'd never had any. He was astounded by how quickly the mechanics of his newspaper, the *Illumine*, came together for its first day of printing. Mayhap, a bit sooner than he was quite ready. Ideas were such a lovely concept; reality was another thing altogether.

A printing press had arrived from Philadelphia within weeks after placing the order. A typesetter had been hired, an elderly fellow from Boston named Zebadiah Smythe. He had much experience in the trade and recently retired on Nantucket to live with his daughter. Marie-Claire had been the one to find Zebadiah and recommended him to Henry. Zebadiah had no plans to go back to work, until Henry offered him a salary he could not refuse. Money could make things happen.

The articles for the inaugural issue had been written by Henry and typeset by Zebadiah. This first issue was only two pages, front and back, and Henry planned to provide this issue free of charge to all Nantucketers. Ten thousand copies, one for each resident. It had to be perfect—compelling and interesting and well-written and void of all typographic errors. Zebadiah had told Henry repeatedly that it was ready to go to bed, but he could not quite pull the trigger. He felt it needed something more, something newsworthy to make people eager to subscribe. The problem was he wasn't quite sure what was missing.

Zebadiah was annoyed by Henry's reluctance to print. "What's the holdup?"

Henry sighed. "I'm not sure it's everything it should be." He raked a hand through his hair. "How do I know?"

"My old editor had a saying: The right information at the right time can make all the difference." He grabbed his hat. "However, I am not sitting around here while you stare at your proof, watchin' the ink dry."

Henry looked up from his desk. That's exactly what he had

been doing. Watching the ink dry, thinking and pondering and wondering what else this paper was missing, so that it would instantly stand out from the *Gazette*. He rubbed his forehead. "Tomorrow. We will print tomorrow."

"Is that a guaranteed promise? I have things to do, y' know."

Henry doubted that. But he did need to get this debut issue printed. He knew that, but it didn't make it easier to do. "Tomorrow. Guaranteed."

At the door, Zebadiah turned and said, "I think y'll know, when it's time."

Oh, *how* Henry wanted to believe that. He pulled open his desk drawer to find a new quill feather and noticed the key to another drawer, the locked one where he kept Great Mary's journal. He picked up the small key, fingering its cold metal. He bent down and turned the lock with it, lifted the journal, and held it in his hands. Old, so very old. How would Great Mary handle his situation? Could she have even fathomed something like this?

Carefully, he opened the journal and read a few entries, hoping to glean some wisdom. He needed it.

Mary Coffin Starbuck

31 October 1692

My brother Peter arrived yesterday with disturbing news of the mainland, especially in towns near Salem. A great furor about certain persons whom the Devil had entered and turned into witches. Eighteen witches confessed and were condemned, and then executed. Mother and the other women felt quite uneasy as Peter relayed the tales of horror involving devilish acts of the Salem witches.

Mother said we should consider ourselves fortunate that no witches have appeared on Nantucket, and all the women heartily agreed. A few, I thought, cast anxious looks around the room, as if looking for devils who might be lurking nearby, but mayhap 'twas my imagination.

I would not dare say it aloud to anyone other than Nathaniel, but I wonder if the women were truly witches, if they had been given a fair trial, or if anyone bothered to ask their defense. At my age, I have known enough people, all kinds, to know that there are two sides to every story. Often more than two sides.

Public sentiment can be an overwhelming tidal wave, without right or reason. I remembered, in Salisbury, seeing a mob grow out of control to attack a woman, an innocent Quaker missionary. She ended up in the stocks during a stormy night and was dead by morning. She had done nothing wrong but to have a differing opinion of how to worship the Almighty. That, and she was a woman, daring to speak out.

Women are so utterly vulnerable. They have no voice, no rights, no means to defend themselves. Especially against a mob.

Did anyone bother to seek out the truth behind these women's stories? To ask why they behaved as they did? To question what made them so fearful that they resorted to superstitious, distorted means to find peace for their souls? I wonder.

8

Henry read and reread the single sheet of newspaper proof. Zebadiah had rolled one paper through the press for him to see, hoping it would give him the confidence to print ten thousand copies. It did not.

Mayhap he should take this proof home to show Hitty and Jeremiah. And Marie-Claire—she surprised him with her insights. He found he did not mind that Marie-Claire resided at the Grand House, as he understood Hitty's enjoyment at having a companion. He knew his sister sorely missed Daphne, and Jeremiah wasn't much company. Marie-Claire was a very intelligent young woman, though he could see she remained wary of him. Or nervous? Or both. Those big brown eyes of hers, they signaled her every thought. And yet those thoughts, when revealed, were often quite unexpected.

This very morning was an example. During breakfast, Henry quizzed Marie-Claire to see if she had found any potential buyers for the Grand House, and if not, why not?

She froze, and her cheeks went rosy. That was a frequent occurrence, for she did seem uncommonly shy, so he was not too concerned. But what she said next did concern him, rather a lot. "Apparently," she said in her quiet way, "the house is considered to be haunted."

"What?" Henry was shocked. "Haunted? That's rubbish!"

"Haunted?" Hitty's face lit up. "I've always thought this house was eerie."

Henry rolled his eyes. "By whom?" he asked. "Who is supposedly haunting it?"

"By . . ."

Henry braced himself, for Marie-Claire tucked her head down at this point.

"By thy grandmother."

"I knew it!" Hitty said, slapping her palms on the table. "I knew it!" She looked up at the corners of the dining room. "I can just feel her pointing her finger at me, scolding and chiding me."

"Sister, that is nothing but bunkum!" Henry turned to Marie-Claire. "Who started such a vicious rumor?"

Marie-Claire's cheeks—her entire face—went from pink to flaming red. "Thy own grandmother. She said she would come back and haunt anyone who tried to live in her house, but for her own family members. She told that very thing, word for word, to the grocer and the baker and—"

"The candlestick maker," Jeremiah chimed in, grinning.

"And they told—"

"Everyone," Henry finished.

Marie-Claire nodded. "There seems to be a consensus on the island to avoid this house. Children won't even walk past it."

"Ah, Lillian." Jeremiah laughed. "That shrewd old bird. She knew exactly what she was doing."

A church bell chimed three times, jolting Henry back to

the problem at present, to his office above the candle factory. His eyes fell to the thin sheet of newspaper on his desk. To the proof, waiting for his approval to print.

Anna! She might know just what this newspaper needed. She'd been enthusiastic when he finally confessed his venture to her, as soon as she recovered from her shock. Was he really as indecisive as she had presumed him to be?

He looked down at the proof. Aye, he was, he sighed, struck by the irony of the moment.

Carefully, he folded the newspaper proof and tucked it into his pocket. He would take this to Anna and see if she agreed it was ready to print. A thought niggled at him. It didn't *feel* ready. But was that because of his wretched indecisiveness or could he trust his gut? He didn't know.

Maybe Anna would.

He hurried to the African School and bolted up the rickety steps, two at a time, to the door, left wide open. Inside, he saw Anna near the front of the room with Eunice Ross, her prize pupil. Henry paused at the doorjamb when he realized they were deep in conversation. Eunice held her hands against her face, and Anna was pacing back and forth, her arms held tightly against her abdomen as if she had a stomachache. Henry stepped back to remain unseen, waiting. He wasn't sure if he should wait to speak to Anna, or leave now, before he was noticed. He had no doubt what Hitty would recommend: stay and eavesdrop.

While still trying to decide what to do, Henry heard Anna's voice, tense but excited. "Tonight, Eunice. It's finally here. We're facing the fulcrum point. This meeting will change Nantucket forevermore."

Henry took in a sharp breath. He spun around and went

down the steps as noiselessly as he could. She must be referring to the monthly town meeting. William Gurrell, a local businessman, was a member of the school committee. Henry had just visited his office to let him know about the *Illumine*'s launch, and William had not said a word about the meeting. Not a *word*. William was a staunch segregationist.

A thunderclap hit Henry. He knew what the first issue of the *Illumine* was missing. *This* story.

Henry stood in the back of the great room of the Atheneum, jotting down notes on the town meeting.

"If it was moved to the Atheneum," Hitty whispered, "why aren't there more people? Usually town meetings have a large turnout."

Henry had asked Hitty and Marie-Claire to attend with him, to have more eyes and ears to record details. So far, there was nothing much to write about, other than its sparse attendance.

"The school committee took care not to publicize the meeting," Henry said.

Marie-Claire frowned. "And I suspect it is held in the Atheneum because no blacks are permitted inside."

Henry snapped his head in her direction. "How does thee know that?"

"Look around," she said.

As his gaze swept over the audience, he noticed. White men and women only. How had he missed that?

Anna rose to her feet, and his attention focused on her. Without even using notes, she politely requested permission of the town to admit Eunice Ross into the Nantucket High

School based on her test scores. "The highest of any island child, white or black," Anna pointed out. "Eunice deserves an opportunity to further her education." Her voice never wavered, never wobbled. She spoke eloquently, with great authority. How Henry admired her!

Anna had not even finished before she was interrupted by spokesman William Gurrell, who strongly objected to her request. "There is already a public school for those children," he insisted. "The African School."

"But 'tis not a high school!" Anna said.

"It could be," William argued. "You are the paid teacher for the school. No one is stopping you from continuing to teach her. So teach!"

Anna did not back down. "But high school provides more breadth of education. I can only do so much when I am teaching more than thirty children, ages five to fourteen."

Someone else interrupted Anna, then another, and another, and another. The debate grew vigorous, divided by those who supported integration and those who did not. Divided, but not equally so.

Edward Gardner, a relation to Anna, rose to his feet and waited until the room quieted. "I wish to make a motion to see if the town will instruct the school committee to permit colored children to enter all or any of the public schools of this town."

One by one, the vote was taken. Henry's eyes were fixed on Anna, on how tightly she held herself, as if she was trying to win the motion through sheer willpower.

The motion failed. Eunice Ross was denied entry. There was a moment of heavy silence. The sound of failure.

Anna's shoulders sagged.

For one split second, Henry was caught between two obligations. Should he stay to console Anna? Or should he hurry to the *Illumine*'s office, where Zebadiah was waiting to typeset this story? His mind was racing, composing the article.

He glanced at Anna. Hitty had already gone to her side, with an arm around her shoulders. *Good, Anna has an ally.* Henry nodded at Marie-Claire, who had been watching him, he realized, and slipped out the door.

Mary Coffin Starbuck

22 March 1692

A fire broke out yesterday morning over at the Husseys', caused by a lightning strike, and the house burnt quickly to the ground. No one died, and for that I am thankful.

I was appalled to learn that no neighbor came to their aid, although the smoke and smell was observed by many. The reason they were not helped, I was told discreetly by one of their neighbors, was because the Husseys have rerouted their creek so that it runs only on their property. No one else can share in this bounty. "'Tis God's way of punishing them," said this neighbor. "Fresh water is scarce on this island. God meant it for all."

The Husseys were wrong to reroute the creek. 'Tis true that God meant for all to enjoy water. Still, I wonder if the punishment of fire came not from God and his lightning, but from cross neighbors. I do not recall any thunder or lightning during yesterday's rain soaking. I said as much to the neighbor and he sharply rebuked me. "Capaum Harbor is miles away from Hussey land." He pointed a long finger at me. "You don't see everything, Mary Starbuck."

At that point, I knew it would be pointless to pursue any more discussion. It would boil down to "his word against her word," and "her word" counts for nothing.

We have no law on this island but for man's conscience. And conscience, it seems, can be a very subjective thing.

17 April 1692

Stephen Hussey hired Indian laborers to rebuild his house. Then he paid them with jugs of rum from his still (which he thinks no one knows of, but everybody does).

How could he? What a terrible thing to do.

Later that day . . .

My father and the other founders believed that they could create a kind of Utopia on Nantucket Island, held strong to its principles through familial connections. (How could any kind of Utopia exist when Stephen Hussey and Christopher Swain were among them? They argue over the shade of blue in the sky!)

It might have seemed possible for those first few years, when families were small and everyone knew each other well. It wasn't long before serious conflicts developed, all based on money and property and assets and shares and half-shares. The conflicts were eventually resolved, but not easily, and they left lasting scars.

There are now seven hundred white people on this island. 700! The store provides more interaction with islanders than most, as well as a peek into their lives: the items they order, the credit or barter they require. I probably am more aware of the conditions of families on this island than any one else. Thus I feel confident in assessing that our island is in danger of decay through sheer selfishness. There is an attitude of "each man to himself" that is greatly concerning to me. That is not what it was like in the old days, when neighbors looked after each other. We all felt allegiance to each other, even Husseys and Swains. Even them.

My husband says I am romanticizing the old days. He reminded me of the first winter on Nantucket, back in 1661, when Stephen Hussey grew increasingly irate that Christopher Swain's children were collecting driftwood on what Stephen considered to be his beach. (What kind of man dares to claim a beach? The sea and sand are God's gifts to all men.) While it is true that any wood is dear on the island, Stephen waved his rifle at Christopher's little children and threatened their lives. Over a few pieces of wood!

"Think also of those early years and the few cattle we had," Nathaniel said. "Do you not remember when our cows went into the wrong field and gorged themselves? We had to provide a summer's worth of hay."

Indeed, I had forgotten those struggles, and many more like them. My recollection of those early years was constant work, heavily reliant on the weather. Summers meant preparing for winters. Winter meant enduring until summer.

And then Nathaniel reminded me of the feud that grew over the half-share concern, not ten years after we arrived. The first proprietors knew the island needed more settlers, more skilled tradesmen, to become self-sufficient. They enticed others to reside in Nantucket but withheld full benefits. The town's business was conducted by majority vote. The original proprietors held two votes, the tradesmen had one. The new settlers were called "half-shares" and had half a voice in town politics.

"Those who retained power only held it more close to themselves," Nathaniel said, and by that he meant my father, who was deeply embroiled in stirring that heated debate.

No wonder I had put all those struggles out of my mind. The half-share debate, in particular, took a toll on our marriage. There were days when we hardly spoke to one another. Edward, Nathaniel's father, sided strongly with Peter Foulger. They wanted new settlers to experience full benefits of ownership on the island. My father felt otherwise. He had in mind a stronghold of family and wanted to preserve a legacy. The half-share means was how it had been set up in the beginning, it had been approved by the English government, the new settlers came to Nantucket with a full understanding of it, and Father was adamant it should remain such.

Nathaniel leaned toward his father's way of thinking, as did I. But I was also caught in a tight spot. My store serves all of Nantucket, not just those with whom I agree. But my father was relentless to try to persuade me to support his faction. He knew that I had some influence on others, and desperately wanted me on his side. I felt torn in two. It really never resolved until my nephew Jethro married Mary Gardner, and the ongoing friction between opposing families settled down.

I suppose Nathaniel is right. There is no such thing as finding a Utopia because the sins of men come right along with them.

Later, I went down to the beach to watch the sun dip

below the horizon. 'Tis my favorite time, those sunsets over the Sound. It never fails to remind me that the Lord is sovereign over all.

14 May 1692

We received word from the mainland that an act of Parliament in London transferred Nantucket, Martha's Vineyard, and the Elizabeth Islands to Massachusetts. But at least Nantucket is our own county.

After all, some think we are our own country.

9

Hitty invited Maria Mitchell and Anna Gardner for tea at the Grand House a few days after the debut edition of the *Illumine* had been published.

"This," Maria said, "has shaken up the island. Rattled people's cages." She tapped the paper resting on the dining room table. "Good for Henry! I didn't think he had it in him."

Hitty opened her mouth to object to Maria's slight on her brother, but before she could say anything, Anna blurted out, "I've resigned my teaching post!"

"What?" Hitty said. "But why?"

"I can't teach under these circumstances."

Maria added a spoonful of molasses into her teacup. She did not care for sugar. "And how did the school committee receive thy news?"

Anna folded her arms against her chest. "They said I had no cause to quit."

Maria snorted at that. "There's plenty of cause! Thee has upset the apple cart with Eunice Ross." She slapped the table with the palms of her hands. "'Tis time for this island to step forward. To be a beacon of light for others."

"Maria," Hitty said, carefully choosing her words, "is it true that the Atheneum is closed to Nantucket blacks?"

Maria kept her eyes on the top of her teacup. "Most visitors are elderly men of leisure. When they talk, I close my book and take out my knitting."

"But is that true?" Anna said. "Is Hitty correct? Are these elderly men of leisure only white men?"

Maria sighed. "'Tis true."

Anna stared at her for a long moment. "Thee has never said anything about it."

"I'm not proud of it."

"Maria! The Atheneum is our town library. Something must be done."

"I don't disagree, Anna," Maria said, "but what can be done?"

"Thee is the librarian!"

"Exactly! I am an employee. 'Tis my only source of employment. Thee knows my family counts on my income."

The unstable finances of the Mitchells were well known on the island, not unlike Hitty and Henry's family situation. It was something Maria and Hitty had in common, and it drew them together. By contrast, the Gardner family was quite well to do, content in a large Orange Street home with a scrimshaw mortgage button firmly attached to the newel post.

"I certainly don't want to teach again. I thoroughly dislike children. Anna, were I to create agitation, I would lose my job."

"Thy father is the trustees' president!"

"I have spoken to him about the barring of Africans." She lifted her palms in the air. "Do not look at me like that. I have!"

"Then what has he said?"

"'Tis not as simple as thee believes it to be, Anna. There are many trustees who are devout segregationists."

Anna slammed her fists on the tabletop, rattling the teacups. "Devout Quakers too, I suspect. They are abolitionists, while remaining segregationists. Politically open-minded but not socially. 'Tis the worst hypocrisy of all." She exhaled a puff of air. "We must be willing to take a stand against injustice."

"Is that what thee did?" Hitty asked. "Did thee quit because thee was taking a stand?"

"Of course! What's the point? If I can't teach a child to reach for more, then . . . what is the point?"

When Hitty asked her if Henry was aware that she had resigned the teaching post, Anna's eyes narrowed, ever so slightly. "Henry did not inform me of his plan to publish Eunice's story."

"Would thee have objected?"

"Nay," Anna said thoughtfully. "But I would have liked to have been prepared. I could have given him the full story. I think important details were missed. Mayhap more information could have made the difference."

"But he wasn't writing from thy perspective alone, Anna."

"Still, I felt rather blindsided."

That was fair enough, Hitty mulled, as Anna and Maria debated the injustices on the island. Anna's logic rested on the premise of all or none. If she couldn't get Eunice into public high school, she wouldn't teach any child.

Henry's first week as a newspaper editor and publisher was full of unexpected moments. He was astounded at the response of the *Illumine*'s debut issue, surprised and overjoyed. It was creating vigorous dialogue, and challenged thinking, and that, he decided, was the purpose of a newspaper. Marie-Claire had said that very thing to him this morning at breakfast. "'Tis not for a newspaper to tell people how to think," she said, "but to get people to think." It surprised him to hear such an astute remark out of such a young woman.

Philemon, his grandmother's solemn butler—who seemed more solemn than usual today—brought Henry a cup of tea, even though he had not asked for it. The tall man paused for a moment, until Henry looked up and said, "Thee seems cast down."

"Nay, sir." Philemon turned to leave the room, then pivoted around. "Aye, sir. It is wrong that my granddaughter has been kept from getting more education." He straightened his shoulders. "But it is right that you tried to do something about it with your newspaper."

Henry rose to his feet. "I will keep trying, Philemon. So will Anna Gardner. And there are others, too, many others, who want Eunice to have a chance at higher education on this island. She deserves a chance. This isn't over."

Philemon's calm response surprised him. "Changing minds takes time. It happens one by one."

Marie-Claire had been at the table, observing their interaction. She watched Philemon leave the room, a thoughtful expression on her face, then must have felt Henry's eyes on her, for she glanced at him and blushed, and quickly turned her attention back to breakfast.

Another surprise came to him when he met with Anna later that day for a walk along the beach and she blamed him for feeling the need to quit. It baffled him, for she was the one who had sought to challenge the school committee. He had only reported it.

Anna stood on the sand in front of him with her legs braced and arms akimbo, reminding him of the way sailors stood on a ship's deck, to keep from getting pitched to and fro. The wind was kicking up and she held on to her bonnet strings. "Why did thee not tell me?"

"I am sorry, Anna. I see now that I should have. But at the time, I was gathering facts about the story, writing it up, and then rushing to get the copy to Zebadiah to typeset. I was thoroughly engaged in the project." Wasn't that what she had wanted in him? Passion, commitment, action?

She gave him a long, hard look. "Thee added quotes by the segregationists."

He rubbed the back of his neck with his hand. "I just wanted to set the record straight, that's all. I felt obliged to include their point of view, even if I don't agree with it. The *Illumine* abides by the equal-time rule."

"Henry, thee is the editor. Thee makes up the rules."

Henry met her gaze. Anna had a clear way of looking at things. The problem was, Henry didn't see it that way and he resented the patronizing tone in her voice. "Not *that* rule, Anna. 'Tis the gold standard of good journalism." He gave the churning sea a cursory look. There was a storm coming, he could forecast by the color of the grayish green water and the whitecaps licking the surface. "Aside from that, did thee approve the story?"

She paused, just long enough for him to know she did not. "There were important details missing."

"Such as?"

"Eunice taught herself to read. She has mathematical skills that astound Maria Mitchell."

Henry fought back a stab of impatience. As it happened, he had sought out the full story on the situation, interviewing many to get a variety of angles. "I did state that her scores were at the top of the class, beyond all Nantucket children."

"Of course, why let the facts get in the way?" Anna cut in sharply.

Henry hadn't meant to challenge Anna, but he could see from her expression that his response had risen her ire.

"I do appreciate the effort thee made, Henry," she added, a little more softly. "I truly do. But it wasn't enough."

Nay, it never was. He could never seem to hit the right note with her. Why did he vex her so?

She started up the beach.

"Anna, hold up a moment. The school committee has paid for an advertisement to hire a teacher for the African School. They are seeking a male teacher. I wanted thee to hear it from me first."

She stopped, and the look on her face made his stomach twist and turn. He could see she was trying not to look as shocked as she felt. Her eyes grew glassy and she bit her lip. He had known she was bitterly disappointed by the Nantucket town meeting over denying Eunice Ross a chance to attend high school, but with this news, he could see she also felt betrayed by it. "I thank thee for telling me, Henry," she said quietly.

He felt an impulse to wrap his arms around her and hide her face against his chest, to do what he could to take away that sadness. "Anna, don't lose heart. There are plenty of opportunities to teach on the island. I thought I might speak to the headmaster of the Admiral Coffin School and see what he might suggest."

"Oh, Henry," she sighed in that voice that made him feel glad he hadn't tried to embrace her. "It isn't about finding a teaching job. I was making such a difference at the African School. Who will they get to replace me? Someone who doesn't have the same vision. Someone who sees the black children as inferior to the white children. It's not enough to just get another teaching job. I wanted *that* job."

Then why did thee resign? he wondered. *Why not stay and keep on making a difference? Why does it have to be all or none? Thy way . . . or no way?* Yet, what was the point of arguing? There was no winning with Anna.

She moved away from him and folded her arms against her chest. Heavy gray clouds scudded across the sun, and Henry felt suddenly chilled.

"Thee has made some good points, Henry, and I'm going to think about all thee has said. Honestly, I will."

She won't, Henry realized, reading Anna's closed expression.

Mary Coffin Starbuck

21 September 1695

Autumn has arrived. The first frosts have come, and with them the leaves have turned a riot of color, from reds to oranges to yellows. Nature is putting on its final show of the year. And oh, the stars! How they shine in the dark.

It was my father who gave me an extraordinary interest in the night sky, and his mother was the one he credited for giving him such a love for stars. The last words his mother told him, as he set sail from England for the colonies, never to return, were to remember that when he gazed upon the night sky, she would be gazing at the very same stars, though an ocean apart.

As a child in Salisbury, I remember standing outside the house on cold, clear nights with my father. He took my hand in his to trace the constellations, as if we were merely connecting one dot to another. "Remembering Mama," he would say, in a voice that cracked slightly as he said it.

And now, living on an island, the stars have an entirely new meaning to us, for they help sailors determine their location and guide them to their destination. They have brought my Nathaniel home from the sea more than a few times.

But what I love most about stargazing is that it reminds me of how very small I am, and how very big the Almighty is. Gnawing worries and troubles seem to melt away, leaving me with a sense of awe and wonder. I often *think of the psalmist who looked up at the very same stars and felt the very same way, thousands of years ago.*

"When I consider thy heavens, the work of thy fingers, the moon and the stars, which thou hast ordained; What is man, that thou art mindful of him? and the son of man, that thou visitest him?"

18 October 1695

A man and his wife arrived from Cape Cod today and stopped in the store to wait out the rain. They are considering a move to the island and had a few questions. A fear of the Indians is always foremost on visitors' minds. They can set their mind at ease, I tell them, as the Wampanoags are friendly. What are the hardships of the island? Isolation, I say. Are Nantucketers friendly to newcomers? Mostly.

And then the man asked a few uncommon questions. Was the population of Nantucket growing? Indeed, I said. Nearly seven hundred settlers now. But with so few trees, the man asked, what did we use to heat our homes? Anything and everything that we could find to burn, I told him. With the one exception of my magnificent oak tree, I thought but did not say aloud.

I offered them both mugs of my mullein tea and a warm spot to sit by the fire. The man sat right down, staring at the flames. His wife sidled up to me to whisper, "Is there any truth to the notion that Nantucket's sea air can improve a sour disposition?"

She was an exceptionally attractive woman, blond and blue eyed, skin like fresh cream, with a pink blush to her cheeks, and she spoke English in an accent I couldn't place. It had an unfamiliar lilt (German, mayhap?) that only added to her charm. By the twinkle in her eye, I gathered she was referring to her husband, for he was the disagreeable sort. He had nothing but complaints about Nantucket. Rain, fog, moors, the lack of civilization, the Wampanoags and their dogs as they came in and out of the store, nuisances all. And he made those complaints while he sat comfortably by my fire and drank tea.

I thought carefully of how to answer, for I did not wish to raise the hackles of her husband any more than they were. "I do believe that for some it does the trick," I told her. "Of course, others might spend an entire lifetime here, and it wouldn't do a thing."

She smiled at me, and I found her quite enchanting.

I hope they decide to move here. I think we could be friends. And then I realized . . . I did not even ask her name!

10

Jeremiah woke before daybreak and dressed in the shadows of his room. Down in the kitchen he drank a cup of strong tea with a slice of bread and butter, then another slice of bread with jam. He slipped out of the house, closed the door behind him, and stood on the porch, relieved. He'd beaten Cook to the kitchen this morning, and even ol' Philemon to the door.

And then there was outfoxing Hitty. His granddaughter watched him like a hawk, convinced he was knocking at death's door. The cough, it was finally loosening up, and he was eager to get out of the house, to fill his weary lungs with bracing sea air. To see the changing colors of autumn in the trees before all the leaves were gone. Best of all, to smoke his scrimshaw pipe in peace, a vice that Hitty would not allow. She claimed it hurt his lungs and filled the house with the lingering scent of tobacco.

Fie! No wonder he never remarried. Women were such fusspots. Most, anyway. Not his darling Angelica, but most.

He stood on the porch for a moment and took a long, deep breath. The air was frigid, a sign of winter's coming. He felt the sharp cold travel deep in his lungs and choked down the coughing it triggered, as he had no desire to wake his meddlesome granddaughter. Slowly, he felt his head clear. It was a fine day to take a walk.

Slowly, he made his way through town and down to the harbor. Nearing the water, he suddenly felt exhausted by the exertion. He spotted his favorite bench and staggered to it, landing with a loud grunt. He sat a very long time, oblivious to the cold, until his heart stopped pounding and his breathing slowed. He didn't want anyone to see him huffing and puffing like an old man. No doubt they would tell Hitty, and she'd never leave him be.

Elisha plopped down next to him on the bench, puffing on his pipe. He was a low-ranking sailor who lived his life at sea, spending his lay before he earned it. "I heard y' been sick. I see yer on deck." Up and around.

Jeremiah glanced at him, then back at the wharf. "How are y' today, Elisha?"

"Above average, I'd say." He nodded to himself with a cheerful air that did seem above average. "I got some news. Someone's donated money to cobble Main Street. The entire street, right up to the bank." He elbowed Jeremiah. "I'm guessing it's one of them hoity-toity captains down on Orange Street."

"Probably right." *Wrong.* Jeremiah knew Henry was behind the cobbling, but his grandson had made him promise not to say a word to anyone else. The cobbles were coming from Europe, but a paving work crew would come from the mainland to do the work.

"Them captains, they's so high and mighty. Thinking they can just sprinkle their pennies and pence around the island," he said, rubbing his fingertips together in the air, "like fairy dust."

Jeremiah took offense at that sweeping assessment, as his son was a sea captain who had once lived on Orange Street. "Y' don't want cobbles on the road? Y' prefer walkin' through mud puddles and who knows what else?"

Elisha ignored him. "Why not just say who's shellin' out the cash? Why does it have to be a big secret? I spent a lifetime bowing and groveling to them sea captains. Now I got to do more of it in m' sunset years."

"Elisha, y' need more on yer mind."

Elisha shrugged. "Now yer sounding like m' wife." He frowned. "So who do y' think this do-gooder is?"

Jeremiah opened one eye. "Mayhap it's more than one. Mayhap 'tis a group of kindhearted folk who want t' remain unknown."

"Them Friends, y' mean?" Elisha huffed. "Sounds like something they would do. Fix the island and not take credit for it." He elbowed Jeremiah. "Y' dinnae think they're from Martha's Vineyard, do y'? Oh, that would be a jab in the pride to them Flat Hats."

Jeremiah considered himself to be one of those Flat Hats, out of deference to his beloved mother, though he was an extremely casual one and took no offense at derogatory remarks. Usually, he agreed with them. "Elisha, why do y' even care? So the island is getting a little window dressing. She needs it."

"More than a little window dressing, Jeremiah! Someone is trying to dress this island up in a fancy frock. And I dinnae like it."

"For heaven's sake, why not?"

"I was born on this island."

"As was I."

"And I'll die here."

"As will I."

"I don't want anything to change."

Jeremiah looked at him, astounded by such a narrow attitude. Change was long overdue on this island. It troubled him greatly to hear Elisha's kind of thinking, because he wasn't alone in it. Plenty of islanders resisted change. He'd long been concerned that Nantucket seemed stuck. Look at the story of Eunice Ross, a story that irked Jeremiah to the very core. A bright young girl like her, unable to get a proper education. *Shame on you, Nantucket Island! Shame on the school committee that denied her.*

But Elisha wouldn't understand that.

"Those Vineyarders . . . wouldn't that be just like them? Come in with a smile, and hit us below the belt. I never liked Old Town Turkey."

"Why not?"

"Because . . ." He gave Jeremiah a look as if it was obvious. "They're not us." He rose to his feet and rambled on.

A few weeks after the *Illumine* debuted, Benjamin Foulger came to the Grand House with distressing news. It was midafternoon; Henry was at his newspaper, Marie-Claire had gone to post some letters, Jeremiah had gone out for a walk despite Hitty's fervent objection that it would tax him. He hadn't listened to her—he never did.

Hitty was upstairs in her room, hiding from the servants. They still made her uncomfortable, for she would barely start to do a little housekeeping and they would whisk in and take over. Moments ago, she noticed that the fireplace mantel was dusty, so she took out her handkerchief to wipe it off and *whoosh!* a housemaid intercepted her handkerchief in midwave and finished the dusting. Ridiculous! There was nothing she could say to stop them. They were determined to be . . . good servants. How could she fault them for that? She couldn't. But she also couldn't sit idle. Instead, she stayed mostly in her room when the others were not at home.

As she took her needlework out of the basket, the brass knocker on the front door rapped once, then twice. Her pulse jumped when she heard a male voice downstairs, then jumped again when she recognized the speaker. She checked the small mirror over her washstand, tucked her curls under her cap, pinched her cheeks, assessed herself with a disappointed sigh, and hurried downstairs. Benjamin Foulger stood in the foyer, dressed in a traveling overcoat with a stark and somber look on his handsome face. "I apologize for the intrusion, Hitty. I've just arrived from Boston with some bad tidings to tell."

Nearing the bottom of the steps, Hitty stilled. Father and Daphne. The *Endeavour* had gone missing. And now they were dead! The mere thought of such an outcome brought a wave of tears to her eyes. "I feared this very thing!" She covered her cheeks with her hands. "I didn't want them to go!"

"Who's gone? What has thee feared?" Benjamin looked confused, alarmed by her strong reaction.

"My father and Daphne! The *Endeavour* has gone missing. That's thy bad tidings, is it not?"

"Nay. Nay! No ship has gone missing. Calm thyself! My tiding concerns Oliver Combs. He has had a stroke. A massive one that has left him impaired. But he lives, for that we can thank God."

"Oh dear," Hitty said, her hands dropping to her side.

"I'm sorry to hear of this." Oliver Combs had been their grandmother's attorney for as long as Hitty could remember. "Will he fully recover?"

"Hopefully. It will take time, of course."

From the look on Benjamin's face, Hitty did not think he had much confidence in that.

"I will be required to spend more time in Boston, at least for the foreseeable future. I'll be handling Oliver's clients . . . until he recovers. Marie-Claire will be able to handle any needs here that arise. I'll be back and forth from Boston to Nantucket, as often as I can return."

"Benjamin, thee is doing just what Oliver would want thee to do—to carry on."

"Thank thee, Hitty. I came to give thee the news in person. I do not want thee to worry. The inheritance is in good hands." He smiled at her and squeezed her shoulder. "I'm off now, to track down my able secretary."

"She went to town to post a letter."

"I know. I saw her from a distance, heading into the post office."

He came to me first! No one ever delivered tidings to Hitty first. Always to Henry. She could barely hold back a grin.

He put a hand on the door and turned back to Hitty. "This arrangement, with Marie-Claire living here, 'tis working out? Thee can be candid. I can seek other lodging for her if thee would prefer."

His concern touched her. "Marie-Claire is . . . she's wonderful, Benjamin." And she was. He gave her a relieved smile, tipped his hat, and hurried down the walk. Hitty watched his long, confident strides, hearing the crunch of his boots on the shell path, until Philemon appeared to close the door.

Hitty went back upstairs, thinking of how Marie-Claire's arrival at the Grand House added the warmth and companionship she longed for, as her brother was rarely at home and her grandfather was not much of a conversationalist. Plus, she had proved herself extremely helpful to Hitty and Henry. Somehow she had learned of an old battleship for sale in a Salem shipyard and presented it as a possibility for Isaac's lightship, saving the costs of building one from scratch. Isaac was intrigued by the notion of outfitting an existing ship and, greatly encouraged, hastened to finish the Fresnel lens he'd been constructing.

It pleased her to think of Marie-Claire staying on longer at the Grand House. She was sorry, though, genuinely sorry about Oliver Combs's ailment. While Hitty did not consider him to have much personality, anyone who could stay long in their grandmother's good graces deserved a medal. Certainly not a stroke.

Anna walked beside Henry, lost in thought. He waited for her to speak first.

Anna had spent most of autumn brooding over the school committee's veto to allow Eunice Ross to attend the public high school, wondering what she could do to change their mind. It was all she could talk about. "I don't understand it, Henry. Islanders are unified in opposing slavery—after all, there are over five hundred fugitive or freed slaves on this island! And many more to come. Yet the white islanders overwhelmingly support a segregated society."

"Not overwhelmingly, Anna. Many islanders support integration. Many Friends do. Changing minds requires patience." Hadn't Philemon, Eunice's grandfather, told him that very thing?

They were standing above the beach as they talked, at a spot on the footpath near a fragrant thicket of bayberry that filled the air with its brisk heady scent. She turned away from him to look at the horizon. Puffy white clouds filled the sky and hid the sun, but suddenly a ray of light beamed down on Anna, limning her hair. Henry's breath was nearly taken away as he was struck by her beauty. And her sadness.

The truth was, he hated to see her wallow in discouragement. The way he looked at it, giving in to discouragement did no good at all. He reached out to her and put his arms around her, and she leaned against him. "Anna, it's going to be all right."

Anna sighed, and he tucked her head under his chin. It was more of a comforting hug than anything else, he knew, but he loved the feeling of holding her close. She pulled away a bit and tipped her head back to look up at him. He had the impulse to kiss her, but then she slipped out of his grasp and the moment was lost.

"It's wrong, Henry. Just so wrong. Last week's town meeting spent more time on debating the installation of gaslights on Main Street than the school committee spent on Eunice Ross."

He knew. He'd been there, taking notes for an article for the *Illumine*.

"The streets of Paris and London are being lit with Nantucket whales," she said. "And because Main Street will be under construction for the cobbling of the road, the selectmen think it's high time for our streets to be lit, as well. And then there was another lengthy and tedious debate about adding cisterns below the street."

"Those aren't bad things, Anna. The cisterns are intended for fire fighting."

She stopped and lifted her hands. "Exactly! The rich islanders take fine care of their own possessions, but do they show concern for those who have less? 'Tis only Main Street that is getting such attention." A pair of screeching gulls arced overhead and she frowned, watching them soar. "Apparently, some rich whale master has donated money to cobble Main Street."

"So I heard," Henry said, rubbing his chin. "Did thee hear who might be the benefactor?" Keeping that information from Anna, he hoped, was not a lie of omission. Friends did not lie. They did omit.

"Who knows? Who cares! Stones are being shipped over from Europe. *Such* extravagance. Why not just pave it in gold?"

Henry felt his jaw drop. He was barely able to hold back his frustration. Once again, he'd run smack up against Anna's idealism, headfirst into a brick wall. He'd hoped she would have been pleased to learn about the cobblestones. Finding those cobbles was no easy task. Marie-Claire had spent months finding a river source in Europe where the stones would have been smoothed and polished by years of rolling along on currents. They were round and greystoned, intended to ease traveling for horses and carts. "The island has no cobbles, Anna. Only sand. They had to be imported from somewhere."

She rolled her eyes. "Thee is missing my point."

"Anna, dearest, I am sorry. I'm sorry. I'm sorry about everything, but I'm not the one thee should be angry with. I know it is disappointing about Eunice. But not now doesn't mean not ever."

Anna was silent for a moment. "Can't thee see, Henry? Islanders will not change, not without some serious provoking. I'd hoped Eunice Ross would be the catalyst for the school committee to allow integration, but I was wrong. Now I can see it won't come from within. There needs to be external pressure."

She grew quiet then; as her expression relaxed a little, a very thoughtful look came over her. He wondered what was going through her mind. Anna's thought process was strident and forceful, and he knew better than to get tangled in the middle of it. His thought process was slow and logical and deliberate—the opposite of Anna's. He only frustrated her when he tried to help.

Anna walked down the path that led to the shore, and he followed a few steps behind. Her commitment, her single-mindedness, her determination . . . they were inspiring. She had a hunger within that could not be quenched, not until every wrong on this island was made right. He did wonder, though, when would it ever be enough? If Eunice Ross had been admitted into the public high school, would that have satisfied Anna? Or would she march on to tackle another injustice?

He caught up with her to ask, "Isn't there something I can do to help you figure out what to do next?"

She spun around to face him, her eyes lit up. "But I know what I shall do next. I know exactly."

"What?"

She smiled, the first smile he had seen on her in weeks, but it lacked warmth. "And have it reported in the next issue of the *Illumine* before I am ready to reveal it? I think not." She patted him on the arm as she passed him, hurrying down the beach. She wasn't waiting for him. *That* was clear.

Mary Coffin Starbuck

14 November 1695

A delightful surprise has occurred! The man and his wife from the mainland (whose names, I have since learned, are William and Elsa Coleman) have moved to Nantucket! They are settling near some marshland that William has leased from the Swains. Apparently, William is a relation to Christopher Swain. (~~That accounts for his sour disposition.~~)

I had to wonder why they would choose such a low, swampy area. Nathaniel said that Christopher Swain has let him stay on the land without rent. William plans to harvest peat from the bogs, dry it, and sell it as heating fuel. Now I understand his peculiar concern about how we stay warm in the winter.

10 December 1695

Elsa Coleman came into the store today with a faded bruise on her cheek, that pale yellow and purple of a healing wound. "It is nothing," she said, when I asked after it. She laughed at herself. "I am very ungeschickt . . . how do I say? . . . clumsy. I am clumsy."

I sat by the fire with her, for the store was quiet and my son was going over the accounting book. (He doesn't like me to hover nearby when he works.) Elsa and I drank tea and talked for more than an hour's time. Suddenly, she jumped up in a panic. "Coffee! Wilhelm sent me for his coffee." I packaged her bundle and watched through the *window as she hurried home. It felt as if we'd known each other for years, yet it had been only a month's time.*

As she reached the bend in the road, Elsa passed Martha Hussey, Stephen's wife. Most likely, she was coming to the store to deliver another complaint.

Strange, isn't it, how some friendships are so spontaneous and easy, and some so laborious.

11

Henry had barely seen Anna over the winter months. Each time he'd dropped by 40 Orange Street, he was told she was working on her project at the Atheneum. He hesitated to interrupt her, because she had been very clear that she would tell him about the project only when she was ready to, and that time hadn't come yet.

On a sunny afternoon, he happened to bump into her on Federal Street, and they chatted a bit. He asked after her project and she said it was coming along swimmingly. She spoke with animation and it pleased him to see her so happy.

Then he told her about the article he was working on for the *Illumine*—about the coming of the first lightship—and she listened for a while, then seemed distracted. "I'm sorry, Henry, but I must be off. I have some letters to post before day's end." She turned and started walking, and he fell into step beside her. He had the urge to take her hand but didn't dare.

"Mayhap thee could come for dinner at the Grand House soon?"

"That sounds lovely. I'd like that, Henry." A church bell

chimed and she turned toward the sound, then started off again.

"Anytime, Anna," he called after her. "Come anytime. Whenever it works."

She lifted her hand in a half wave to acknowledge the invitation, adding "Soon! I'll come soon!" and that was some consolation. Henry watched her hurry down the street with that telltale stride she had—he would know her particular gait anywhere—and wished he could get rid of the funny hollow feeling in his chest. Much of what he found appealing in Anna was her commitment, so what right did he have to get upset when she put other things first?

Most mornings, Jeremiah would walk from one end of the village to the other and back again. He'd take his spot on his favorite bench near the waterfront, pack his pipe, have a long, satisfying smoke, and watch the Pass. All kinds of people strolled past, including fair maidens. It wasn't like back in his day, when maidens dared not walk too close to the wharf. Nowadays, young maids had more freedom. And he wasn't so old that he didn't enjoy the view of a pretty girl.

Throughout the morning, groups of fishermen gathered there, setting out for their workday on the water. He listened to them talk about boats or boast about the size of a catch. He heard them argue and complain, compare prices, or guess when Maine lobsters would swim down from cold waters. Jeremiah listened, grateful he was near them but not with them. He'd had enough of coaxing a living from the sea. It was no wonder the sea was oft likened to a fickle woman. Men fell head over heels in love with her, yet she loved none of them back. He knew that truth now, but he'd had to learn it for himself. All seamen did. The wise ones, like his son Reynolds, learned it young.

Jeremiah looked up, squinting against the bright sunlight that shone down on the buildings of Main Street. He was there to check on the cobbling, to see its progression over the last few days since the cobble-bearing ship had arrived from Europe. This was a significant stride forward on the island, to have a road cobbled. Martha's Vineyard, he noted with pleasure, had none.

The part of the street where the crew worked had been sectioned off so no horses and drays or carts could get through. A mere foot of cobbles had been laid, with many crewmen standing around arguing while only one or two actually laid the cobbles. He saw piles of smooth rocks set around the marked-off section. This would be a painfully slow venture.

A dory came in from a schooner and dropped a fellow off on the wharf. Something about the way this man jumped from the dory to the wharf struck an oddly familiar chord, but Jeremiah couldn't recall whom it belonged to. He watched him as he strode down the wharf, but when he passed not far from Jeremiah on the bench, he turned away before a good look could be had. It left Jeremiah with a vague uneasiness, a feeling he'd had quite a bit these last few months. A nameless, gnawing worry.

Maybe it was the feeling of coming in from the cold, or maybe that long bout of grippe had taken more of a toll on him than he had expected; it certainly had stolen his strength and not returned it. As he approached the Grand House, he felt a keen gratitude to be going there, rather than living alone in the cramped, drafty Easy Street cooperage.

The softly glowing lamplight, the scent of good cooking that wafted through the house, the warm welcome by his granddaughter.

Somehow, Hitty had done this. She had turned the large, cold house into a comforting home. Some people were just born with a certain buoyant spirit that didn't desert them, no matter what. Hitty was like that. And with that pleasant thought, Jeremiah put any lingering unsettled feeling from the stranger in the dory out of his mind.

It was more difficult to give away money than Henry could have imagined. Through Benjamin and Marie-Claire's help, he'd tried to anonymously provide money to different organizations on the island to help them with their projects. To his surprise, the organizations were delighted to receive money but didn't want to be told what to do with it. For example, he'd noticed that the Atheneum's main room floor was in seriously poor condition—rotting boards that sagged and splintered. He tried to quietly donate funds to replace the old floor and discovered, quite accidentally—only because Hitty had spoken to Maria Mitchell, the librarian—that they hadn't used it for a new floor at all, but for a rare collector's edition of *King Lear* by William Shakespeare. While Henry was a proponent of reading fine literature, he still worried about that sagging floor. It was an accident waiting to happen.

But Henry had learned an important lesson from the Atheneum's sagging floor. Careless generosity was not particularly helpful. Since then, he'd grown savvier, adding tighter parameters to each donation.

On his mind was the next benefactor project: Isaac's lightship.

Earlier in the week, he had interviewed Isaac to write a story about the lightship with the Fresnel lens, soon to launch. Isaac came to the *Illumine*'s office and settled into a chair across from Henry's desk.

"I'd like to get some background for the story," Henry said.

"I don't have much time. Hitty offered to watch Bitsy into the noon hour, but I don't want to take advantage of her kindness."

"My sister speaks fondly of Bitsy," Henry said, watching carefully to note Isaac's reaction. Well, well, look at that. The man's cheeks flamed red! How about that. Mayhap Isaac Barnard did have a beating heart, after all. He took out his quill and uncorked the ink bottle. Dipping the quill in the ink bottle, he glanced up at Isaac, all business. "So what is thy motive behind the lightship for Nantucket?"

"My motive?" Isaac blinked once, then twice. He took off his spectacles to polish them.

"Aye. What has spurred on this unique concept?"

"'Tis not entirely unique. There are other lightships. The Fresnel lens, that has not been installed on a lightship before." He cleared his throat and put his spectacles back on. "So then, my motive." His hands clasped the brim of his hat in his lap. His eyes were fixed on the hat as he turned it round and round. "My father was a fisherman. He knew these waters like the back of his hand. But one day, thick fog settled in—you know that heavy, dense fog—and his ship foundered on shoals. He was not far from land, yet"—he hesitated and his voice quavered—"he did not survive."

"I'm sorry, Isaac. I did not know." But he should have.

Henry set down the quill and stopped taking notes. "What of the fire alarm thee has worked on?" When Isaac looked up, confused, he added, "Hitty mentioned it to me."

"That invention is still . . . well, it requires more consideration."

"But why a fire alarm?"

"Why?" Isaac kept his gaze on his hat, planted on his knees. "My wife, she died in a fire." He lifted his head to gaze out the window. "We were living in Truro, over on the Cape, near my wife's family. There'd been a storm that day, and so I had taken Bitsy down to the beach to scavenge. To see what the storm had turned up on the shore. While we were gone, the hearth fire . . . the broom had been set too close to it. The broom caught fire. My wife was upstairs, resting. By the time she realized a fire had started below, it was . . . too late. She died of smoke inhalation. If there had been some kind of warning system, mayhap she could have gotten out." His eyes returned to his hat, turning, turning, turning the brim. "My wife, she was resting because . . . she was great with child." He glanced at the door, as if he wanted to leave. "I returned to Nantucket . . . for a fresh start."

Henry had no idea of this man's story, only that he had been born here, left the island, then returned suddenly and inexplicably with a child, and that he tinkered with inventions while everyone else was involved with whaling. He doubted even Hitty knew Isaac's story. He doubted anyone knew. How could they? Isaac kept himself to himself. "So, that is thy idea for a fire alarm? To warn of smoke?"

Isaac nodded. "As I said, it has not yet been successful."

Henry looked at the man with admiration. Isaac Barnard wanted to make the world a safer place. He kept persevering at different inventions, all with a theme of safety. Henry had never noticed that theme, only the theme of failure. He felt ashamed for belittling him.

"Is that all?" Isaac seemed quite uncomfortable.

"Nay. Nay, I'd like to hear more about this lightship, Isaac." Henry picked up the quill.

"Lightships are floating offshore lighthouses," Isaac said quickly, far more at ease with a less personal conversation, then launched into the benefits of the lightship on an island like Nantucket, with shallow and dangerous shoals.

As Isaac opened up, Henry wrote as quickly as he could. He had greatly underestimated this man. Hitty had not.

As he listened to the thoughts of the gentle, reserved man, Henry thought it was rather unfortunate, for his sister's sake, that Isaac Barnard was not a Quaker.

Hitty watched Isaac swing Bitsy up on his shoulders as they headed down Centre Street, an ache in her heart. She knew Henry had asked him to come to the newspaper office to be interviewed about the lightship, so she'd offered to watch Bitsy after the Cent School ended for the day. Afterward, she had asked him how the interview went, hoping he might stay and share details with her, but he seemed in a hurry. Mostly, he seemed all out of words for the day. He barely gave her thanks for staying late to watch Bitsy.

That man. Isaac had such a small amount of words to share with others in a day's time; no doubt Henry used them up. It was slow going, this relationship. *There is no relationship*, she could hear her brother insist.

Give it time, Henry, though she wondered. Mayhap she

should accept the facts. Isaac did not care for her as she cared for him, and for Bitsy.

"Hitty, how fares thee?"

She whirled around to face Benjamin Foulger, looking dashing in a charcoal-gray wool long overcoat. "I'm . . . fine." She hadn't seen him in quite some time. The weather had been inclement, and she knew he'd been absorbed with Oliver's work.

"How has winter gone?"

"Cold," she said. He gazed around the keeping room in a way that made her feel self-conscious. "How is Oliver?" From the look on his face as she mentioned his name, she could tell the elderly lawyer was not in good condition. "He is not recovering?"

Benjamin shook his head. "Unable to speak intelligibly. 'Tis quite a sad thing."

"Can he not write his thoughts? Or point to letters to communicate?" Hitty had an elderly cousin who suffered a stroke, but she was able to hold a pen and print out her demands and opinions. Quite a few of them, as Hitty recalled.

A surprised look flittered through Benjamin's eyes. "I hadn't thought to ask his attendant." His voice trailed off on a vague note. "The sounds he makes . . . they are jibberish . . . I assumed his thoughts were equally tangled." He looked away. "I will seek an answer to that question when I return to Boston. I thank thee, Hitty, for mentioning it." He smiled, and his eyes rested on her face. He seemed pleased by what he saw. "Thee is a constant surprise to me."

She smiled to mask an oddly familiar feeling—how a sparrow felt near a popinjay.

Henry had to admit that Marie-Claire was everything Benjamin had promised her to be—competent, astute, intelligent, determined. Artistic too. She had a sketchbook filled with remarkable likenesses.

What he hadn't expected was that she was also deeply religious. He found her each morning at the small desk in the parlor, the one beneath the east-facing window, where the morning sun would contour her young profile in light, her high cheekbones and wide mouth, the soft curls that framed her face—unlike Hitty's curls, which were more like unruly corkscrews. Marie-Claire's Bible was always open, and she studied it diligently.

When had he ever read the Bible diligently? Never.

This morning at breakfast, Hitty commented on how attendance was dwindling at First Day Meeting. "Did thee hear how long this week's list was for the Book of Objections? The disownment for absenteeism went on and on."

Henry nodded. Anna Gardner's name was on that list, as was Maria Mitchell's. Soon, who would be left? Only a few cotton tops, along with Henry and Hitty. "I fear the Friends are becoming irrelevant."

"But God," Marie-Claire said in that calm and confident way that had become familiar to him, "he is always relevant."

A jolt went through Henry with those words and left him with a pounding heart. He spent much time criticizing the Society of Friends, even while sitting in Meeting. But God was not confined to a square room, nor a certain way of worshiping. God was not a Quaker, though Anna and Maria and others seemed to think he was. When they dismissed the

Friends, albeit for good reasons, they mistakenly dismissed God.

"Brother Henry, is thee not well?"

He glanced up to see Marie-Claire peer at him with a worried look on her youthful face. "I am very well, Marie-Claire. Thee has given me something more to chew on this morning than a piece of toast."

Mary Coffin Starbuck

17 February 1696

'Tis a winter of sorrow after sorrow.

In early January, a French sloop arrived with four sailors, three of whom had the grippe. Many on our island have succumbed, though the three sailors survived and sailed off. In one month's time, we lost Sarah Macy Worth, an old friend. And then my darling daughter Mary died, followed by daughter Elizabeth's husband.

I must be strong for my family, especially for Nathaniel, for he is suffering greatly over the loss of our firstborn. He loved her so fiercely, and held on to the very end with a confidence that she would rally, even when it was apparent to the rest of us that she was losing the battle. He had done all he could to protect her from the moment she took her first breath on that cold March morning, so many years ago. He simply could not accept the reality that he could not protect her from her last.

My dear friend Elsa Coleman came, in a snowstorm, to help me prepare Mary's body for burial. When I learned that her husband was off island to purchase supplies, I insisted she stay in our home. Her cheerfulness is a great help to me during these dark days.

I labor to be cheerful, but my own heart feels fragile. If one more grave must be dug this winter, I don't know how I shall bear it.

25 March 1696

I have not had the strength to write this winter, and it is not just because the cold has made my fingers clumsy. The fog of Nantucket has settled deep, deep in my soul, affecting my outlook. I know Nathaniel worries about me, and I worry about him. Our hearts have been broken and are slow to mend.

Oh spring, please hurry.

17 April 1696

Elsa Coleman and I took a long walk through the marsh today, hoping to see signs of spring with the return of birds.

Last spring Nathaniel and I took many walks through this marsh, and counted hundreds of different species nesting among the highbush cranberries.

I had claimed there were a thousand varieties of migrating birds. Nathaniel agreed, but said that because I am prone to exaggerate, 'tis best to underestimate and have others believe us, than overestimate and be less credible. A window to our temperaments.

Elsa was enraptured with the nests we found, filled with small and smooth eggs. Some speckled, some colored, all perfect. "Such hope," she said in her German accent. "God must take great pleasure in springtime. Everywhere we see life begin again."

As we walked home, I felt my spirits lift a little. 'Tis a lovely gift to have such a friend as Elsa.

18 May 1696

Tonight, I read Scripture aloud before bedtime, as is our nightly tradition. "Let there be light," I read from Genesis 1. "Let there be an expanse."

Nathaniel asked me to read the passage again, start to finish. "How interesting."

"How so?" 'Tis a very familiar story.

"The very first words out of God's mouth are 'Let there be light.' And then his next action is to separate the atmospheres."

"I'm not sure I follow you," I told him.

"God lifted clouds so that we may walk clearly. Think, Mary. Think of the fog that drenches our island, and how it feels when the sun breaks through and the fog disappears. Our paths are cleared. He miraculously lifts clouds . . . clouds of depression, of aimlessness, of helplessness, of inferiority. It's as if . . . as if we move to a new atmosphere."

This, this is why I love that man.

12

The bright day had darkened into a steely gray afternoon. A pale orange sun began to sink, lighting up the bank of clouds that clung to the horizon. It would rain tonight, Jeremiah knew, for his trick knee was aching. He considered it his own personal weather forecaster and, unlike the *Farmer's Almanac*, never wrong.

He took his time as he strolled, noticing the changes in the seasons as he walked down to his cooperage on Easy Street. There were a few things he wanted to fetch—a favorite old sweater and his best pair of woolen socks. It was apparent that his vigilant granddaughter was never going to let him vacate the Grand House to return to his humble abode. The Grand House, it was a big house. But sometimes, not quite big enough.

Truth be told, he didn't mind so very much. There were moments when he missed the peace and quiet of his cooperage, but not many.

There was something else he wanted to look for in the cooperage. He'd had a thought of making a sign to hang outside the door to Henry's newspaper office. There was a piece of walnut wood he'd saved that might be just the thing.

When he reached the door, he saw that the latch was undone. Was he slipping? He was sure he'd latched it. As he walked inside, he stopped abruptly, and a shiver went down his spine. Someone had been here. He could sense it, as real as his achy knee.

He walked around the small rooms, slowly and carefully, absorbing the sights, sounds, and familiar scents of shaved wood, looking for evidence of thievery. Everything was orderly and in its place, high up off the damp floor, just as his father had always taught it must be. His staves sat in a hoop, the partially constructed barrels lined the far wall, his drawknives still hung above the grinding stone, waiting for him to sharpen them. His shaving horse rested on the floor near the window. His broom leaned against the bench. He remembered sweeping curls of freshly shaved wood when the call sounded for the shipwreck. He'd set it right there and run from the shop.

He turned in a small circle once, then twice. No tool had gone missing, no personal items had been used, nothing had been disturbed.

Why did he feel so sure someone had been in here? Mayhap it was Hitty's endless twaddle about the haunting of the Grand House—making him squirrelly. He loved that girl, but my! she was a high-strung lass.

He shook off his strange feelings—sheer claptrap—and found his sweater and socks. He checked on the piece of walnut, but left it where it was. Suddenly, he felt exhausted. That project could wait for another day. He latched the door and checked it twice.

Late one spring afternoon, Benjamin Foulger dropped by the Grand House with papers to sign. Henry was not at the *Illumine*'s office, he explained to Hitty, so he hoped to find him at the house.

Marie-Claire joined them in the front room and volunteered to go seek Henry, for she thought she knew where he might be. "I believe he said he would be at the Atheneum this afternoon."

Hitty was surprised by Benjamin's hesitancy, as it was most unlike him. He seemed to lose his train of thought, dropping his head to his chest, and didn't answer her. Then he took a deep breath, lifted his head to look right at Hitty, and said that it mattered not whether Hitty or Henry signed them, so long as one of them did. "To keep things moving along," he said, taking the quill from the desk and dipping it in the inkpot.

Hitty hesitated. Henry had been the one to sign the documents that liquidated Grandmother Lillian's assets, for Hitty hated to read, and the details of the documents confused her. But it embarrassed her to confess as much to Benjamin, so she signed without reading them.

When she finished, she gathered them together to hand to Benjamin. He'd been watching her closely, which both pleased her and made her nervous. Was there something on her face? A smudge of charcoal? Before Benjamin had arrived, Marie-Claire had been teaching Hitty how to draw with a piece of charcoal. Awkwardly, she pointed to the sketchbook, left on the desk, just to divert his attention. "Look. See how talented thy secretary is."

But Benjamin was not so easily distracted. He took the

papers from Hitty, looked through each one to make sure they were in order and properly signed, tucked them in his satchel, and latched it. It was only then that he picked up the sketchbook and glanced through each page. "Thee made these drawings, Marie-Claire? They are quite realistic."

Hitty saw her cheeks blush pink. "In my spare time," she said.

Benjamin closed the sketchbook and placed it back on the desk. "So I see," he said, though Hitty wasn't sure what he saw.

After Oliver Combs's stroke, Henry noticed a change come over Benjamin. He lost his affability and seemed brittle, short tempered, even with Marie-Claire. He would come on island for a few days, give Marie-Claire a mountain of corrected paperwork to copy over into legal documents, then leave for Boston and not return again for weeks.

Earlier this afternoon, Henry had stopped by William Geary's hat store to go upstairs where Benjamin had let space in the loft, and was just about to open the door to the loft when he heard Benjamin's raised voice, taut and hard. "Twist not my words!"

"Benjamin!" Marie-Claire sounded upset. "Why is thee so tetchy of late?"

Henry froze. Should he stay? Should he go?

"Thee pummels me with questions. As if thee no longer trusts me."

Henry stayed.

"Not trust thee? Of course I trust thee! How could I not? But I am concerned, Benjamin. Thee seems cast down, exhausted. Ought thee work so constantly? Even on First Day. When was the last time thee went to Meeting?"

"Meeting? I have no time to spare, Sister. Not like thee, who seems to be growing fond of hobbies like the idle rich."

"Hobbies? What hobbies?"

"Thy sketching, for one."

Their voices dropped in intensity, so low that Henry couldn't discern what they were saying, though he did try. He pivoted and went below, careful of his booted steps on the narrow staircase.

William Geary, a gloomy man even on the sunniest of days, looked up from his work desk and gave him a woeful nod.

Hearing Marie-Claire express worry over Benjamin left Henry with an unsettled feeling for the rest of the day, for he had the same concerns. Henry had many plans brewing for the inheritance, particularly for the second portion of it. If Benjamin quit, or if Oliver Combs didn't recover—worse still, if he passed away—then what would happen? He didn't know. He didn't even want to think about it.

The next afternoon, Benjamin dropped by the Grand House for coffee and asked Hitty to show him the cove. "The weather is unseasonably warm today," he said. "It hints of summer." He gave Marie-Claire a kind smile. "My secretary has reminded me to slow down. She is right. And I've long been curious to see thy grandmother's estate from the waterfront." He shook his head. "Forgive me. 'Tis no longer thy grandmother's, but thy property. And thy brother's." He reached a hand out to Hitty. "Would thee mind showing it to me?"

"This afternoon?" Hitty hesitated, not because she had something to do but because the idea of being with Benjamin was strange to her. Alone with him? Might she not bore him, say something stupid or ignorant?

"There's no time like the present."

Hitty turned to Marie-Claire. "Do come with us."

Benjamin cut in. "She has some pressing matters to take care of."

Marie-Claire looked a little surprised, but then her head bobbed up and down. "I do have quite a bit to do. I thank thee for including me, Hitty. Another time."

Hitty looked at Benjamin. "Let me run upstairs to change, then I'll be ready to go."

"Good." He sounded genuinely pleased.

She hurried upstairs to her bedroom. She untied her cap and her hair sprang free. She brushed it back nervously with her fingers, then surveyed herself in the mirror, frowning.

Too plump. Too short. Too . . . everything.

A long dark curl flopped across her face, and she blew it away like a feather.

Oh, what's the point?

She changed her dress, smoothed her hair with her fingertips, and placed her cap back on. That would be enough primping for Benjamin Foulger. As she came downstairs, she saw him waiting for her in the foyer. The look in his eyes dispelled her self-doubts. "The color of that dress suits thee nicely," he noted with an admiring smile. His praise made her feel suddenly shy. When had Hitty ever, ever felt shy? Never!

They walked down the path to the water's edge. She felt awkward, at a loss for conversation. That was strange; talking had always been easy for her. Mayhap this wasn't such a good idea.

A dock jutted out in the cove, with a small sloop tied to it.

"Should that boat be there?"

She'd asked Philemon to have it brought out of the boathouse, to be ready for a day such as this. "'Tis my aunt Daphne's boat. My father's wife. She's an able sailor, the best on the island, says Papa." Hitty felt a sudden sweep of missing Papa and Daphne. Only one letter had arrived, passed along in the Azores to a ship returning to Nantucket. It sounded as if they were having the time of their lives, in no hurry to return. No mention was made of whale hunting.

On the beach now, Benjamin turned in a wide circle. "I find myself rather . . . dazzled by all this."

"All what?"

He lifted his hands up. "Nantucket. The extravagance of it. Its beauty, its history, its people. What has been carved out of this small pork chop–shaped island, thirty miles out to sea . . . it's more than I ever expected."

She watched him as his gaze swept the houses along the cove and landed down at the dock. There was an unusual look in his eyes—and they were truly remarkable eyes. Intensely blue, fringed by dark lashes. Watching him, her stomach did a somersault—there was . . . what was it? . . . stark longing in those eyes. Almost a hunger.

"It must have been wonderful, to grow up with all this."

The tender tone in his voice made her smile. "But I didn't. All this, it belonged to my grandmother, and she rarely included us in her life." He looked surprised, but Hitty was accustomed to that reaction.

"I gathered she was not a particularly agreeable woman—"

Hitty smirked at him.

"—but I didn't realize she hadn't embraced thee as a grandmother should. May I ask why?"

"It had something to do with my mother marrying my father against Grandmother Lillian's wishes."

"Yet I've only heard good reports about thy father."

"Indeed. He's a fine and honorable man. But my grandmother held very strict and old-fashioned notions about people, and he did not suit her taste."

"Even more of a reason for thee and Henry to use the inheritance to indulge thy desires. 'Tis a way of evening the score with thy grandmother. Savor the irony."

She took her time framing her answer. "My father and Daphne may not ever have had much wealth, but they have more than enough love. That was how Henry and I were raised. 'Better a warm cottage than a cold castle.'"

"That was the Centre Street cottage? I've heard it referred to as Petticoat Row."

"Aye. That's my true home." She pointed to the Grand House. "And that has been one cold and lonely castle."

For a split second, he stared at her as if she had suggested the moon and stars had fallen from the sky. Then he recovered and his charming smile returned. "Best of all, I suppose, is to have a warm castle."

She laughed and turned to Daphne's sloop, bobbing in the water. "This weather today is a sailor's delight. Just enough wind but not too much. I haven't gone sailing since last autumn."

"What does thee think? Shall we try it?"

She grinned. "Can thee swim, in the event that we capsize?"

"If anything goes wrong, I'm trusting thee to rescue us."

He feigned worry, but she saw the light in his eyes and knew he'd been hoping for an invitation.

The sloop was in fairly good condition after the winter. Hitty was an able sailor, taking her turn at the tiller as the mainsail caught a strong, steady breeze, and the boat skimmed along quickly, heeling gently to one side as she maneuvered it out of the cove.

As the shoreline receded from view, Hitty didn't think at all about the Grand House or Isaac Barnard or Grandmother Lillian. She felt far away from everything, surrounded by water, sky, and wind. No wonder seamen arrived home only to sign on again for another voyage. A life at sea was a complete escape.

They sailed for hours, much longer than Hitty expected, but Benjamin didn't seem to have any desire to return to shore, and she was relishing the day. As they drifted past the harbor of Nantucket, he said softly, "'Tis so beautiful."

"It is," she said. "The early settlers hoped to create a perfect place, far and away from all the troubles on the mainland. It didn't take long to discover that was impossible. But 'tis a fine island, with good people." Mostly.

"What kind of troubles were on the mainland?"

"Religious ones, mostly."

"The early settlers . . . those are thy ancestors?"

"Macy, Coffin, Swain, Starbuck. Those names belong to my family tree. Most everyone on Nantucket is related to each other, to some degree."

"So that's what thy grandmother meant by ancestral alliance."

Hitty nodded. "Grandmother Lillian used to frighten children by grabbing their chins and turning their faces to observe their profile. She wanted to 'See the Look.' The Coffins, for example, have a very aristocratic nose. The Husseys lack much of a chin. The Foulgers have high foreheads to hold their brains. Mitchells too. My friend Maria is an example. She is both a Foulger and a Mitchell. 'Tis no wonder she is brilliant."

He smiled and she stopped suddenly, realizing she'd been talking a blue streak. Where had her shyness gone?

"So then, what about the Macys? What are they known for?"

"Well," she said, pleased that he asked, "the men are not overly tall, though they are lean and lank. Henry is a fine example of a true Macy, at least in appearance. Less so in temperament. The Macy men, they are on the go. Henry prefers to ponder."

"Then that quality must be changing in him, it seems. This newspaper takes up much of his time. I have difficulty locating him on island. When I go to his office, he's never there. Always off, chasing down stories."

"So true! He's rarely at home."

Benjamin's eyes smiled. "And the Macy women?"

"They do not share the men's lean stature. Instead, for the most part, they are amply endowed. And then there are combinations. I seem to have the Starbuck curly hair, the Coffin nose, and the Macy plumpness."

"I 'See the Look' in thee," he said with an admiring glance. "Lovely in face. And a warm and gentle character."

She kept her eyes on the tips of her kid leather slippers, embarrassed by his compliments. She wasn't accustomed to men praising her appearance. Frankly, she wasn't accustomed to compliments of any kind, for it wasn't the way of the

Friends. The inner life was the focus of Quakers, not worldly exteriors. And yet she found she liked the compliments. She liked them quite a bit.

Benjamin rose to reel the mast in, just in time, as he noticed they were heading toward an anchored boat. Graceful as a cat, he slipped under the mast to avoid getting hit. He'd had some experience on a boat, she could see that. Just when she thought she had Benjamin figured out, he would show her some new aspect of himself.

For some inexplicable reason, she found her thoughts wandering back to Isaac. Staring at Benjamin across the sloop, she couldn't help but compare the two men. Benjamin's sandy hair, blue eyes, and broad shoulders were almost the physical opposite of Isaac's dark coloring and lanky build.

The strange thing was that even though Isaac had given her no reason to believe he had feelings for her, being with Benjamin—enjoying his company—seemed terribly disloyal.

Back at the house, Marie-Claire sat at the desk in the parlor, writing a letter. She looked up and smiled at Hitty when she came back to the house after the sail. "I wondered what had happened to thee!"

"We went for a rantum scoot."

Her eyes went wide. "A what?"

Hitty shook her head. "I keep forgetting thee is a coof."

"A *what*?"

"A coof. A stranger. An off-islander. Benjamin and I went for a sail. Just to take advantage of the good weather. He headed back to his office."

Marie-Claire blew on the wet ink, then put the stopper

in the ink bottle. She glanced at Hitty. "There is a happiness in thy voice."

"Is there? I haven't sailed in a long time. I'd forgotten how much I enjoyed it."

"Did the company have anything to do with thy enjoyment?"

Hitty plopped down on the settee, trying to find the right words. "There's no denying Benjamin is a thoroughly charming man, but we are not well suited." She let out a deep breath. "I am not well suited to him."

"How so?"

"Because I am hardly the type of woman that a man like Benjamin Foulger would be interested in." She laughed, but Marie-Claire did not join in.

Benjamin was an attractive man. Easy to talk to, she thought. Not at all what she'd expected. They seemed to have much in common too, and he asked many questions. So unlike most men. *Isaac.*

And so very attractive, she noted again. No doubt about that. *I wonder why he hasn't married?* He must have *somebody* in Boston.

Don't even give Benjamin Foulger another thought, Hitty, a sour little voice advised her.

Marie-Claire came over to sit on the chair next to the settee, leaned forward, and put her hand on top of Hitty's. "Thee is a remarkable woman, inside and out. Full of light and joy. Thee deserves to be with a man who makes thy heart sing."

Something in Marie-Claire's touch made Hitty feel as if she understood her, deep down. "Thee is kind, but I think thee knows what I mean."

"It distresses me when I hear thee think so little of thyself, Hitty. Any man on this island would be blessed to earn thy affection. And if he didn't consider himself blessed, then I pity him for what he is missing." Marie-Claire sat in the same chair her grandmother used to sit in. How strange, that something could be so different now. Hitty avoided that stiff armchair. As a child, during the annual visit to the Grand House, her grandmother would interrogate her from that chair, pointing out Hitty's flaws, starting with her size. Somehow, Marie-Claire made that same chair seem soft and welcoming, almost cozy.

Another strange thought occurred to Hitty. This young woman, only sixteen years old, was more inspiring to her than any other woman Hitty knew, bar Daphne. It was unfortunate, for Henry's sake, that she was so young. More to the point, that his heart was claimed by Anna Gardner.

The next morning, Henry rose earlier than usual and was startled to find Marie-Claire at the dining room table, breakfasting alone. This might be awkward, without Hitty or Jeremiah. Should he stay? Should he go?

"How goes the newspaper?" Marie-Claire asked, offering him a plate filled with hot biscuits, and he caught a whiff.

Cook had made the most amazing flaky butter biscuits—bacon, cheddar cheese, and chives. He pulled out a chair to sit down. He would stay. "Today is printing day. I want to get to the office early and go over the proof one more time." This attention to detail drove Zebadiah crazy, but Henry felt a great responsibility to print accurate news with a minimum of typographical errors.

"'Tis a fine and noble venture, thy newspaper," she said.

He felt so too, and it was wonderful to have someone else acknowledge it. The *Illumine* provided another viewpoint to the islanders, and he could see it was making a difference.

"I think thee has a talent for remaining objective."

"That's what good reporting is all about." He reached out to grasp the teapot and pour himself a cup, then thought to pour a cup for her first.

As she held out her cup and saucer, she said quietly, "The pen is always mightier than the sword."

Henry froze, midpour. "What did thee say?"

"The pen is mightier than the sword." She looked up at him, her brown eyes open wide. "'Tis a saying coined by a British playwright. I read it just the other day and thought of thee. Of thy noble venture."

The pen is mightier than the sword. Henry rolled the saying over and over in his mind. He liked it. He liked it quite a bit. It was just the kind of catchphrase he'd been searching for, a way to capture the heart of his newspaper. He was eager to share it with Anna, to convince her he *was* doing something significant to right social wrongs. She had never actually said so, but he sensed she thought that he was merely dabbling in the newspaper business, frittering away his grandmother's inheritance. That it was a lark.

Nothing could be further from the truth.

He glanced up at Marie-Claire and she looked quickly away, as if she did not want to be caught looking at him. He noticed a becoming shade of pink rise on her cheeks. *Sweet.* He rather liked Marie-Claire's admiration.

When Henry reached the *Illumine*'s office, he found a sealed envelope pushed under the door. He waited until he sat at his desk to open it and read the long letter. It was a well-written essay about how the Bible never mentioned any differences between races, and it called on the island to allow African American students to attend the high school. The letter was signed only with the initial "B."

B. Could the letter writer be Anna? Mayhap this was what she had in mind when she told him on the beach that she knew what she would do next. The handwriting didn't resemble her careful script, though she could have disguised it.

He leaned back in his wooden chair. This letter lacked Anna's fervent tone. It developed a balanced, thoughtful argument, one that would be difficult to object to. He couldn't tell if it was written by a Friend or not, but the author knew Scripture well. He reread it, looking for clues. Man? Or woman? Old or young? He just couldn't tell.

His grandfather Jeremiah came into the office with a wrapped bundle. He set it on Henry's desk, a pleased look on his face. "What is it?"

"Open it and find out," Jeremiah said, pulling out his pipe.

As Jeremiah filled his pipe with tobacco, Henry unwrapped the bundle. Inside was a wooden sign, with *Illumine* carved into it.

Henry took in a deep breath. "Jeremiah. Thee made this. It's . . . beautifully crafted."

"T' hang over yer doorfront. No one can ever find this place."

Tears pricked at Henry's eyes. He was at a loss to tell his grandfather how much this meant to him. The hours he'd spent on it, the precise and careful carving. Each letter that spelled *Illumine* was painstakingly perfect.

"'Tis nothing."

"'Tis a great deal to me. I'll hang it this very day." Henry could see Jeremiah was embarrassed now. He didn't even trust his own voice to express how grateful he felt. Jeremiah knew, though, and avoided meeting his eyes. Henry broke the silence with a mundane remark. "I received a letter to the editor." He handed him the "B" letter and waited for him to read it. "Any idea who might have written it?"

Jeremiah finished reading it, looked up at Henry and said, "None. But what does it matter? Print it."

"Print it? As it is? Signed as 'B'?"

"Print it."

So Henry did. The letter went on the second page of the *Illumine*.

That night at dinner, just as Jeremiah, Marie-Claire, Hitty, and Henry sat down for dinner, Benjamin arrived at the door with some work for Marie-Claire, and Henry insisted he stay and join them.

Benjamin told everyone that he overheard customers in the hat store buzzing with one question: Who was "B"?

"So, Henry," Hitty said, "do tell! Who is this mysterious 'B'?"

Henry's eyes were fixed on Philemon as he offered Benjamin a bread roll. Was it his imagination, or was Philemon's countenance lighter this evening? Could "B" be Philemon? Then his gaze slipped to Benjamin. *B.* Could he be the letter writer?

"Who, Henry? Who?" Hitty wanted an answer.

Henry could only respond with a shrug. He had no idea. For one strange moment, he wondered if the author could possibly be Mary Coffin Starbuck, letters found somewhere, for "B" sounded like her way of thinking. He shook that thought right out of his head, glad he hadn't said it aloud. He'd stayed up too late last night reading Great Mary's journal, and in his head the two worlds, a century apart, were colliding.

Mary Coffin Starbuck

22 August 1696

Something happened today that has greatly distressed me. I went to pay a visit to Elsa Coleman, to bring her some fresh-baked bread. When I arrived at their settlement, I found Elsa outside, cutting peat (which is no easy task for a man, much less a woman). Leaning against their modest wooden cabin, William was drinking rum from a Hussey jug.

Who knows how long he'd been at it, for he was senseless, staggering as he walked. He yelled at me, waving a jug of rum in the air, shouting at me to get on home and leave his wife to her work.

Elsa was quite embarrassed by him, but she did not contradict him. "You'd better go," she said softly.

I was loath to leave, for I have no fear of a drunken man. Plenty of them have stumbled into the store, white and Indian both, and I have learned how to manage them.

"I brought Elsa some fresh-baked bread, William," I said in a calm and friendly voice. Offering food to a drunk man always seemed to douse his spit-and-fire.

But not THIS drunken man. Kindness only flared his anger. He took the Lord's name in vain and told me again to get off his property.

"Please, Mary," Elsa whispered. "Please go."

I put the bread in Elsa's hands, gave her a reassuring squeeze, and went home.

When I told Nathaniel what I had witnessed, he warned me to stay out of it. How infuriating! That kind of passive response was exactly how bad men grew worse. "Women deserve a voice, Nathaniel," I told him.

"Mary, this is between a man and his wife."

That annoyed me even more. A man and his wife. Harrumph! As if she were a possession, like a horse or a sheep, instead of a human being. I told him just that.

He seemed baffled. "But you've told me before that you don't like the word husband, for it implies animal welfare. So what should I call a married man?"

The whole discussion made me so upset that I didn't speak to him for the rest of the evening. I do not think he even noticed.

13

Henry unlocked the door to his office and inhaled, relishing sights and smells that had become dearly familiar to him: the printing press, the ink, the stacks of paper. Shafts of morning sunlight filtered through the windows, bathing the room in soft light. The day felt full of possibilities. He set his satchel on his desk, a contented man.

"Henry!"

He spun around to face Anna, standing at the doorjamb with a mortified look on her face. "What's happened?"

"Does thee know what I have discovered? The North Congregational Church, the very place where the women's Anti-Slavery Society has been meeting this past year . . . I have learned that they bar black women from the church! I had no idea, not until I saw a black woman turned away, with my own eyes. I am outraged! We will not meet there any longer. Fortunately, Obed Macy has offered an upstairs room in his store for us to meet." She pointed to the large printing press that took up most of the room. "I came to thee to report the story." She put an envelope on his desk.

"Here it is. Facts, quotes. Thee must use it." She frowned. "Not bury it like thee did in the last issue."

A few months ago, Anna had been voted as secretary of the Anti-Slavery Society and had since used her post to supply regular articles for him to print. He incorporated them as often as he could. "Anna, I told thee—in that last issue, the launch of the lightship took full coverage." From the look on her face, he knew she did not accept that excuse, but it was the truth. "Thee seems to have an abundance of ideas for the *Illumine*," he said, then instantly regretted it.

"That I do." Her tone was light, but her expression more serious.

"I'll do the best I can, Anna."

"Thee is sidestepping."

Henry didn't like her tone now, distant and analytical. That subtle note of warmth was gone. He felt the chill as if someone had opened a window. He wished he didn't feel he always needed to be on his guard, to live up to Anna's expectations. "Let's not argue." He reached out to take one of her hands in his. "I've missed thee," he said, and he had.

She glanced up at him. "I've missed thee too."

He waited for her to say something more. When she didn't, he said, "We haven't had much time together. Come to dinner tomorrow night at the Grand House. The latest edition will be printed and delivered. 'Tis a good night to relax."

The edges of her lips curled, and he could see her soften. "First, I have something to tell thee. It's the project I've been working on, Henry. In fact, I need thy help." She dropped his hand and picked up a fat leather folder, filled with letters. "Come summer, the Atheneum will be hosting the first Anti-Slavery Convention to be held on Nantucket." Her eyes glowed with excitement as she showed him all the letters from significant individuals who had agreed to come and speak. "William Lloyd Garrison has agreed to attend!" She leaned close to whisper excitedly, "And William Coffin has invited Frederick Douglass."

"Who is he?"

The smile left her eyes. "Frederick Douglass is a runaway slave, Henry. He has a powerful story." She took a paper out of the folder and handed it to him. "I have prepared a press statement for the *Illumine* and the *Gazette*, both, so thee can make a full and accurate report on it for the next issue."

He read through the press statement, impressed by her diligence and attention to detail. Anna Gardner was one of a kind, a force of her own. How he admired her. And yet, there was a part of him that felt a tweak of disappointment too. She hadn't involved him in this venture, she hadn't shared any details with him, she hadn't sought his opinion. And when it was time to announce it, she provided press information to both newspapers. He felt rather insignificant to her.

Anna was doing something very important; he needed to shake off his injured pride. He lifted his head and gave her an approving smile. "This is tremendous, Anna. I will make sure it gets plenty of space."

"Oh, that would be wonderful, Henry! And I accept thy invitation to come to thy house for dinner." She leaned over to kiss him, right on his lips, right in his office. "I'll see thee tomorrow night."

He could barely keep a smile off his face for the rest of the morning. It didn't slip away even when Zebadiah arrived at work to discover that much of the typesetting he'd done to prepare for tomorrow's printing had to be scratched. That was part and parcel of the newspaper business, and the reason Zebadiah threatened to quit on a weekly basis. Even then, Henry kept his smile.

The evening found Henry sitting at his desk, reading through the proof for tomorrow's edition of the *Illumine*, caught in a quagmire. He had intended to lead the news with the convention, but a fire had broken out in a warehouse; two workers lost their lives. Fire posed a serious danger, as casks of the whale oil, sitting in warehouses, were tinderboxes.

For a moment he allowed his doubts to surface. What if he was wrong? This was going to be harder than he thought. He stared at the paper a long moment. *Hold it to the Light.* Henry lifted his eyes to the ceiling. Where in the world did that thought come from? It sounded like something Marie-Claire might say.

He bent his head over his desk, closed his eyes, and folded his hands in prayer. *Oh, Lord,* he prayed silently, *light me the way.*

He tried to hear the voice of the Spirit, speaking inside him. Nothing, nothing but the clatter of his own confusion.

He paused, reviewed the proof one more time, then with a frustrated crumpling of the paper, threw it on the ground. He picked up the graphite pencil, considering how to start. As he wrote out the lead sentence, a sense of peace settled over him.

The next evening, the family had gathered in the parlor to examine the latest edition when Anna arrived at the Grand House for dinner. Right away, Henry could tell she didn't look happy; her pretty face was drawn into a tight frown.

"The convention was not even mentioned. Not a single word. Not in the *Illumine,* not in the *Gazette*. Thee promised me it would be a headline."

"I tried, Anna," Henry said, though he never had promised her a headline. "The fire—it was of immediate concern to islanders. There's plenty of time to advertise for the convention."

"Advertise? Henry, the convention is not to be advertised. 'Tis *news*."

"But the convention isn't until Eighth Month," Marie-Claire said. "There is still time."

Exactly. Henry flashed Marie-Claire a grateful look before turning to Anna. "The *Illumine* must report news of the entire island. Two men died in this fire, Anna. Think of their families."

"I don't deny the importance of the fire's impact. But these ongoing concerns—they need attention too."

"What more could I be doing?"

"Thee should be agitating public opinion. After all, thee is the editor. Where is thy voice?"

"I report the news, Anna. I don't create it." Henry folded the newspaper and put it away.

"There are some who think that objectivity is the proper perspective for reporting," Marie-Claire said.

With a quick, sharp glance in Marie-Claire's direction, Anna replied, "Objectivity can be an excuse for inactivity."

An awkward silence fell over the room.

Jeremiah enjoyed the freedom old age brought to him. He could sit in a chair, feigning sleep, while he was actually listening in on conversations. Just now, for example, after an oddly uncomfortable dinner, Jeremiah excused himself and went to the parlor to sit by the fire.

A bit later—though he wasn't sure how much later because he drifted off, cozy from the warmth of the fire—Henry and Anna came in and sat down on their settee. Jeremiah heard their voices but kept his eyes closed, curious. Anna questioned Henry about some letters he'd written to her while onboard the *Endeavour*. Henry claimed to not yet have found those letters, as he'd been so absorbed with responsibilities for the *Illumine*.

Bunkum and balderdash! Henry was stalling and Jeremiah wondered why.

Jeremiah had known Anna since she was a little maid, and knew her parents well, a notable family. When Anna was a child, her parents had hidden a runaway slave in their attic. What was his name . . . ah, what was his name? Arthur Cooper. *There, y' old salt dog! Still as sharp as a tack.*

As impressive as Anna was, Jeremiah had never been a fan of Henry and Anna's romance—if anyone would call it that. They couldn't quite commit to marrying, they couldn't quite give each other up. Love shouldn't be so complicated.

If he were to put the situation in sea terms, Anna would be a bluefish, bold and dramatic, fighting the fisherman to its last breath. And Henry would be a cod, carefully evading the fisherman's net. He yawned, starting to doze off again. The two together, they didn't match.

On chilly days, Hitty and Marie-Claire ate the noon meal together in the parlor, in front of the fire, as soon as Hitty returned home from the Cent School. "I know it sounds petty," she said, carrying her plate into the room, "but one reason I like to eat in here is because I know it would annoy my grandmother."

Marie-Claire smiled. "What was she like, thy grandmother?"

"Disapproving. Severe. Daphne says that she was quite beautiful as a young maiden, considered even by Friends to be the most beautiful woman on Nantucket . . . and thee knows as well as I do that Friends do not encourage such prideful assessments. But I remember Grandmother Lillian as always wearing a sour expression."

"How curious. Surrounded by all this." Marie-Claire glanced around the room. "All these frills and ornamentation. And yet she sounds rather unpleasant. Mayhap . . . she was lonely."

"Lonely? If she was, 'twas her own fault. Daphne tried to include her in everything." Hitty lifted her palm in a circle. "All *this* only gave her the sense that she had the right to control the destiny of others. Like she's trying to do with Henry and me."

"Did. She tried to. Thee is *not* letting her."

Someone cleared his throat.

The two women turned their heads to find Benjamin at the doorjamb. "Marie-Claire, might I speak privately with thee?"

Hitty noticed an irritated expression cross Benjamin's face, then disappear so quickly, she thought she'd imagined it.

Marie-Claire excused herself and the two went outside. Waiting until the front door clicked shut, Hitty hurried to peek out the window. Benjamin was clearly upset, speaking animatedly to Marie-Claire. Although she couldn't hear what he was saying, she could read his emotions in the rigid set of his body. Hitty never imagined he had a temper. What could have caused Benjamin such upset?

Hitty leaned closer to the window to try to open it, but her elbow tipped over one of her grandmother's prized Ming vases. The vase exploded on the floor. Benjamin heard—everybody heard!—and stopped talking to Marie-Claire to tilt his head toward the house. Had he seen Hitty? She jumped back from the window, tiptoeing around the broken shards. Benjamin and Marie-Claire came back inside, just as Philemon walked into the foyer.

"What in the world happened?" Benjamin said, eyeing the shattered vase.

"The cat!" Hitty blurted out. "It tipped over the vase." It was a bold-faced lie, Hitty's first. They had no cat. She was surely going straight to Hades. Hot with shame, she bent down to pick up some large shards.

Philemon returned with a broom. "Allow me, Miss Hitty."

"That was an extremely valuable vase." Benjamin sounded distressed, then confused. "I didn't even know there was a cat in this house."

"Oh, he's an awful cat," Marie-Claire said quickly, picking up some broken shards. "He's always getting into things. Then, *poof!*" She snapped her fingers. "He disappears."

From that moment on, Marie-Claire earned Hitty's heartfelt devotion. Here was the sister she'd always wanted.

Henry walked around the section of Main Street that had been cobbled. He'd spent the entire day trying to fix a jammed roller on the printing press, and after finally getting it to work, he needed fresh air. And something upbeat to fill his mind. It pleased him, seeing this work, slow as it was. A Scripture verse came to mind, something Marie-Claire had said months ago on the morning that construction began: "The Lord delights in small beginnings." Something like that. Marie-Claire reminded him of Daphne—finding her in the mornings with her Bible open, reading Scripture. "Seeking Light for the day," Daphne would say, and he thought Marie-Claire might say the same thing, if asked.

He came to the end of the cobbling, pivoted, and started back to the Candle Street office when he heard a familiar voice call to him.

"Working hard?" Anna said, walking out of Obed Macy's store.

"Actually, I have been. Just stepped out to get some fresh air."

She moved closer and touched his arm, looking regretful. "Henry, it did not go well at dinner the other night. I apologize. I was disappointed in the situation and aired my feelings to thy household. It was wrong of me."

Henry's spirits lifted. He couldn't remember a time when Anna had ever apologized to him. "Apology accepted. And I thank thee for it, Anna."

"Who is this Marie-Claire?"

"Who is she?"

He could see that Anna was holding herself very still, waiting for him to answer. "She is . . . the law clerk's secretary. Hitty invited her to be a tenant at the Grand House last summer."

"Who is she . . . to thee?"

"To me? Anna, thee jests! She is but a girl!"

"A comely girl." An eyebrow lifted. "A comely girl who is smitten with thee. Surely thee has noticed."

Henry felt insulted; worse still, his cheeks felt hot. Mayhap he had noticed both of her assertions. "Thee sounds . . . jealous! What a ridiculous notion. Marie-Claire works very hard on our behalf."

"Doing what?"

Henry had to think of how to respond. Anna was not aware of the details of the inheritance and he still wanted to keep it that way. The slow pace of liquidating assets was mind numbing. Handwritten documents had to be created—bills of sales, transfers of titles, all kinds of legal recording was required. If changes were made, signatures from both parties were required—adding lengthy delays. And that was all before the documents could be returned to Boston to be filed. He took in a deep breath. "Well, currently . . . Marie-Claire is trying to find a buyer for the Grand House."

"And how is that coming along?"

"Not swiftly. There is the rumor that the house is haunted."

Anna rolled her eyes. "Oh Henry, that's sheer piffle."

"Haunted *by* my grandmother. She told others she'd return from the grave to spook them."

"Who would believe such a thing?"

"Everyone, apparently."

"Henry, I doubt Marie-Claire is trying particularly hard to sell the house. I think she rather likes living there. It seems to suit her quite nicely."

Strangely enough, Henry was growing rather fond of the Grand House too, and it shocked him to realize that. Hitty still couldn't stand it and was eager to leave. He chose to ignore Anna's slights about Marie-Claire. "I think the house will sell when the right buyer comes along."

"Just how long will Marie-Claire remain on Nantucket?"

"I don't . . . I don't really know." Nor did he want to think too far into the future, especially as far as the second portion of his grandmother's inheritance. Each time he did, it made his stomach churn. To avoid relinquishing his grandmother's remaining assets to Tristram Macy, he would need to be married to a Friend in good standing. So would Hitty. And right now, with Anna shockingly unconcerned to be disowned by the Friends, and with Isaac being a Methodist as well as . . . being Isaac . . . they weren't even close to satisfying the conditions of the will. Oliver Combs was a stickler for detail; Henry knew he would uphold Grandmother Lillian's will to the very last jot and tittle. That was exactly why Grandmother Lillian had hired him.

But that worry was still a few years away. There was time. "Anna," he said, "we should try to have another evening together soon. Alone, this time."

A soft expression came over her, the Anna he loved best, and she smiled. "I would like that."

Mary Coffin Starbuck

27 September 1696

I didn't see Elsa Coleman for another month, but then, one sunny afternoon, there she was, standing at the store's door, left open for the sea breeze. "Elsa! Welcome, welcome. I have missed you. Do come in. I'll get you a cup of tea."

She came for William's coffee, she said, acting as if nothing strange had happened when I last saw her and her ~~horrible~~ husband, so I took her lead and did the same. We visited for a long while, laughing and having a fine time. And she was in a talkative mood, thus I learned more about her today than I had in all our other visits.

She said she had immigrated to Pennsylvania with her first husband, a German man who died soon after the ship left Rotterdam. She was at a complete loss, she said. She knew no one on the ship, or in the colonies, and did not know where to go or what to do. The captain of the ship had a brother in Boston, a fisherman who was seeking a wife, preferring a German one for they were known to be hard workers. Elsa agreed to marry the captain's brother, sight unseen.

When I asked her how she could have done such a brave thing, she replied, "Not so brave, Mary. Desperate." She said she had a hope that William's disposition would be similar to the captain's, for he was a good man who was trying to help her. "And then," she said, eyes cast downward, "I was told Wilhelm was a pastor."

William Coleman? A pastor? That was a stretch for the imagination. "What has happened to his church?"

"No church yet has called him. Last summer, his cousin, Christopher Swain, he wrote to him. He said there are many lost on this island who need salvation. He asked William to come to Nantucket and start a church."

My heart started pounding. Here? THAT MAN? William Coleman thinks he will be our first clergyman? ~~A man mad as huckleberry chowder?~~ Oh . . . I think not.

And what had Christopher Swain presumed to do? Sneak a clergy onto the island in an underhanded way! I felt my blood start to boil. Those Swains! They were always trying to pull the wool over Nantucket eyes.

The clock struck noon and Elsa rose from the chair to leave. "Wilhelm is out fishing today. I should return before he does." She smiled at me. "You give me such joy, Mary Starbuck. I have not had a friend like you since I left Germany."

I reached out to hug her and she flinched. It was then I realized that she'd been holding one arm against her belly during the entire time we'd been visiting. I reached out to gently touch her arm and she pulled back. "Oh Elsa, what has he done to you?"

Her eyes went wide with fear, and she shook her head. "I must be getting home." She left the store then, forgetting William's coffee.

29 September 1696

I'd hoped Elsa might return for the coffee, but by the second day, I took the forgotten coffee out to the Colemans.

When Elsa opened the door to my knock—an ever-so-gentle tap, she quickly stepped outside and closed the door behind her. "Mary," she whispered. "It is not a good time for a visit."

I didn't doubt that. There never was. There never would be.

I handed her the coffee she had left in the store. "Elsa . . . if you need to get away, I will help you. Come to me, anytime. I will help."

Then I left. And I prayed.

6 October 1696

In the middle of the night, I woke to the sound of someone knocking on our door. I flew out of bed, as if I had been expecting her.

"Elsa! Come in. Come in out of the cold."

As the light from my candle flickered over her lovely face, I gasped. An eye was blackened, her lips were swollen. And her teeth! Beautiful white teeth . . . the front two were chipped! I sat her down by the fire, and quickly went to work to clean up the blood and get some cold water on her bruises.

Nathaniel came downstairs and assessed the situation. Suddenly, we heard a commotion outside, a man shouting and yelling awful accusations. William had come to claim his wife. Nathaniel and I exchanged a look.

"I'll take care of him," he said.

He went outside, facing a torrent of ugly words from William. Elsa and I heard a crashing sound, and then silence. Nathaniel poked his head inside the door. "I'll take him home. He won't bother you any more tonight, Elsa."

But what of the morrow?

7 October 1696

Early this morning at high tide, Nathaniel and I settled Elsa on my brother Peter's sloop as he hoisted the sails for the mainland. Wisely, Peter asked no questions, and assured me he would get her on a ship bound for Rotterdam, safely back to her family. As I carefully hugged her farewell, I pressed ten pieces of Spanish silver into her hand. It is from the treasure, some leftover pieces from when I last dug it up. Saving Elsa is the best possible use of that silver.

15 October 1696

William Coleman set sail for the mainland today, fit to be tied. He is furious with me, but frightened of Nathaniel (I do believe my gentle husband knocked him out cold!). He said this island was only good for devils and dogs.

I did not answer him for his insults. I wanted to. I nearly did. I wanted to say that pigs seem to be on the island, too, but I had read that very morning in Scripture of a warning not to put pearls before swine. And so I held my tongue.

30 October 1696

While it was a very good riddance to see William Coleman sail away, I have wondered if I have made a grave error in discouraging any and all clergy to put up a church in Nantucket. For they will come, even if uninvited.

I've also come to realize that, without a church, our island does not heed the authority of God but replaces it with their own authority. We settled Nantucket with the common thought that God did not need a church, only true believers. What I had not realized until now is that believers need a church nearly as much as they need God.

14

As the summer of 1841 approached, every edition of the *Illumine*—now up to eight pages—carried "Letters to the Editor" about two heated topics: the Anti-Slavery Convention to be held during Eighth Month at the Atheneum, and the ongoing debate about school integration.

One afternoon, Anna briskly entered the newspaper's office, holding up the latest issue with a shocked look on her face. "Henry, thee allowed this to be printed?" She read, "'There is a danger of contagion spreading from black students if they sit in classrooms with white students.'" She was practically shaking with rage. "'Tis appalling!"

"I heartily agree, Anna."

"Then *why* did thee publish it?"

He didn't even try to explain. "It is the best written of the letters by the segregationists, and the least appalling."

"There are worse?"

"Much, much worse."

"Why did thee give credit to it by publishing it?"

"A newspaper must be fair, Anna. I hope others read it and see the folly of their thinking."

She crossed her arms and clasped her elbows. She let out a puff of air. "I will be eager to see what 'B' has to say in response."

He felt the same way. The "B" letters had arrived irregularly, averaging one a month, and were highly anticipated by readers. Last month, he had to print a second edition of the paper, as so many copies were requested to cut out and send the "B" letter to the mainland.

"Henry," Anna said softly. "I'm sure thee must know who the author of the 'B' letters is." She gave him her sweetest look. "I won't tell a soul."

"I do not! Don't look at me like that. I truly have no idea. I'm not even sure it's one person. The envelope arrives in the office without rhyme or reason. Once, Zebadiah and I were even in the office and hadn't noticed it had been slipped under the door. 'Tis a mystery to us." He smiled. "A good one."

She tipped her head. "I have oft wondered if the author is thee."

"And I have wondered the same thing of thee!" He laughed, and then she joined in, and all was well between them again.

Late one summer evening, nearly nine o'clock, Hitty was up in Maria Mitchell's cupola observatory to peer through the eyepiece of a telescope at the night sky. "Look to the moon, Hitty," Maria told her, "and follow the star patterns. To the left is the planet Jupiter. Peer closely."

Hitty did as she said but always had trouble finding what she meant. Maria had tried to teach her how to locate stars and planets by knowing constellations—Sagittarius, Cat's Eye, Scorpius, Pleiades, and so many others—but stars and planets all looked alike to Hitty. Spine-tinglingly beautiful, but not distinctive. So many of them! Like grains of sand on the shore. She stepped back to let Maria take a turn at the eyepiece. "It makes me feel so small, looking up at the stars."

"As it should! There is such great beauty and order in the heavens. By comparison we are small and insignificant."

"Small but not insignificant to God, I hope."

Maria did not answer. "There is much buzz in town about the convention," she said, squinting into the eyepiece as she refocused it. "Anna hopes for three hundred to attend, but I am doubtful. She has such high goals for others. I fear she is often disappointed."

"Anna cares so much," Hitty said. "It seems as if those who change the tide of public opinion must walk a hard path. A lonely one."

"Oh, I daresay she won't be lonely for long. Things seem to be moving swiftly along for Henry and Anna. I saw them together on Main Street just the other day, heads together in a serious conversation. I'm sure they'll marry soon." She stepped back to look at Hitty. "Does thee not agree?"

"He has not shared any such thought with me," Hitty said, a little shocked by Maria's assumption, though she shouldn't be. She knew that Anna was important to Henry. Did she think that life would never change?

It was good that Henry was in love. It was good that he might be thinking of marriage. Hitty felt glad for him . . . and a sense of loss for herself.

On the way home, the wind gusted through the trees and flapped her skirts like sheets on a laundry line. She heard the hoot of a short-eared owl, and another hoot back, but not even birdsong could cheer her spirits.

She felt so strange inside. Sad and lonely. It was not a common feeling for Hitty, for she'd always had somebody—Daphne, her father, but mostly Henry, who listened to her thoughts and gave commentary. What would life be like with her brother married? She wondered if others would pity her for not marrying, and she would grow old and odd, like Cousin Lucinda, talking to parrots and make-believe cats.

On the day of the Anti-Slavery Convention, the Atheneum was packed, standing room only. Henry estimated over five hundred men and women were squeezed into the lecture hall of the library like sardines, eager to hear Frederick Douglass, a fugitive slave, speak of his former life. Henry sat at the back of the room, furiously jotting notes, trying to keep his expression interested but neutral. It was not an easy task, for he was not at all neutral on this topic. A fresh wind was blowing through Nantucket, and he knew Anna Gardner deserved much of the credit.

Frederick Douglass cleared his throat and took a sip of water. He stood very straight and looked out at the audience. He was tall, almost stately, with high cheekbones and intelligent eyes. He was also reluctant to speak. Anna said he was very shy, and he could see others urge Douglass to speak, until he finally acquiesced. Henry found out later that this was Douglass's first public speaking engagement to a white audience. He spoke of his slavery with a quiet authority, having experienced it and run away from it. Henry was astounded by his wisdom, his intellect, and his power of persuasion. The audience had stilled, listening carefully to every word—not a cough nor sneeze, not a rustle of a skirt. Utter silence.

Not a moment after Douglass's speech concluded, William Lloyd Garrison stood and raised his hands, turning in a circle to face the entire assembly. "Have we been listening to a thing, a piece of property, or a man?" he asked.

The entire room shouted back, "A man! A man!"

Garrison continued. "Shall such a man be held a slave in a Christian land?"

"Nay! Nay!"

"Shall such a man ever be sent back to bondage from the free soil of old Massachusetts?"

With that, every man and woman in that lecture hall jumped to their feet, continuing to shout, "Nay! Nay! Nay!"

It was the most remarkable experience Henry had ever witnessed. Everyone, everyone in the room, united by the conviction that all men should be free.

As soon as the convention wrapped up for the day, Henry made his way over to Anna. She saw him and grabbed his hands. "Wasn't it . . . amazing?"

"It was! An historic day that will not soon be forgotten. Anna, I am so proud of thee."

"Credit must go to so many. William Coffin was the one who invited Frederick Douglass to Nantucket. And then . . . William Lloyd Garrison. Why, he was heroic."

He grinned. "I will quote you on that."

A worried look came over her face. "Thee will get all the details straight, Henry?"

"Of course! In fact, just this once, I will let thee look over the copy first." He leaned in. "Do not breathe word of that to anyone else."

She laughed, then her lovely face settled into a broad smile with a happy sigh. "Today will always be the best day of my life."

Not so fast, Henry thought. There might be other best days.

Mary Coffin Starbuck

18 August 1697

I had not thought Boston would ever welcome Quakers, and yet my son Nathaniel and his wife Dinah just returned from a visit and reported that they saw Friends throughout the city. Carrying on with their daily life like everyone else—making a living, buying bread at the baker's, apples from the corner vendors. Just raising their families and living their life.

When I was a girl, two young men were hung on Boston Common for the sole reason that they professed to be Quakers. In just a few decades, the Quakers have triumphed over grisly persecution and stood their ground in Massachusetts.

So strange, how public favor rises and falls so quickly. 'Tis so fickle.

25 August 1698

Rain fell all day long and the store was quiet. My son Nathaniel came in to work on accounts, and he was in a chatty mood, for the Quakers he observed in Boston were much on his mind.

Nathaniel said that Penn's Woods has been filling up with Quakers from England, along with all kinds of those from remnant religions from Germany (like my dear Elsa Coleman). William Penn, himself a converted Quaker, has opened his arms to those who have been persecuted elsewhere for their beliefs.

I asked Nathaniel what they looked like, for I remember

seeing a few Quakers in Salisbury and they dressed like peasants.

"Nay, nay, not peasants any longer," he explained. "Just the opposite. They are making a name for themselves as worthy citizens of the Crown—honest and reliable. In fact, I heard that Quaker merchants refuse to barter, for they believe their word should be true at all times and under all circumstances. As for their clothing, the men are in flat-brimmed hats, the women wear large black bonnets that hide their faces. They're very distinctive. Apparently, they eschew excess, and that is why their clothing is intentionally modest. It's as if they want to be identified by their outward appearance, like a beacon, to draw people to their inner Light. That's what they call it, the Spirit of God within. It's their inner Light. Everyone has the Light, they say. Everyone."

Stephen Hussey came into the store then, interrupting our interesting discussion to complain about the lumber my brother Peter had delivered to him. Too knotty, he said.

I left his problem to Nathaniel to sort out and went to the back room to tidy up. But my thoughts remained on those Quakers whom Nathaniel described.

Years ago, a Quaker missionary named Jane Stokes came to Nantucket to seek converts. She spoke of similar beliefs, and I remember feeling a deep stirring within my soul. At the time, her beliefs seemed far-fetched, radical. Or mayhap my experience with Quakers has never impressed me. (Stephen Hussey, for example.)

Mayhap the years have mellowed my judgments. My strict notions seem to have blurred. These peculiar people no longer seem so peculiar.

15

Hitty went into the parlor to glance out the windows at the falling snow. It was only Tenth Month! Big fat white flakes slowly drifted from the sky as if shaken loose from a goose down pillow.

She saw Benjamin Foulger open the gate and walk up the shell path, leaving footprints in the freshly fallen snow. In his hand was a thick satchel, filled with paperwork for Marie-Claire.

"Funny how he always seems to turn up right at the supper hour," Jeremiah muttered as he peered over Hitty's shoulder.

"Jeremiah!" Hitty said. "Benjamin Foulger is doing a great service to us. Thee must not act cranky and crotchety around him."

"I'm never cranky," he said, sounding crotchety.

Benjamin stopped abruptly, halfway up the walk, and looked up at the house with a frown. Hitty went to the door to welcome him before he knocked, so as not to bother Philemon. "So many lights are on in the house," Benjamin said before even saying hello. "'Tis wasteful."

Hitty took his coat, surprised by the scolding tone in his

voice. She hadn't thought of lighting the house as wasteful, only as chasing away the darkness. Before she could respond, Marie-Claire came downstairs and the two went to the library to go over paperwork he'd brought to her. It was Hitty's least favorite room—dark, small, and full of books. Henry loved that room best of all.

No sooner had the library door shut than the brass knocker rapped. Hitty opened it to find Isaac Barnard standing on the threshold, with Bitsy in hand. How exciting!

"Welcome," Hitty said, trying to sound as if this was an everyday occurrence. Isaac had never before come to the Grand House. Though Hitty saw him each day, it was brief moments, and Bitsy was a chatterbox.

"Come aboard, come aboard!" Jeremiah said, his voice much more welcoming than to Benjamin. "Hitty, let them in."

Isaac glanced briefly at Hitty. Was she imagining it? Then his attention was quickly drawn to Jeremiah as he greeted him. "Sorry news about that wreck. Too bad y' don't have more of those lightships in place."

Earlier in the week, a fishing vessel had wrecked in a furious storm on Nantucket's west shore. "I agree," Isaac said. "A terrible tragedy. In fact, I've come to speak to Henry about the lightship."

"Henry is not at home," Hitty said, trying to hide her disappointment that he hadn't stopped by to see her. "'Tis always a late night before this week's edition is printed."

Bitsy yanked her hand free from Isaac's hold and ran into the parlor. "Look at all the pretty things!"

"Bitsy!" Isaac said. "Mind thy manners."

Bitsy stopped in her tracks, then turned around to face her father. "I just wanted to see them, Papa." She pirouetted in a circle and clapped her hands. "I've never seen such prettiness!"

Settling into a chair by the fire, Jeremiah chuckled. "She means me."

Bitsy walked around the perimeter of the room, fingering each vase, candlestick, and porcelain figurine. She stopped to peer at a delicate crystal bell, used by Grandmother Lillian to call for a servant. Just as Bitsy was about to touch it, she was reprimanded. Not by Isaac, but by Benjamin.

"Do *not* touch that!" There was an angry tone to his voice that surprised everyone. He had a stern look on his face, a look that Hitty had never seen on him.

Embarrassed by the sharp rebuke, Bitsy rushed to Hitty's side and buried her face in her skirts.

"Benjamin," Marie-Claire said, "there was no need to speak harshly."

"My apologies," he said, embarrassed. "I did not mean to frighten the child. But the room is filled with priceless antiques. After the cat debacle, I felt concerned something else might be broken."

Jeremiah's eyebrows lifted in surprise. "We have a cat?"

Quickly, Hitty jumped in. "These antiques have survived much more over the years than the curiosity of a child."

"Nay, he is right," Isaac said. "I should not have brought Bitsy. I'll speak to Henry at his office."

"Bitsy is welcome here," Hitty said. "She is worth much more than these antiques." She rushed to add, "Mayhap thee would like to have supper with us."

Isaac declined until Jeremiah insisted that Bitsy must stay and sit by him to sample Cook's cranberry jam. He had a concern it was too tangy. Or was it too sweet? He couldn't recall which and needed Bitsy's help to discern. The mention of cranberry jam swayed Isaac, and Hitty silently blessed her grandfather for suggesting it. Isaac's own kitchen cupboard was sparse; such a sweet treat was rare.

But it was unfortunate that Bitsy ended up seated next to Benjamin, for she had taken a strong dislike to him and glared at him frequently during the meal. Hitty asked Isaac to explain the mechanics of the Fresnel lens, and while he stumbled at first, he seemed to be in an answering frame of mind, for he soon forgot to be shy and spoke of the lens with keen enthusiasm.

Hitty had never seen him so animated nor heard him string so many sentences together. He was positively elated—for Isaac, she thought. It was like watching a flower bloom.

Jeremiah quietly used his napkin to play poke the bunny with Bitsy, and Hitty could not have been happier. This was exactly how she had imagined her life with Isaac to be. This was *it*.

Suddenly Benjamin yelped, jumping up from the table. He held one hand in the other and pointed to Bitsy. "She bit me!"

"He put his hand near my mouth!" Bitsy bellowed.

"I was trying to wipe cranberry jam off thy face before it got on the linen tablecloth!"

Isaac jumped up. "We'd best go," he said. "My sincere apologies." He scooped his daughter up with one arm and made for the door—Bitsy screaming all the while.

Disappointed, Hitty returned to the table.

"Well," Benjamin said with a sympathetic smile, "*that* child has a flair for drama."

"She does," Hitty said. And she loved her for it.

Early the next day, at Hitty's insistence, Henry went along with her to Isaac's house to follow up on the reason he had stopped by the Grand House last evening. Isaac opened the door after Hitty knocked only once, as if he had been waiting for her to arrive, and gave Hitty a shy smile. More than that. Isaac couldn't take his eyes off her. "Thee is early."

"Henry is with me," she said, stepping to the side.

Isaac looked past her in surprise.

Henry lifted one hand in a wave. "Hitty said there's some concern about the lightship."

"Ah, last night. I apologize again for a hasty departure. Come in, come in."

Henry had never been inside Isaac's home. It was modest, in serious need of a woman's touch. They remained standing in the front room, for there was no place to sit.

"If Bitsy is in the kitchen, I'll go see to her," Hitty said, excusing herself to head down the hallway.

His sister knew her way around this house, Henry could see that. He turned to Isaac with a questioning look. "Did thee want to request funds for a second lightship?"

"'Tis a good idea, especially after the recent shipwreck. But there's something to figure out first." He crossed his arms over his chest. "A few days ago, I sailed out to the lightship to do some maintenance on the lens. It was then that I learned of a brewing problem among the crew."

"What's that?"

"The crew wants to quit."

"Why?"

"They have long watches, and they grow bored."

"Bored." Henry sighed. "Too much idle time. How well I remember it on the *Endeavour*."

Isaac's head snapped up. "What did you do to keep from boredom?"

"I read books."

Isaac frowned. "That would be my choice too, but most of the crew is illiterate."

"Same as on a whaler. So the sailors carved scrimshaw." After a whale had been caught and butchered, the captain would give the crew the teeth of whale to keep their hands busy. "Mayhap I could find a sympathetic captain who would be willing to share his scrimshaw." He doubted it, though. Scrimshaw was dear. "Better still would be to find something for the crew to do that used local materials."

Hitty walked into the room with Bitsy. "What about Abram's baskets?"

"Baskets?"

"Wampanoag baskets. Indigenous to the island. Thee must remember the baskets, Henry. Daphne had one that she kept by her chair, to hold her knitting. They're oval-shaped and tightly woven, very durable. Goodness, they last forever. There's plenty of material for staves on the island, and I can think of a few shopkeepers who could be persuaded to sell them."

Henry and Isaac exchanged a look. "It might work," Henry said. "Sister, can thee find me a sample? I'll get some materials gathered and take them out to the lightship. See if they'll give it a go."

"Better still," Hitty said, "Abram Quary is an expert basket maker. He's a Wampanoag. I believe his mother taught him to weave. Take Abram with thee. He can teach the crew."

"Would he come?" Isaac said.

"If thee made it worth his while."

"Let's give it a try," Henry said, shrugging. "Good thinking, Hitty."

"I'll go out to the village today and see if I can locate this basket maker," Isaac said. Henry noticed he still kept his eyes on Hitty, as if spellbound.

Hitty looked pleased, almost embarrassed. "Bitsy and I are off to the Cent School. We are starting work today on a singing program."

"I don't want to sing," Bitsy shouted, as Hitty tugged on her hand to head out the door. Henry could hear the child's loud protests as she went down the steps.

"I must say, Isaac, thee wastes no time." He walked to the door to leave, but Isaac stopped him.

"Henry, if you have a moment to spare, there's something else I'd like you to consider."

Henry hesitated, then pivoted. "I have a moment to spare." Truth be told, he didn't, for today was printing day for the *Illumine* and he planned to check the proof one more time before giving Zebadiah the go-ahead, just one more time, but he was intrigued by whatever Isaac had on his mind. It would not be trivial.

"Has thee heard of Humane Houses?"

"Nay."

"In 1785, the Humane Society of Boston created small shelters. They're like fishing shacks, built along the coast, equipped with blankets, lanterns, wood for heat. And a cache of food."

"Whatever for?"

"To aid shipwreck victims."

"But I thought that was what lightships and lighthouses were for. So there would be no more shipwrecks."

"As long as there are oceans, there will always be shipwrecks."

True enough. Henry nodded.

"I believe that the fatalities of the wreck this week might have been avoided if shelter had been available."

Henry had written the story about this wreck after interviewing the sole survivor. The captain on the schooner had two sons on board with him. They made it ashore, but then his boys' strength gave out and the captain carried them over a mile looking for shelter. Finally, he spotted the glow of lampshine coming from a house, but both boys died before reaching it. The captain crawled the final distance to the house. It was a haunting image.

Henry took off his hat and ran a hand through his hair. "Isaac, what kind of funds would these Humane Houses require?"

"It wouldn't be much, I think. More materials than anything else. Helpers to build them. I can supervise and manage construction." Isaac looked directly at Henry. "But I think all of Nantucket should be involved in this project, Henry. The islanders, there's a long history of helping each other. Your generosity, it's a fine thing, a good thing, but it can also . . ." He stopped himself. "Well, I'm sure you haven't intended to erode community spirit."

Those words startled Henry, and he felt a little offended by Isaac's remark. Had he been taking something vital from the island? It wasn't his intent. He'd been trying to improve this island, not splinter community. A vague sense of unease set in.

On the walk to the office, Henry thought more about the Humane Houses, and about inspiring the Nantucket community. By the time he arrived, he had a decision, and told

Zebadiah to hold off. "I want to write an editorial about the shipwreck. For page 2."

Zebadiah's eyes bulged. "But I've already set the type for page 2! It's ready for the ink rollers."

"I know, I know. I'm sorry. But the wreck is foremost on islanders' minds. Now's the time to call for a way to save lives." In the editorial, Henry called for Nantucket to donate money and materials to provide Humane Houses. He gave full credit to Isaac Barnard for spearheading efforts to save as many lives as possible.

Over the next few days, donations arrived at the office earmarked for Humane Houses, as well as promises of labor and materials. By week's end, the envelope had grown fat. Henry went to Isaac's house to personally hand it to him. "Here it is. Cash for the Humane Houses. And a list of those who will help build."

Isaac opened the envelope, stunned. "Just like that?"

Henry beamed. "Just like that." Nay, more than that. So much more. He was finding his voice, as an editor. As a man.

Mary Coffin Starbuck

3 November 1698

My son Nathaniel confessed to me today that he and Dinah want to know more about the Society of Friends and their way of thinking. He believes they have discovered something in God's Word that the rest of us have overlooked. He hoped I might have an interest too.

As I mulled that over in my mind, my son added something that gripped my heart, mayhap because Elsa Coleman has been weighing on my mind after receiving her letter last week. She wrote that she has arrived in Germany. She feels safe, she said, and free to be. She didn't say what she was free to be, but she didn't have to. I knew what she meant.

Nathaniel said, "Think on this, Mama. Armed with the Bible, all believers are elevated above any earthly authority. Everyone, Mama. Including women. A shoemaker, smithy, farmer, a goody wife. All eligible to act as ministers. All considered worthy to speak, to have a voice. Think on that, Mama."

I have thought of little else since.

16

On this gray and dreary March afternoon, Hitty walked home from a particularly tiring morning at the Cent School, hoping to get to the Grand House before rain started up again. The children were full of pent-up energy today and couldn't go outside to play. They seemed as eager for the school day to end as she was.

Her mind replayed the conversation she'd had with Isaac earlier this morning. She had stopped by his house to fetch Bitsy, and he walked along with them to school. It was something he'd started to do since the new year, quite regularly. They'd each hold Bitsy's hands between them, like a family.

Her relationship with Isaac definitely seemed more than a friendship these last few weeks . . . but less than a romance. She admired him so much, loved him in a way that made her heart hurt. It actually hurt.

This morning, Bitsy had run ahead to peer at a robin's nest, tucked away in a low-lying branch of a tree. They all stopped to admire the blue of the eggs. At one point, leaning close to the robin's nest together, Isaac's face lingered so close to Hitty's, for a moment she could almost feel his breath on her skin. She smelled soap made of bayberries and a hint of coffee. He stepped back and the sound startled her; she'd been *that* caught up in the moment.

Self-conscious again, he quickly put his hand back in his pocket and gazed straight ahead. He cleared his throat and said, "Now where did Bitsy run off to?" He realized she was about to knock on Lovinia Bunker's door and rushed off to stop her, a second too late.

The moment was over . . . but they'd *had* a moment. Hitty was sure of it. She felt as if she were floating inches off the ground.

And then she came tumbling back to earth with a thud. Lovinia Bunker opened the door and gasped when she saw Isaac standing in front of her house and Bitsy at the door's threshold. "Why, 'tis thee! I was going to bring it to thee today." She held out Bitsy's doll.

Bitsy grabbed it and returned to her father's side. He bent down to remind her to say thanks, so Bitsy yelled, "THANKS FOR DINNER!" Lovinia giggled, gave Isaac a little two-finger wave, giggled again, and closed the door.

By the time Hitty caught up with Isaac, she noticed two red spots burning on his cheeks. She waited for an explanation as to why he had dinner at Lovinia Bunker's house, but none seemed to be forthcoming. He avoided her eyes and bent down to give Bitsy a goodbye hug. Then, still carefully avoiding Hitty's frowning gaze, he gave a slight nod of acknowledgment and went on his way. Tears had balled up in her throat as she watched him leave.

She felt a drop of rain on her bonnet, then a few more, and picked up her pace toward home. *Lovinia Bunker.* Lovinia, a few years younger than Hitty, was beautiful and dainty, with an immensely thin waistline. She was smitten with Isaac, even Hitty could see that. She wondered how many more maidens had grown keen on Isaac, after Henry had made him such a hero over the Humane Houses. Dozens and dozens, she feared, ignoring the warning voice in her head—sounding eerily like her brother Henry's voice—that accused her of gross exaggeration.

Early in the afternoon, Benjamin came to the Grand House with documents for Hitty to sign.

"What are these for?" she asked.

"They are showing proof of ownership for the island that thy grandmother owned. Before a buyer can be found, the title must first be transferred to Henry's name and thy name. Everything must be in order."

"It goes on and on, this paperwork!"

Benjamin smiled. "Thee doesn't know the half of it."

"I hope Oliver Combs is compensating thee well, Benjamin. Thee looks tired. All this running back and forth between Boston and Nantucket must take a toll. And I'm sure thee has other clients to tend to for Oliver as well."

He glanced away, as if embarrassed by her concern for him. "Worry not on my account, Hitty." He handed her the documents and she went to the desk to sign, feeling his eyes on her. When she finished, he put the papers away in his satchel, closed it up, and then surprised her by asking if she would like to take a turn. The rain had swept through, leaving only white puffy clouds against an azure sky. "If thee is available."

Available? An image of Lovinia Bunker waving two fingers at Isaac popped into her mind. Hitty was available. She had never felt more available in her life. She put on her bonnet, grabbed a shawl, and off they went.

Hitty waved hello to Sister Alice, a neighbor across the street, and Benjamin turned and flashed a smile at her. "That woman, she can talk a blue streak. She caught me the other day and I felt like a pinned butterfly." His comment surprised her. She enjoyed finding humor in ordinary moments, and felt a bond with others who brought levity. A good sign, she thought, reflecting on the kind of person Benjamin must be. She didn't really know, for he did not reveal much about himself.

Hitty smiled. "Henry will often peer out the window to see whether Sister Alice is in her garden before he ventures out. I don't mind her so very much."

"From what I have observed, I think thee will talk to anyone."

Hitty avoided his gaze, feeling a jolt at the thought that he'd been observing her. She had assumed he took no notice of her. "I guess I do," she said with a shrug. "Most people have a story to tell. I find their stories to be interesting."

"I consider it charming." His voice went soft, though he kept his eyes on the road. "Thee has a nice way with others, Hitty. I wish I were more like thee."

He took her elbow to steer her around a mud puddle and she felt keenly aware of his touch. They talked and walked until the sun had dropped low on the horizon and lamps were lit inside homes. When he said goodbye to her, it felt as if something had subtly shifted between them. The notion made her feel light-headed—in a good way.

What an odd day. It started with her feeling joyful and happy, took a nosedive in which she felt downhearted and hopeless, but ended with her feeling buoyed and full of cheer.

The last few weeks, all but on First Day, Henry had been working from dawn until midnight, home for a few hours' rest, then back at dawn to put in another day's work. Yet it never felt like work to him. Since last summer's convention, the newspaper had expanded from eight to twelve pages. Each month, he gave Benjamin an accounting of expenses. Benjamin would draft a check to deposit in the Pacific Bank. Henry would then pay Zebadiah's wages and all outstanding bills. Benjamin had recommended keeping a limited amount of cash available in the Pacific Bank, the balance to be retained in other investments as long as possible, so that money was not left sitting idle. It made sense to Henry, and he was grateful to have the law clerk's financial acumen to guide him. He'd rather put his time into developing the newspaper than into the accounting books.

He set down his graphite pencil and leaned back in his chair, stretching his arms. It had been two years since his grandmother had passed. So far, so good, though he did not want to worry himself too far into the future. The second portion of the inheritance troubled him when he thought on it, so he tried not to think on it.

To date, the inheritance had been used wisely. He hoped his father would be proud, whenever he did return to the island. It would not be soon, if Daphne's latest letter was any indication. Whales were shockingly scarce, she wrote.

Letters! He rubbed his face. Anna had stopped asking to see the letters he had written her. He had not exactly lied to her when he told her that he hadn't located them yet, for he could not tell a lie. But he had not opened his sea chest, and he was fairly confident they were tucked in there. Two years later. Why did he feel such a reluctance to show them to her? He had no answer to that question.

A knock on the door startled him back to the present. "Come in," thinking it was Zebadiah, but nay, it was Marie-Claire. She poked her head around the door. Henry jumped out of his chair and raked his hair with his fingers. "What brings thee here?" He felt his cheeks grow warm and willed them to stop. What was wrong with him? Not enough sleep, that's what.

"I have some news. About the Grand House. At long last I have found a buyer. A cousin, Lucinda Coffin."

He pulled a chair out for her to sit down. "Crazy Lucinda . . . the one who talks to her parrot?"

Marie-Claire stifled a smile. "She is . . . a bit colorful. She is strongly attached to the Grand House, she says, and believes it should be hers."

"Does she not care about the haunting rumor?"

"She said it only adds to the house's appeal."

Henry smirked as he settled into his chair. "And does she have the cash to buy it?"

"Well, in a way. She has asked thee and Hitty to be the mortgage lenders."

"The Bank of Henry and Hitty," he said, rolling his eyes. Many relatives had broached him with similar requests. He sent them all to Benjamin and Marie-Claire, and never heard from them again. "I'm surprised thee hasn't shut her down like the others."

"This might be a little different," she said. "She does have a down payment to provide, a sizable one, and she has offered to pay an additional percentage point above what the bank charges for a mortgage." She set out the document in front of him. "Henry, there are no other offers. Soon it will be two years since the house went on the market. I even tried to advertise on Martha's Vineyard and on Cape Cod. Not a single bite. Since thee has been firm about the price—"

"I won't budge on that. It's worth that and more."

"—then this is the best offer." She lifted her shoulders in a shrug. "'Tis the only offer."

He picked up the paper and saw that Hitty had already signed it. "My sister, she is in favor of this sale?"

"Very much so."

He nodded. "I'll look it over and make a decision. Hold it to the Light."

Marie-Claire looked at him with concern. "I'll pray for a clear answer."

Their eyes met for a long moment, and Henry felt as if everything stopped—the wind outside, the sound of the surf, the very air in the room stood still—until in stomped Zebadiah.

"Look at this! Another one of them 'B' letters." He held an envelope in the air, grinning. "Found it tucked right under the door, just like always." He dropped it on Henry's desk.

Marie-Claire rose. "I'll be off, then, and let thee get back to work."

He smiled. "My thanks, Marie-Claire." He watched her until the door closed.

Zebadiah stood by his desk. "Fancy type."

"Marie-Claire has a refined composure, I'll grant thee that. But she's quite remarkable. Astonishing, really, for she is young. Only seventeen. Quite intelligent, with strong opinions, though she comes across as shy and reticent. I've seen her handle some of my worst relatives with a quiet determination. Rather than the fancy type, the kind who needs a lot of attention, I'd say she's the very opposite. She's quite an encourager to others."

"I meant the letter." Zebadiah pointed to the "B" envelope. "The handwrit script. It's a fancy type."

Ah.

Mary Coffin Starbuck

15 December 1698

An English sea captain named Thomas Chalkley has come to the island to preach, and he has created quite a stir. He is a Quaker missionary, a vivacious speaker, and has held meetings each day. My son Nathaniel has attended each one and wants us to go with him tonight. He said that over two hundred people have turned out to listen to Chalkley. Imagine that! There are but six or seven hundred people on the island.

I told my son I will attend, though not to expect his father to join us. Nathaniel takes more of an interest in spiritual matters than his father, for whom he was named. He looks much like his father, but he is my child through and through.

21 December 1698

I did not return home until very late last eve and then I could not sleep. I was enraptured by Thomas Chalkley and stayed afterward to converse with him, and ever since my mind and soul have been stirring. Chalkley's message resounded in me, though it is difficult to grasp. Baptism and other sacraments, the Quaker insisted, even the Lord's Supper, were empty transactions, nothing but outward ceremonies. "Look inward!" Chalkley told me. "Turn within to find the Christ. The Light resides within thee."

Light.

Light is a theme that vibrates throughout Scripture.

The very first words of God recorded in Scripture were, "Let there be light."

Jesus Christ is known as the "Light of the world."

Believers are told to let our light shine bright.

Light.

On a bleak, dark winter day, the darkest night of the year, that thought is especially appealing.

17

Hitty heard Isaac's voice when Philemon opened the door and she hurried to the foyer. "Good evening," she said, trying to sound as if her heart wasn't pounding like a drum. "Thee is welcome to come in, but I fear Henry is not at home."

Isaac was dressed up, she noticed, or as dressed up as Isaac got. He was wearing a dark overcoat that appeared to be somewhat new. When he took off his hat, she saw that he had a haircut too. Normally, he wore it shaggy. It was trimmed and neatly combed. He had a coy look in his eyes, Hitty thought, excited and wary at the same time.

"I only have a moment. Might I speak to thee?"

Me? He came to see me! She joined him on the porch steps.

"I came to tell you that I'll be off island for a week. Mayhap two."

"Oh, right . . . the fire department," she said, forcing a brightness in her voice she didn't really feel. Isaac's current mission was to create a municipal fire department, and Henry was sending him to interview some departments on Cape Cod, to glean from their experience. Nantucket had privately organized fire companies that would respond only to houses and businesses that carried a plaque of insurance.

Isaac was constantly worried about the safety of Nantucket citizens. Sometimes Hitty wished he would worry about her. Benjamin certainly did. Whenever he was on island, he would arrive at the Grand House to pay a call on Hitty. Was Benjamin interested in her? He seemed to be lately. Or was he just being friendly?

She was not particularly good at reading signals from men, nor women. Never had been good at it. Either she made something out of nothing or missed the signal entirely. "Thee must be keen to go."

"Indeed, I am keen for this project. Bitsy will be staying with Sister Hannah."

"But . . . but she doesn't like staying with Sister Hannah." The night had grown colder, and their breath mingled in frosty clouds that hung in the air. "Last time, she said that Sister Hannah made her sit in a chair for hours and hours."

Isaac smiled. And he hardly ever smiled, at least the kind that bursts forth from amusement, so when he did it was a little overwhelming. Small lines fanned out at the corners of his eyes, deep creases etched his lined cheek. She felt herself staring at him, then tried to hide her reaction. "Bitsy probably did not confess that she had hidden Sister Hannah's walking cane. My daughter tries to pull the wool over others' eyes."

"I've never quite understood that expression."

"It comes from the powdered wigs worn by British judges. If their wig tilted down over their eyes, they could not see what was going on."

"Oh! I thought it had something to do with Nantucket sheep."

A laugh burst out of Isaac. She looked at him quickly to see if he mocked her, but the look on his face was not unkind. Not the way Henry would tease Hitty when she said something that revealed her ignorance.

"Sister Hannah will care well for Bitsy in my absence. I . . . just wanted thee to know . . . for Bitsy's sake." He paused, tucking his head, as if he had something more on his mind and was gathering the words to say it. All at once, he lifted his head to meet her gaze. His face was shadowed by his hat, but she could see his eyes. Those eyes! There was so much going on behind them. "Hitty . . . ," he took a step closer to her, "there's a matter I'd like to discuss—"

She would never know what "matter" he meant—a declaration of affection? a kiss?—because, in the next moment, the gate opened and in strolled Benjamin, calling out, "Surprise! I've just come in on the tide."

What could she do? She greeted him as he joined them. Benjamin turned to Isaac and boldly shook his hand, then he took his place by Hitty's side. She felt as if a lion had just pounced on the porch, declaring his territory.

Isaac nodded briefly to Hitty, then turned and left without another word.

Hitty stood still for a moment, watching Isaac stride away. Benjamin left her side to head into the house, looking for Marie-Claire.

Hitty felt a twinge of sadness. A sense of losing out on something that *could* happen—but never would. *So near and yet so far,* she thought with a sigh.

A few days later, Hitty sat at the desk in the parlor on a rainy evening, trying to replicate a sketch of a bird made by Marie-Claire. She held it up and thought it looked like a hideous rat, not a bird. Frustrated, she crumpled the paper and took out another to start again, when someone pounded on the door, shouting frantically. Hitty went to the foyer as Philemon opened the door and there was Bitsy, bonnetless and capeless, drenched from the rain and shivering from the cold. When she saw Hitty, she ran to her and threw her arms around her. "Don't make me go back!"

The little girl seemed overwrought, gasping so she could hardly catch a breath. Hitty waited until the sobs tapered down before asking, "Bitsy, what has happened to make thee run away? Sister Hannah must be worried sick."

"She's not! She sleeps in her chair all day and all night. And she forgets where she's put her wooden teeth. She leaves them all over the house. I went to butter my bread and found them in the crock just now! Hitty, I'm sure they moved!" She squeezed her fingers to her thumb, like a clamshell snapping shut. "I *hate* it there!"

Bitsy looked up at Hitty, a pleading look in her eyes, a gaze so much like Isaac's that the resemblance made her lose her train of thought. "Please, please, please let me stay with thee until Papa comes back."

By this time, Henry had come downstairs, curious to see what the ruckus was all about, as had Marie-Claire, Philemon, Cook, and two housemaids.

Henry gave a nod to Hitty. "Let her stay. I'll tell Sister Hannah that Bitsy is here."

Sister Hannah seemed greatly relieved, less so on the news that Bitsy had been found—for Henry was not entirely convinced she had realized the child had left the house—and visibly delighted when he told her that Bitsy would stay with them during the rest of Isaac's absence. The poor old dear. She looked positively worn to a frazzle by the girl.

The rain had stopped and Henry savored the walk home. He felt his spirits lift at the sight of the Grand House. Every window glowed with light, the large downstairs rooms filled with movement and life. Henry recalled walking past the Grand House when his grandmother had lived there. The house was usually dark, deserted looking, except for a small square of light in an upstairs window. His grandmother's bedroom.

Tonight, the windows were open to the fresh spring evening air and the sounds of happy voices floated out, including the peal of a child's laughter. *Bitsy.*

A decision, one that had troubled him greatly, one he had held to the Light, was suddenly as clear as day. He would not sell the Grand House to crazy cousin Lucinda. Not to anyone. This house was his home.

Hitty stared out the window to the cove. Every time she looked at the sea, it reminded her of Isaac. He'd been away two weeks and it felt much longer. Her feelings seesawed between missing him and savoring this time with Bitsy, for she had grown exceedingly fond of the little girl.

Although it was late in the afternoon, the sun was still bright and strong, so Hitty took Bitsy down to the cove. As children, she and Henry would run backward across the sand to spy their own footprints, amazed at how quickly they vanished with the next wave that rolled in. Bitsy reminded her of those happy days of childhood, chasing seagulls as they swooped and dove in to find their evening meal.

Hitty had always loved the sea at low tide, with the wide, flat shoreline. The smooth, wet sand took on a silvery sheen. As she watched Bitsy dance after the waves, she felt someone touch her shoulder. "She looks happy."

Isaac!

"How did thee find us?"

"Sister Hannah told me. I hope Bitsy has not been a bother to you. I came directly here, and Philemon sent me down to the water."

"She is never a bother to me."

He dipped his chin, so Hitty could not see his eyes. "When Sister Hannah told me that she had run away, I felt . . . grateful to you, Mehitabel. Grateful that my daughter had a place to run to." He paused. "Someone to run to."

"As did I." When he met her gaze, Hitty noticed two spots of color tinge his cheeks. They shared a private smile, a brief one, for Bitsy caught sight of her father and ran to him in a gallop, and he opened his arms to catch her up.

He tipped his head back to survey the sky. "'Tis a fine day—the weather cleared up nicely, no wind. Just the right circumstances to build a sandcastle, don't you think?"

They built a sandcastle on the beach, spending a long time on its construction, and it was a sight to behold, tall and sturdy, with drizzles of wet sand to soften its edges. The tide started to come in, nipping away at their castle.

"'Tis time I get my daughter home," Isaac said finally.

"One last splash in the water!" Bitsy ran down to the water's edge to dip her toes.

Hitty watched her, startled that the sun had dropped below the horizon and the blue sky was darkening. How could time go so quickly?

Isaac stood and offered her his hand. Hitty took it, holding on lightly as she came to her feet. She met his gaze for a long moment, then let go. Isaac's hand came up, and she thought he was going to touch her, but instead he let his hand drop. "We should be off," he said, though Hitty got the feeling that he didn't want the day to end.

Progress! she thought, with a satisfied smile. *We are making progress.*

A whaling ship, *Olivia*, had returned to port during the night, and most Nantucketers would take time from their obligations this morning to welcome the crew in off lighters, eager for news of the voyage. At breakfast, Henry asked who might like to go to the wharf with him, right now, before the town came to life and crowds crammed the quay. It took no persuasion for Hitty. She met every incoming ship, always hopeful for a letter from Daphne and Papa. Henry did his best to convince Jeremiah to come too, but he adamantly refused. Hated crowds, he said. "Love m' morning tea in peace and quiet."

It was a warm morning as Henry, Hitty, and Marie-Claire made their way to the waterfront. Hitty nodded to people as they opened their weathered wooden doors, turning them back to signal the start of the workday. The scent of woodsmoke drifted through the air from the blacksmith, then the clanging sound of his hammer, pounding, pounding, pounding, as he crafted iron hoops for coopers to fit staves for barrels. Fishermen peddled oysters, clams, and fresh cod off the back of drays. Farmers sold crocks of butter and baskets of apples from big-wheeled wooden carts. Hitty took a moment to absorb the many sounds and smells and sights. She loved this island.

They should have come even earlier than they did, and it was Hitty's fault for the delay. She had trouble with her corset, and it took Marie-Claire's patience to untangle the strings and start again. How she hated corsets! By now, the crowds had already gathered. They were nearly to the wharf, moving along in the throng, when Henry yanked on Hitty's arm to stop.

"Where is Marie-Claire?" he asked, concern in his voice.

Where was she? Somewhere, they'd gotten separated.

Henry stood on a bench, caught sight of Marie-Claire, and waved and shouted to catch her attention. She smiled, her eyes wide with relief, and quickly wove her way through the crowd toward him. Hitty's stomach growled, so she excused herself to buy crispy sugared buns from a vendor's cart next to the bench Henry had jumped up on—one for each of them to eat while they waited for the lighters to come in. After paying the vendor, she couldn't resist sampling a bit of the warm bun from the bag. Ah, sheer heaven! When she turned around, she stopped short. Benjamin Foulger stood not a rod away, his arms crossed over his chest as he took a long, appraising look at her. So long, in fact, it made her feel self-conscious.

"Oh! Um, hello," she stammered, swallowing, brushing sugar from her mouth. She smiled nervously and tucked a stray curl of hair behind her ear.

"Good morning, Hitty." He paused, looking thoughtful. Then he took the bun out of her hand and popped it into his mouth in one bite. He looked incredibly attractive as he chewed. It was downright annoying.

After swallowing the bun down, he said, "Thee looks quite fetching sprinkled in sugar."

She looked down at her dress. Sugar dusted her fichu. "Umm—thanks." He was laughing, but the flash in his gaze was more than friendly. Brushing it off, she lifted her chin in the direction of the wharf. "I'm here with Henry and Marie-Claire. We're going to the wharf to welcome the sailors."

"May I join thee?" In a gentlemanly gesture, he put his elbow out for her to hold on to as they moved through the crowd. Hitty felt her stomach flip-flop as others made way for them. As they walked, her schoolgirl silliness over Benjamin's nearness vanished, and she laughed over something he said. She caught sight of Isaac Barnard at the edge of the crowd, Bitsy in hand. Isaac noticed Hitty almost the second she noticed him. Her breath caught in her throat as their eyes met, and she felt her cheeks grow red. She put up her hand to wave, but he turned away, crouching down to listen to Bitsy.

Why did he not acknowledge her? He must have seen her wave to him. Was he bothered with her? Had she done something?

No sooner had that thought circled around to settle in her mind than another one arrived as they approached Henry and Marie-Claire. Although Marie-Claire was fairly tall, she looked almost petite standing beside Henry, whose dark good looks seemed a perfect contrast to her fair complexion. They were laughing over something that amused them, and it suddenly occurred to Hitty that she often found them together like this—at the breakfast table, by the fire in the parlor—heads together, talking and laughing.

They looked so happy, so right together. It was a startling thought to Hitty.

In June, to celebrate the coming of summer, Hitty taught songs to the children at the Cent School. Inspired by Marie-Claire's encouragement, she decided to host an event for the parents. Ten songs were sung, all from the Friends' tradition, for those were all Hitty knew.

Bitsy, unlike the other children, had an ability to sing on key, so Hitty gave her a solo to conclude the event. When it was time for her to step forward from the row of children and sing her solo, Hitty held her breath. She met Isaac's gaze and knew he shared the same thought—would Bitsy change her mind at the last moment and refuse to sing? Hitty half expected it.

But the little girl surprised Hitty, relishing the center of attention. She stood in front of the other children, peering out at the parents until she found her father and locked eyes. Then Bitsy opened her mouth to sing. When the last note sounded, applause suddenly roared through the keeping room of the Cent School.

Isaac turned to Hitty, looking awestruck and very proud.

After the parents gathered their children and headed for home for supper, Isaac lingered. Hitty went over to him; she could see he was at a loss for words.

"Bitsy did a wonderful job. So calm and composed."

Bitsy was turning into a different child than the one who had burst into the Cent School a few years ago, like a clap of thunder.

"Indeed," he said, sounding stunned. "I wish . . ." He stopped himself midsentence. Hitty saw a faint flush cross his cheeks. "I wish I could hear it again," he finished quickly.

Hitty nodded, fairly confident that wasn't what he'd meant to say at all. She had thought about the enjoyable afternoon she'd had with Isaac on the beach when he returned from Cape Cod to fetch Bitsy. She had thought about Isaac.

Things were not as easy between Isaac and Hitty as they had been a few months back, though she still saw him nearly each day. He hadn't walked to school in the mornings for weeks, not since . . . well, not since the *Olivia* sailed into port. She didn't know what had happened to ruin the ease that had been growing between them. It caused her great concern, and sleepless nights, and endless worries about Lovinia Bunker.

Hitty wondered if she should ask Isaac if he and Bitsy would join them for supper at the Grand House. But that might seem too forward . . . wouldn't it? Before she could figure it out, Marie-Claire beat her to it. "Isaac, would thee care to join us for a celebratory supper?"

Before he could respond, Hitty heard someone clear his throat in a very intentional way. She saw Benjamin at the door, flowers tucked in his arm, watching them with a frown on his face. "Did I miss the performance?"

Why was he here? Hitty hadn't invited him, for she didn't think he would be interested. Henry certainly wasn't, nor was Jeremiah.

He strode over to join them in that confident way he had. "Not too late for dinner, I hope. I'm famished."

"We were just discussing that very thing," Marie-Clare said. "Isaac and Bitsy will join us."

Isaac looked at Hitty briefly, glanced at Benjamin, then back at Marie-Claire. "Thanks, but I need to finish up a few things. Some other time." He called to Bitsy, who had taken the lid off the cookie tin and was reaching in for a handful.

As Hitty watched him turn and hurry to stop her, she felt a sweep of disappointment and sadness. Bitsy's birthday was not far off; she would be finished with the Cent School and eligible to attend public school. Not only would she miss that little girl, but what would happen to her relationship with Isaac? *There is no relationship with Isaac!* She could hear Henry's voice in her mind. She dipped her nose into the bouquet of flowers, sadly realizing he was right.

Henry sat by the fire and read aloud to Jeremiah the letter that arrived today from his father on the ship *Java*. Near Greenland, the *Endeavour* had gammed with *Java*, on its way back to Nantucket, and his father penned a quick letter to be delivered. The letter was dated just last month. It was a treat to read the thoughts of Reynolds Macy, Henry thought. Normally, Daphne was the letter writer. While he certainly enjoyed reading Daphne's news, his father had a different perspective on the voyage. A before-and-after view, for he hadn't been whaling in over twenty years. Much had changed.

"'The *Endeavour* sailed far north,'" Henry read in a clear voice, "'in time to see the whales make their way into the cold sea they loved. 'Twas always a magnificent moment to me as the ship sailed into the Arctic Sea. Some might say that one ocean is just like another, but I see the differences between them. It wasn't long before we found the slow-moving creatures. And that was when my heart sank. In the early days, when I crewed as a boy, I would've seen some hundred thousand of these noble animals as they swam their way through the northern seas; now there was less than ten thousand. Massive hunting has taken a severe toll.'"

The rest of the letter had to do with the weather, always top on the mind of a whalemaster. Henry finished reading, then dropped the letter in his lap. "Jeremiah, what would thee think if I were to publish a portion of this letter in the next edition?"

Jeremiah's bushy eyebrows lifted. "Why?"

"I think it would be a beneficial perspective."

"It might cause a rise in the price of whale oil. You'll be accused of causin' a gouge."

"The whaling industry is not going to survive if this keeps going. Whales will become extinct. Thee knows how brutal some of the captains can be—killing the mothers and their calves. There has to be some kind of balance, some rules of the sea, before it's too late."

Jeremiah shrugged. "Just get ready for some backlash. Even Samuel Jenks won't touch criticizing the whalers."

"Nantucket led the whaling industry. Why can't we lead still?"

"Aye, we led it right into the mess we've made for ourselves. For greed is what led us, boy."

That hasn't changed, Henry thought. *Greed leads us still.*

Mary Coffin Starbuck

1 January 1700

I woke at dawn, eager to see the sun rise on a new century. I dressed warmly and walked along the shore, my favorite place. 'Twas cold but not windy, not foggy. The sea was calm, almost glassy. A perfect morning for reflection. The surf broke on the sand, the seagulls arrived to search for food. Just an ordinary winter day. And yet such an extraordinary day. A new century!

I stood for a while, watching the water, thinking of that day Father brought us to this island, over forty years ago. Mother thought we would only last a year, at best, and then Father would pack us up and off we'd go, to another imagined paradise. She was wrong, for Father rarely left the island after that, and never will again. My life has been here, and now my children are raising their children here.

Most of the Indians have been Christianized and we have been fair in our dealings with them. They remained loyal to us during King Philip's War.

I turned in a circle, looking back at the houses that dotted the harbor. The new harbor, that is, for Capaum Harbor is no longer open. Sand is always shifting and moving this island around, like a woman in a tight-fitting dress. It seems a metaphor for the island, for islanders have had to adjust, then readjust, then readjust again. The town has been moved, laid out to contour the edge of the harbor that will not be closed again by a sandbar. We hope.

I thought of the year when our own house was dismantled, piece by piece (for lumber is so dear), and rebuilt closer to the new town. Nathaniel took the opportunity to enlarge it to fit our growing family and might have gotten carried away. My father dubbed it Parliament House for its grand size, and the name stuck.

The sound of sheep bleating in the distance pulled me back to the present. That, too, is in the midst of a change. We had hoped raising sheep would be the path to prosperity, to sell wool on the mainland, and for food. That does not seem to be the case. Peter Foulger forecasted that very thing, long ago, when he warned that sheep would keep people clothed and fed, but they would not make anyone wealthy.

But whaling would, my Nathaniel insisted. He was not a farmer or shepherd by nature, but a man made to live off the sea. He spent much time with the Wampanoags when we first arrived on the island, taught by the local Indians to hunt whales. The island is ideally suited for whaling, as its location is close to the migratory routes of the whales.

After a particularly bad year with the sheep, when much of the flock died, Nathaniel brought Ichabod Paddock over from the Cape to teach others to catch whales. And now, as 1700 dawns, anyone who can hold an oar is involved in the whaling industry.

We have settled this rugged island and made it something to be proud of.

18

Jeremiah had a bad feeling about Benjamin Foulger, though he couldn't come up with any reasonable explanation for it. He'd given much thought to it, and came up with . . . nothing. The young law clerk had never done anything to offend Jeremiah, not remotely. He was impeccably polite and well mannered, attended to his work quite diligently. Henry certainly had no complaints.

And now Benjamin was showing an inordinate amount of attention to Hitty, and she seemed rather smitten by it, judging from the amount of time she spent fussing and fiddling with her hair and dress when she knew he was coming round to the Grand House.

What *was* it about Benjamin Foulger that got under Jeremiah's skin? The only thing he could point to was the way he would walk around the parlor while he waited for Hitty, as he was now, carefully examining each treasure Lillian had collected. Such a small thing, but it irritated Jeremiah. It was like the man was tallying up the knickknacks in his head, considering their cost.

Ridiculous, he knew. But Jeremiah always trusted his gut,

and it had never proved him wrong save once—his cousin's son. He settled back in his chair, almost shrinking, and watched the flames of the fire. *Tristram Macy*. He'd never been so wrong about anyone in his life.

When Hitty came downstairs, she found Benjamin waiting in the front parlor. He sat in Grandmother Lillian's stiff armchair, staring at the fire, his expression pensive.

"Sorry to keep thee waiting," she said.

At the sound of her voice, his expression brightened, and he rose to greet her.

"Is everything all right?"

"Nay. Well, aye. Hitty, I don't think thy grandfather approves of me."

She was confused; Jeremiah wasn't even in the parlor. "Of course he approves thee. What makes thee say such a thing?"

"He was here but a moment ago and snapped at me for examining that crystal bell on the mantel. As if I were a child like that wild urchin, about to drop it, without a care for its value."

Bitsy, he meant. She was *not* a wild urchin. A child with a mind of her own, a bit impulsive, blunt to the point of rudeness. But not wild, and not a raggedy urchin. "Jeremiah sounds more gruff than he is. It's just his way."

Benjamin reached out for her hands. "I hope thee is right. I wouldn't want us to start off on the wrong foot."

Us? There was an *us*? What did he mean by that? Did that mean she fit into his future? That he was making plans that included her?

Henry would scold her; he would say she shouldn't try

to read too much into offhand remarks. And yet, even she couldn't deny that her friendship with Benjamin was growing deeper with each passing visit. He was very attentive to her, unlike Isaac, who seemed inordinately preoccupied with his work. Why, Isaac hardly went out of his way to speak to her anymore. She had to face facts on that front, as well. Nothing was brewing with Isaac, and something was definitely brewing with Benjamin. Simmering!

Why was she thinking about Isaac Barnard when Benjamin Foulger was right here, holding her hands? She shook off thoughts of Isaac and tried to focus on this fine and handsome man in her parlor, a man so sophisticated and erudite that he could have his pick of any beautiful maiden on this island.

Benjamin leaned forward and kissed her, just a light, gentle brush of his lips on hers. Then he released her and stepped back with a fond smile. "Shall we go in to dinner? It smells delicious."

Flustered by the unexpected kiss, she followed meekly behind him into the dining room. Something was happening between them, even if she wasn't sure how she felt about it. She tried to shake off the feeling of life being a weather breeder. But she didn't want to get her hopes up. It was all too good to be true. It couldn't last.

Almost near midnight, Henry left the office and walked to the Grand House. He had signed off on the proof for tomorrow's edition and left it for Zebadiah to roll the presses, come morning. He wished he could see the look on Zebadiah's face when he walked into the office. How shocked he would be!

I'm making progress, Henry realized, as his boots crunched up the shell path that led to the front porch. His stomach didn't twist and turn nearly so much when he finally approved the proof. Decisions were coming easier to him. It was practice, he supposed, that made them easier. Even when he made the wrong decision, which he certainly did now and then, though far less often than the first few months of the *Illumine*, he had discovered mistakes were not fatal. Failure did not have that sweeping, paralyzing sense of regret over him like it once did. He could get over it.

But for tomorrow's edition, he had no hesitation. Just the opposite. He felt elated to sign off. It was a momentous occasion for a newspaper. The kind of a day when Nantucketers would read the newspaper and tuck it carefully away into their chests for safekeeping, to be saved for future generations. This edition would not serve as kindle for the fire!

Henry wasn't sure how Anna did it, but through her dogged persistence, the public school integration issue had stayed on the front burner of Nantucket politics. Tonight, school committee chairman Nathaniel Barney presented a motion to integrate the public schools, which would allow Eunice Ross to enter the high school. And it passed. It passed! *What* a victory!

As he went into the house, he noticed a flicker of light coming from the parlor door, cracked open a few inches. He poked his head around the door and saw Marie-Claire at the desk, concentrating on something. "Thee is still up?"

She looked up in surprise. "Benjamin is leaving for Boston at high tide. He needed these letters prepared to send."

He walked into the room. "What are they about?"

"Benjamin has found a buyer for the island that thy grandmother owned."

"An island." Henry sat down by the fire and stretched out his legs. "An island! Imagine that. I doubt she ever set foot on it." He let out a huff. "She was constantly collecting things. I remember one time when Daphne opened the door to the Centre Street cottage to find two burly men, sent to deliver furniture from the Grand House. Grandmother Lillian had purchased new furniture and sent the old to Daphne, without asking her first." He smiled at the memory, as real to him as if it were yesterday. "Daphne did not want the hand-me-downs. The cottage was small and cozy, and Grandmother's furniture was like her, stiff and formal and imposing."

He remembered listening to the conversation Daphne had with his father as the two men stood impatiently at the door—that children would not be able to sit or eat or talk or move around Grandmother's furniture. She was trying to turn Henry and Hitty into little soldiers, Daphne had said. To take away their childhood, as she had done to her own two daughters. As Henry's gaze swept the parlor, he realized Daphne had been right. This room, the main gathering room, was a painfully prim and proper room. Children did not belong here, it said.

"So Daphne refused the men entry. Grandmother did not take kindly to being rebuffed." He wasn't sure why he was telling Marie-Claire that story, wasn't even sure she was listening, but then she blotted the letter with the ink blotter, folded it, tucked it in an envelope, and said, "Done."

She swung around to look at him with a certain smile that made him know she had heard him. "Henry Macy, thee looks quite content."

"I am. Quite, quite content. Tomorrow's edition is ready to print. Zebadiah will be shocked when he arrives in the morning."

"Has thee eaten yet?"

"Eaten? Nay."

"Come. I can make thee some supper."

"Thee cooks?"

She lifted a hand in the air and seesawed it back and forth. "Not really, but I can warm up some leftover potpie."

"That sounds safer."

She laughed and he felt happy. "Follow me," she said, walking out of the room to head to the kitchen.

Not much later, she served him a plate of warmed chicken potpie and crusty rolls lathered with butter. They sat together at the kitchen table, the only light came from one candlestick, for they took care not to alert Cook that they were in her sacred space. They lingered long after Henry had finished the impromptu meal, talking first about the newspaper, about the passing of the integration vote and what it would mean for Nantucket. They went on to other topics, all kinds. And they laughed about silly things, muffling the sound with their hands. With Marie-Claire he laughed quite often. He liked to make her smile.

Henry slept late the next morning and woke feeling well rested. He dressed and hurried downstairs, eager to see Philemon, for he must have heard the results of the school committee vote by now. It was abuzz all through Nantucket Town last night.

Philemon gave him a brief nod as he brought him a cup of tea. The smile on Henry's face faded. "Why the long face, Philemon? Surely thee has heard the good news."

"Your printer came to the house an hour ago, Master Henry."

"Zebadiah?"

Philemon nodded. “He said not to wake you, but to let you know that the town reconsidered its vote this morning. He said he would hold the press, waiting for your rewrite.”

Henry’s smile faded. “Because . . . ,” but he knew the answer. He could read it in Philemon’s face.

“The vote was overturned.”

Mary Coffin Starbuck

20 February 1700

'Tis funny how our mind plays tricks on us. We think we are so right about something, so absolutely sure we are right, only to discover that we are so very wrong.

Today is the day of my birth. A cold winter day with bright sunny skies—my favorite! Dinah brought the children over midday to have supper with me, for she knew Nathaniel was away. They had made a sticky toffee pudding, knowing how I love it. Dinah said they had to make it twice, for the first time it overcooked and the house still reeked of burnt sugar.

As we sat around the table, one grandson asked me how old I was, and I answered, "Twenty-two," without thinking twice.

"Surely you jest." Dinah, my dearest daughter-in-law, gave me a shocked look. "Nay, you are not jesting!"

And I was not!

Nay, I am not twenty-two. Today I am fifty-six years old. Where have the years gone? Aging is a sticky thing for me to grasp, for I am full of vigor and good health, and am barely aware I have grown older.

But then I remembered that I have borne ten children—though I must say that each time I sneeze or cough, I am reminded of that truth! (My mother had the same dilemma and made use of the potato as a remedy. Father never did know why the potato barrel emptied so frequently.) And then there is my husband's appearance.

His hair is salt and pepper, and not as thick as it once was. His shoulders stoop ever so slightly, his trick knee plagues him, he cannot stretch out his fingers for they remain bent. Nathaniel is nearly a decade older than I, and as his dear body changes with age, I watch him and realize that I behold my future.

But inside, inside . . . I still feel like a young girl. That is the strange thing. I believe Saint Paul might have felt the same way about aging. Could it be that very pondering about aging was what prompted him to write to the church in Corinth? "Though our outward man perish, yet the inward man is renewed day by day." I wonder.

I said as much to Nathaniel last night as we readied for bed. He had a different view on the topic of aging, which was no surprise, for we think very differently. He said he felt like a man in his midsixties because that's how old he is. "But you, Mary, if you believe something strongly enough, you're sure it's true. Some things can't be ignored, can't be simplified, try as you might."

Things like growing older.

As I blew out the candle and lay in the dark, I felt a bit melancholy.

19

Anna Gardner planned a second abolitionist convention, larger than the first one, to take place in the Eighth Month of 1842 at the Atheneum. Henry hadn't seen much of Anna in the last few months but for a turn around the block once a week or so; she was completely engrossed in the details of the event and spoke of nothing else. He was amazed at her determination. Somehow she was able to convince Nantucket-born-and-raised social reformer Lucretia Coffin Mott to return to the island to speak at the convention. William Lloyd Garrison agreed to return for a second time and planned to bring the Reverend Stephen Foster with him, a fiery abolitionist speaker.

Day one started off quite well. The weather had been stormy earlier in the week, and Anna worried the speakers might be delayed in arriving. But nay, they had all come in on the tide, each one, as promised, and the skies were blue. A good boding, Henry thought, of the days to come. Anna, as host, was first to speak, something Henry knew she was nervous about, as she had practiced her speech on him a half-dozen times as they walked around the block. He knew the speech so well he thought he could recite it himself.

Henry had arrived early to claim a seat on the far side of the large room, close to the front but with a good vantage point to observe the entire room. Anna sat up front, along with the other dignitaries, and gave him a smile when she spotted him. When it was time to begin, she rose, took off her bonnet, shoulders held very straight as she looked out at the audience. The room quieted down as it became apparent that she was waiting to speak. Anna started, then stopped, started, then stopped. Henry could see her struggling to keep a controlled expression and his heart went out to her.

But then, something shifted in Anna. Instead of looking at the audience, she lifted her eyes up to the ceiling, as if she was searching for the words. She found what she was looking for—whatever that was—lowered her head, and started to speak again, this time with authority. She didn't falter again, her voice never wavered nor wobbled. Her confidence was something to see.

Henry jotted furiously in his notebook, for this was not the speech she had practiced on him. This went far beyond that, from the abomination of slavery to the degradation of women. She delivered a rousing lecture that brought many to their feet in applause.

Next to speak was a reformer from Boston, a man who probably had much worthwhile to say, but coming on the heels of Anna's dynamic speech, he seemed pallid and dull. Bored, Henry scanned the audience and noticed Isaac Barnard, whose head was cocked at an odd angle. Who was Isaac staring at? Henry leaned forward for a better look. Ah! *Hitty.* Next to his sister sat Marie-Claire, and he wondered what she thought of Anna's address. His thoughts continued to drift, until he heard angry shouts of protest coming from outside. Not so loud that the speaker could not be heard, but distracting, like a buzzing mosquito in a closed room. He wrote it all down.

The next day, the Reverend Stephen Foster spoke forth, and he did not mince any words. "By refusing to witness against their own denominations condoning slavery in the South," he thundered, "the northern clergymen are nothing but a brotherhood of thieves." And then he began to denounce Nantucket's clergymen, name by name by name. The eyes of the audience went wide with shock. Henry wrote that all down too.

Outside, the shouters of yesterday had grown to a mob, in size and volatility. When word traveled to them that the Reverend Foster had insulted the clergy of Nantucket, the mob doubled in size, then tripled. As the day wore on, over two hundred Nantucketers gathered to throw eggs and beans at the Atheneum's walls, windows, and door.

The following day, the convention took place in the evening. Again the protesters gathered, this time both in and out of the Atheneum, with the goal to shout down the speakers, so loudly that no one could be heard. Inside, they stomped on the floor. Outside, they threw eggs and beans and cobbles, and broke several windows.

The trustees of the Atheneum huddled together in the corner of the lecture hall. Walter Mitchell, Maria's father, president of the trustees, emerged from the huddle to announce that due to concern for the defacing of the library, the convention would not be permitted to continue to meet there. Henry wrote it all down.

Another location was attempted the next day, but in the middle of the Reverend Stephen Foster's speech, mobsters burst in to pelt rotten eggs. The sulphur smell was so noxious that everyone had to clear the room. Henry took careful notes.

The convention was moved to the Quaker Meeting House for First Day, referred to as August 14 by non-Quakers. Again, the mob gathered outside and shouted down Reverend Stephen Foster. The elders asked Reverend Foster to leave the old meetinghouse to protect the building from damage. The convention wound up in a boat-building shop on the edge of town, and there the convention was able to continue in peace. Henry's pad was thick with notes.

The conventioneers tried to meet again the next day at the boat-building shop, but several eggs sailed into the shop through doors and windows, and some protesters broke in to beat Foster and then chaos erupted. One of the speakers, the dull and pallid one, Henry noted, jumped out a window to avoid getting hurt. The day's meeting adjourned, and the sheriff was sent for to safely escort Reverend Foster to his lodging.

Things settled down the next day, and the day after that, and then the convention concluded, and the off island conventioneers departed on the boat to the mainland.

Henry had barely slept all week long, for he stayed up late each night to shape his notes into articles that followed the day-by-day events of the dramatic convention. That week's edition of the *Illumine* spread to sixteen pages. He could hardly wait to see it roll off the presses.

Henry hadn't had a chance to speak privately to Anna throughout the entire convention. He'd been absorbed in reporting for the newspaper; she was immersed in the convention and in providing hospitality—and safekeeping—for its speakers. He prepared himself to see her today, for he knew she'd be disappointed by the turbulence of the convention. It had been shocking to see the depth of hatred among the protesters, to visibly see the island's polarization. On the surface, Nantucket seemed like a tolerant, forward-thinking place. But scratch that surface—try to bring needed reforms—and its societal conflicts were no different than the mainland.

To Henry's complete shock, Anna was not at all disappointed by the convention. She was elated, practically glowing. "Henry, Nantucket is facing change! Of course there is backlash. 'Tis expected, 'tis always expected. But this issue will not go away. Nantucket will be known as leading the charge to a world without slavery. A bastion of anti-slavery sentiment! Nay, I do not feel disappointed. I feel . . . triumphant!"

Henry gazed at Anna while she spoke of her enthusiasm for the other speakers, about their dogged determination to persist to abolish slavery, no matter what. *No matter what.* Deep feelings for Anna welled up inside him, of love and admiration and loyalty. He thought of what his father and grandfather often told him, when he stood at a fork in the road: *If there is no wind, row.*

"Anna," Henry blurted out, "marry me. Be my wife. I'm ready. More than ready. 'Tis long overdue."

"Ready? For marriage?" Her pale blue eyes went wide with shock. "Marriage?" Her voice rose an octave on that word. "But Henry, I'm . . . I am not . . . ready. Far from it." She swallowed. "Dear Henry, there's something I must tell thee." She kept her eyes on her grasped hands, as if they held what she needed to say. "Lucretia Coffin Mott . . . she wants to hire me as an anti-slavery lecturer. To speak at other abolitionist conventions." She looked up. "On the mainland. I'll be under way next week."

Henry felt stunned, couldn't speak. He could only stare at her.

"Please don't look so distraught," she rushed to say.

He looked distraught because he was distraught. He felt as if the wind had been knocked out of him. "Thee is leaving the island?"

"I feel I must do this, Henry, to strike while the iron is hot." She gave a slight nod. "Surely, thee can understand."

"I'm not sure I do." He fought for control, unable to know how to respond.

"I'd hoped thee would support me."

"What am I supposed to do? Clap my hands and exclaim with delight?"

She stepped closer to him. "I do love thee, Henry."

He didn't doubt that she loved him. But he realized now that she was not in love with him. There was a difference.

"I won't be gone long. We can pick up this conversation again when I return."

"How long?" he said. "How long will thee be away?"

She hesitated. "I'll return next summer to host another convention."

"A year?"

She reached out to squeeze his hands. "There's much work to be done."

"Indeed, there is. I do understand that." And he did.

"Henry, I feel a calling to end slavery. A lifelong calling, something so powerful I cannot ignore it. I thought, I'd hoped, that thee shared this calling with me."

"I do, Anna. I share the calling. But it's not the only commitment I have. I am committed to the island. To my sister and grandfather, to my father and Daphne. To the newspaper." It suddenly seemed so clear to him. He and Anna wanted the same things, but they went about it in very different ways. "Our timing." He sighed. "It's always been off."

"But there will be a time for us. I'm sure there will, Henry." When he didn't respond, she added, "Why must thee make this so hard for me?"

He pulled his hands out of her grasp. "Why does thee have to make it so hard for thyself?" he asked in a low, quiet voice that held just an edge of anger. He felt her staring at him for a long moment, but he didn't dare look up. When he finally did, he noticed her eyes had a glassy sheen to them.

"If thee could just be patient and wait." She drew closer to him and added, more softly, "As I did for thee. I waited for thee to return to Nantucket those three long years."

This was hard to accept, harder to say. "I'm afraid I cannot make that promise, Anna. I do love thee. I've always loved thee. But I can't promise I will wait for thee. And I am not asking thee to make such a promise to me."

She sighed and touched his cheek. "Thee could come with me, to help me. Travel alongside me. We could do this important work together."

He envisioned a life known as Mr. Anna Gardner. He had worked so hard to find his own voice. Everyone deserved their own voice. "Nay. It wouldn't work." He pulled away from her. "I belong here. And thee belongs"—his gaze shifted to the direction of the harbor—"out there. Changing the world. I think I am meant to change only this island. My own small world."

Now her eyes did fill with tears. "Changing the island, Henry, that is a good thing too."

"Indeed." He tried to smile but gave up. This was their goodbye.

Later that evening, Henry found Jeremiah sitting in the shadows in the parlor. They sat for a while, watching the cold fireplace. It was out of habit, Henry supposed, to stare at a fireplace, whether there be a fire in it or not. Easier than talking.

Finally, Jeremiah broke the companionable silence. He asked how Anna felt about the convention. "Created quite a lot of ruckus, I heard."

"It certainly did." Henry stretched out his legs, one ankle crossing the other. "Anna felt surprisingly pleased about it. She said that the protests were only evidence that the island is shifting in the right direction."

"Well, I hope she's right on that and not just her wishful thinkin'. I've sensed the opposite. After that first convention, I'd never seen such dividin' lines get drawn on this island. I fear 'twill get worse before it gets better."

Henry had the same concerns. There was increasing strife and discord on the island, he could see it in the letters to the editor. Integration supporters versus segregationists. Abolitionists versus preservationists. The tone had been changing in the "Letters to the Editor," from a discussion about differing opinions to an intensely personal conflict.

"She'll be plannin' a third convention next summer, I suppose."

Henry nodded. It still shocked him, what she told him today. He wouldn't see her for a year's time. "Jeremiah, I asked Anna to marry me today."

His grandfather didn't respond for a long moment. "From the sorrowful look on yer face, I'm guessing she turned y' down."

"She did." Henry swallowed down the lump in his throat. "Said she had to change the world first."

"She did y' a great favor by setting y' free, Henry."

"How's that?" He didn't feel set free, not at all.

"I was in a similar spot once in my life. Hard to believe, but I loved two women. And I had to make a hard decision. I broke somebody's heart, and I'm not sure she ever really mended." He glanced around the parlor, then turned his attention back to Henry. "Y' shouldn't be marrying Anna Gardner, boy. She's a fine lass, but she's not the one y' should be thinking of marrying. Not with the way yer face lights up when yer around Marie-Claire."

Henry had been settled comfortably into the corner of the settee, listening attentively to Jeremiah's confession—his grandfather did not often reveal much of his past, nor his feelings—but then those last few sentences made him sit bolt upright. "Jeremiah! She's but a lass."

"Aye, but lasses grow up to be fair maidens."

Shocked at hearing those words spoken so openly, Henry sat silent, his thoughts tangled in a new turmoil.

The day had started off sunny, but now clouds were gathering to block the sun. Seabirds dipped and dived, and the wind chilled Hitty as she stood on the beach, watching the waves crash. She let out a long breath. The water looked so dark now, with the sun behind the clouds, and the waves in the cove had grown rough and choppy.

She hugged her arms around herself and took a deep breath. She didn't want to start crying, right here, but she felt tears in her eyes when she blinked the wind away. Bitsy's birthday was today, which meant that tomorrow she would start at the public school. Isaac came to fetch her at the Cent School's end, waiting until the room emptied out, and prompted Bitsy to hand a large box he'd brought to give to Hitty. Inside was a long rope, tied in knots at eighteen-inch intervals. Each knot had a rope handle attached to it, with a numbered wooden tag. Fifteen small wooden tags. Hitty looked up at him, confused.

"It's for when you take the children on an outing. So they won't get lost."

Oh. *Oh!* Last week, Hitty had taken the children down the block—one little block—to watch the last few cobbles get set into place on Main Street. A historic moment. The lengthy, tedious cobbling of Main Street, with cisterns now in place below it, was complete at last.

Unfortunately, Josiah Swain had wandered off and Hitty didn't realize he'd gone missing until his mother brought him to school about an hour later, saying he had shown up at home and how in the world had *that* happened! Hitty was mortified. She'd hoped the children hadn't reported the incident to their parents. Alas, Bitsy had told Isaac.

"Thee must think I'm a fool," Hitty said, hurt and embarrassed by this gift of rope.

Isaac looked baffled. "Nay! Not a fool, Mehitabel . . . I had hoped . . . I thought . . ."

She glanced at him, wondering what he was trying to say, for whatever it was, it was not coming out well. And just at the moment when Isaac had taken a deep breath and started again to explain the gift, who should interrupt them but Lovinia Bunker. She stood at the open door of the Cent School, yoohooing to Isaac and Bitsy to come to her home for a slice of fresh-baked apple pie. Did that woman not have more to do?

Bitsy jumped up to go, and Isaac rushed to catch his daughter by the arm, and the next thing Hitty knew, they were crossing the street behind Lovinia Bunker, with scarcely a look back. Was Isaac courting Lovinia? Was he fond of her yoohoos? And Bitsy! Always running off to Lovinia, as if Hitty did not matter to her in the least.

"Sister Hitty . . . thee will catch cold."

Startled, Hitty heard Marie-Claire's gentle voice and felt the shawl being placed around her shoulders almost simultaneously. "Oh, thanks."

Marie-Claire looked at her with concern. "Thee is crying."

"It's nothing, really." She felt embarrassed, and wiped her eyes with the back of her hand.

"It must be something."

"Bitsy's last day at the Cent School was today. She starts tomorrow at the public school. I will miss seeing her each day."

"Thee will just miss . . . Bitsy? Mayhap her father as well?"

Hitty stared at her—was it so obvious?—then shook her head. "If something hasn't happened with Isaac by now, it's not very likely."

"Anything can happen, Hitty. Nothing is impossible for God."

They turned to go back to the house and noticed Benjamin, watching them, standing at the top of the path that led to the cove. Hitty was surprised to see him, for last night he'd said he was sailing to Boston today. When they reached him, he answered her question before she could ask it. "The weather is turning ominous," he said. "The sailing has been delayed until morning." He looked from Hitty to Marie-Claire. "What could have been such an important topic of conversation that even the wind and the cold did not deter thee from standing by the water's edge?"

Hitty hesitated, unsure of how to answer him. Marie-Claire spoke up. "Some conversations are meant to be private, Benjamin." Her tone was most unlike her, almost a challenge. And from the look on his face, he did not like it.

"Who is thee to censure me?" he said, crisp and terse.

Hitty was dumbfounded for a moment, for he seemed eerily like her grandmother. The way he glared at Marie-Claire, even the sharp intonation of his words, it all reminded her of Grandmother Lillian.

Benjamin and Marie-Claire stared at each other for a painfully awkward moment, and Hitty's mind spun to try to find a way to break the tension and lighten the mood. Ask if anyone has seen the cat lately? Point out the dark clouds overhead? Before she could think of something that didn't sound like twaddle, Marie-Claire lowered her eyes and turned to head to the house.

As Henry walked to the office on this cold and foggy morning, his mind rolled through the shock of last evening.

During dinner, Benjamin had announced that he was

taking Marie-Claire back to Boston with him, for the first portion of the inheritance was almost entirely dispensed. "Nearly all assets have been liquidated and disposed of," Benjamin explained, filling the stunned silence that fell over the table. "The second portion of the inheritance remains tied up, under tight conditions."

"Hmph," Jeremiah grunted. "So yer saying 'tis all gone."

"Nearly gone." Benjamin looked at Henry. "The cobbling of Main Street, that was a costly endeavor, with costs that kept rising. And then the lightship. Two lightships, as I recall."

"Three," Hitty said quietly.

"The newspaper, while a worthy venture, has never turned a profit. Quite the opposite."

True. Paper and ink were costly, the printing press broke down so often that Henry ordered a new one to be delivered, never giving thought to the expense of it. It's just that . . . to be perfectly candid, he did not expect to go through the first portion of the inheritance so quickly. He thought it had been more substantial. He thought it was . . . a bottomless pit.

It seemed as if Benjamin could read his thoughts. "Henry, I have tried to reserve cash for what the newspaper will require, based on costs of the last two years. If thee does not intend to marry anytime soon—"

Henry didn't.

"—it might be wise to reduce the amount of pages, or consider advertising."

Advertising. Ugh. Henry rubbed his forehead. He spent much time reporting stories. He spent no time finding advertisers.

"Why must Marie-Claire leave?" Hitty said.

Indeed. Henry glanced at Marie-Claire. She had her chin tucked down. He thought she might be trying not to cry. He put his fork down. He'd lost his appetite.

"Boston is not so very far," Benjamin said, with an appeasing smile. "I will still come back and forth. Mayhap Marie-Claire will join me sometime." He turned toward her. "Wind, weather, whales permitting, prepare to leave at morning's high tide."

"So soon?" Hitty said. "But why?"

"Until the second portion of the inheritance is released, our work here is coming to an end. It would be wrong, quite wrong, for Marie-Claire to take advantage of thy generosity and remain without purpose."

Marie-Claire rose from her seat. "Please excuse me. I'll start packing." She hurried from the room. Henry's and Hitty's eyes followed her.

"She has grown so dear to me," Hitty said, her voice faint.

"When the conditions are met for the second part of the inheritance, and funds are released," Benjamin said, "she will be needed here again. Forget not, that portion is far more extensive." His eyes were on Hitty, Henry noticed. "But first, thee must marry a Friend in good standing."

Jeremiah had huffed, leaning back in his chair. "Who's left? Just a bunch of old biddies and geezers."

How well Henry knew.

An angry shout snapped Henry back to the present. He stopped abruptly to let a horse and cart pass by, ignoring the scowl of the cross farmer. He'd been so preoccupied he hadn't even seen it coming. He started across the street again, his footsteps plodding as he walked. He'd risen early, hoping to have a moment alone with Marie-Claire. But Philemon met him in the foyer and informed him the horse and carriage had already come for her, to take her to the wharf to meet Benjamin. The schooner was leaving at high tide, he reminded Henry.

She'd gone. She'd left without saying goodbye.

Henry felt quite empty inside. His father and Daphne were gone. Anna was gone. Now Marie-Claire was gone. The island seemed a lonely place.

Mary Coffin Starbuck

8 April 1701

A Quaker named John Richardson has arrived on the island, sent as a missionary from England. He sought out lodging at Dinah and Nathaniel's home, for he had heard my son was in some degree convinced of the Truth. I suppose that is valid, for Thomas Chalkley's visit inspired Nathaniel and Dinah to search out spiritual matters. We have had many stimulating conversations about the hearth this winter, and I am grateful for them.

I took a loaf of fresh-baked bread over to Dinah's this morning. I admit that I had been hoping to meet this visiting Quaker. He rose when Dinah introduced me to him as if he'd been expecting me. As if he'd recognized me! He crossed the room and clasped my hands together in his and I noticed that his eyes twinkled, almost as visible as sparks from a fire.

We had an interesting conversation round the fire. As I prepared to take my leave, John Richardson said he had felt greatly moved in his heart when I entered the room. "I sense a kindred spirit in thee, Mary Starbuck."

As did I.

Part Two

1843–1846

20

Weeks had passed, then months, and then came the new year. Hitty scarcely saw Isaac anymore. When she did, he was distant and cool, grave and somber, and not in a good way. She didn't know what the trouble was, truly she didn't. She missed the feeling that they understood one another, but she began to think she had misunderstood their relationship. Henry had been right all along; she should have listened to him. There was no relationship with Isaac Barnard.

But Hitty did see much of Benjamin. He sailed to Nantucket quite regularly, sometimes as much as once a month. Once, he brought Marie-Claire with him, quite unexpectedly, just for a day, and Henry monopolized her time for much of the visit. Hitty noticed, annoyed. So did Benjamin. And he did not seem pleased by it.

It ended up to be a very frustrating day, for she had longed for time alone with Marie-Claire. Maria Mitchell was a poor confidante compared to Marie-Claire. Whenever Hitty did try to talk to her about personal matters, Maria seemed distracted and worse, disinterested and bored. The king of Denmark was offering a handsome prize to the first who sighted a meteor or comet or some such thing, and Maria was determined to win the prize. It was all she could talk about—she could bc like Anna that way. They sang one note.

Today, Hitty tried again. She'd gone to visit Maria after the Cent School had ended for the day. Maria was blathering on and on about this comet, and finally Hitty burst into the monologue to interrupt her. "Maria, can thee think of any reason why Isaac Barnard would not be overly fond of me?"

A surprised look came over Maria, and that did not happen often. "Nay, but I can think of many reasons why thee should not be fond of him. He is an older man, a widower, with a thoroughly irascible child. And then . . . there is Isaac himself."

Hitty knew all that, but none of it deterred her. "Does thee think Isaac is smitten with Lovinia Bunker? She is a Methodist." Maria could see the goings-on of Centre Street from her observatory, if she ever looked down. Mostly, she looked up, to the heavens. Hitty could not fault her for that.

"Lovinia Bunker? Hmm, I do not know. But I will keep a lookout on the situation." She peered out the window down at the street, as if it just now occurred to her that there was something below to observe.

It was nice of Maria to say, but Hitty doubted she would remember.

How she missed Marie-Claire! She was the one who could actually help Hitty sort out her confused feelings and give her guidance. Henry was hardly home, working long hours at the newspaper. The only one left was Jeremiah. If she thought Maria's advice could be useless, Jeremiah's was even worse. He offered up ridiculous platitudes, like "Never put your hand between two snarling dogs" or "Do you want to run from the water or hide from the wind?" He was no help.

She needed Marie-Claire to help her discern whether she should follow her head or her heart.

Henry sat by the fire in his bedroom, reading some entries in Great Mary's journal. It gave him solace to read of her doubts, for he had so many himself. Like Mary, the doubts were not of God's existence, but of how best to worship the Almighty. Lately, he had struggled to sit through First Day Meeting with a heart open to receive the Light. Each week, the same elders rose to give the same weary testimonies. If Sister Hannah spoke one more time about her infirmities, he felt he might scream and run from the building.

Nay. It was not the fault of dear old Sister Hannah. His dissatisfaction had more to do with Marie-Claire's absence from Meeting than from rehearsed testimonies. When she had been in Meeting, he would sit in a certain pew to watch her unobserved. Her face . . . it nearly seemed to light from within. He felt inspired by her to be wholly present at Meeting, with an open heart.

He missed her. He hadn't realized how much until she arrived on Nantucket, with Benjamin, out of the blue, for an all-too-brief and thoroughly unexpected visit. The first thought that popped into his mind when he saw her standing at the door next to Benjamin was: *Who is this stunning woman?* Followed by: *Oh my. Oh my, my, my. Marie-Claire is no longer a lass.*

But the last thought he had of her, after spending much time talking and laughing together and being sorry to see the day come to an end, was this one: *She makes me a better version of myself.*

He closed Great Mary's journal and put it in a box in his wardrobe, deep on the top shelf, far too high a reach for Hitty to find it. Probably a silly thing, not really necessary, but it was a habit from childhood he had yet to shrug off. His knee hit something hard and he looked down to see his sea chest, tucked in the bottom of the wardrobe. He crouched down and pulled it out, then lifted the lid.

Ugh. He should've done this years ago. His salt-caked hat, his slops, his moldy books—all should be burned. Down at the bottom was another metal box. Inside were the letters he'd written to Anna, those three years while he was at sea. Those never-to-be-read letters. As he gathered them up, he wondered if it would have made a difference to her if he'd given them to her when she asked for them.

Maybe the better question was: Why had he *not* given them to her?

He took them over to the fireplace and crouched down. One by one, he fed them into the fire, unopened.

He watched the flames flare up, then settle down again. It reminded him of a time he'd been gazing at the parlor fire, in this same way, and Marie-Claire came into the room. She told him that he looked like a poet in deep reflection, standing there by the fire. A poet! What a thing to think.

Oddly enough, he *had* tried his hand at poetry. In those letters to Anna. But he never felt confident to share the poems with her, unsure of her response, and in the end, he never did.

Was there something romantic between Benjamin and Marie-Claire? Could that have been the reason he wanted Marie-Claire to return to Boston? As the last unread letter caught fire, the thought occurred to him that Marie-Claire came to mind far more than Anna.

He heard the dinner bell ring and went down the stairs. Hitty was seated at the dining table, waiting for him. Philemon stood at attention by the dining room door. "Where is Jeremiah?"

"He's gone on a walk. He said not to wait supper for him. Henry, does thee think 'tis normal, for a man his age to wander so much?"

"I think it's normal for a man who likes to smoke his pipe and his granddaughter won't let him."

Hitty took that in. "Well, I won't. The stink is awful."

"It was thoughtful of Benjamin to bring Marie-Claire for a visit."

Hitty looked at him in surprise. "Don't give him undue credit. 'Twas a long overdue visit. I had asked him to bring her many times, but he always had a reason it would not work." She sighed. "I never had such a friend before."

"What of Maria? Of Anna?"

"Thee doesn't understand, Henry. Having Marie-Claire here, it almost felt like I had a younger sister." She struggled for a smile that just wouldn't come. "Though in my imaginations, a younger sister would come to me for advice. Instead, I sought out Marie-Claire's opinions."

"As did I," he said softly, recalling how he would share story ideas for the newspaper with Marie-Claire over breakfast, and ask for her thoughts about which angle to use in an editorial. She had an uncommon amount of common sense.

"When I first met her, I thought she was as shy as a rare bird," Hitty said, pouring tea into her teacup, "but she is not. Just the opposite. She's remarkably sturdy, savvy to the ways of the world. It's almost as if she has a way of being aware of the world's filth but somehow remains clean."

Henry stared at her. He'd had that same impression, though he'd never given it to words. "Hitty, could there be something between Benjamin and Marie-Claire?"

"Something what?"

"Something romantic."

Hitty's gaze jerked over to Henry and then away again, and two bright spots of color blossomed on her cheeks. "What a silly thing to say, Henry." She dropped her chin and lifted the teacup to her lips, but her hand trembled so that the teacup rattled in its saucer and tea slopped over the edges.

It suddenly dawned on Henry why she seemed so acutely embarrassed by the question. "Oh Hitty . . . nay! Don't tell me thee has gone soft on the law clerk! I just assumed he came here for that . . . endless paperwork. I never thought . . . I mean why . . ."

She sighed, mopping up the spilled tea with her linen napkin. "I know, I know. Why would a man like Benjamin Foulger pursue someone like me?"

"Nay, Hitty. Twist not my words. I just assumed . . . he was here to see to the inheritance." Henry thumped his forehead with the palm of his hand. Why hadn't he seen this? How could he have missed it? It had all happened too fast—his return to Nantucket, Grandmother Lillian's death, the will, Papa and Daphne's departure, the money, getting rid of the money, the newspaper, Anna leaving, followed soon after by Marie-Claire. And now *this* news. Too fast. He wasn't good at fast. He needed time to consider a circumstance from every angle. "Tell me, Sister, is it serious between thee?"

She kept her eyes on the balled-up napkin in her hand. "I believe so. He has hinted at a future together."

"When did this romance start?" And more important, why didn't she seem more excited? He wished she looked more confident, more eager. Normally, Hitty withheld nothing from Henry. Nothing. She drove him crazy with trivial thoughts and piffling stories he had little interest in hearing. It didn't seem at all like his sister to neglect . . . or avoid? . . . telling Henry that she was being courted. By Benjamin Foulger, of all people!

"I suppose . . . quite some time ago. After Marie-Claire left. It has progressed rather slowly. After all, he is not on island very often." She twisted the napkin in her fingers. "He is a Friend in good standing, Henry. His last name comes from a Nantucket founder. Even Grandmother Lillian could not find fault. Would it be such a bad thing if I were to marry Benjamin?" She looked up and then down again. He noticed her eyes were glassy. "Were he to ask me?"

Henry was at a loss for words. Finally, he said, "If thee loves him, then 'tis not a wrong thing." He smiled and patted her shoulder. "Thee deserves to be happy."

Hitty looked enormously relieved. Henry felt considerably less so.

Henry assumed Hitty was in love with Benjamin. Was she? Sometimes she thought she might love him. Not in the same way she felt about Isaac, she admitted as much to herself. But look where that kind of head-over-heels love had gotten her—nowhere!

Her feelings for Benjamin had always been different. She

wondered if it might be due to the fact that Isaac remained so remote, while Benjamin made it clear that he had plans for Hitty's future. Yet there was something about Isaac . . . some strong and inexplicable feeling she had for him. She had felt it from the moment she'd first met him, when he had arrived at the Cent School to shyly ask if there might be a spot for his daughter. Sister Hannah, he said, had told him that the Cent School was the very best place on Nantucket for children to be. Of course! Hitty had said. And deep inside, she sensed her heart had been holding a spot for this man, as well. There was just something about Isaac.

Hitty had not seen Maria Mitchell in a very long time, and she could use a heart-to-heart talk with someone who could help her sort out her tangled feelings. Maria may not be much help, but she was all she had to choose from. Today, after the last child had been picked up from the Cent School, she walked over to the Mitchell residence above the Pacific Bank. She found Maria in the observatory-like cupola, pencil in hand, working through a long mathematical formula. Maria welcomed her in, moving a stack of books off a stool for her to sit on.

"I've been meaning to ask thee," Maria said, "what's happened to those letters?"

"What letters?"

"Those 'B' letters. Henry's newspaper stopped printing them. I thought they were beneficial to the island by stirring up conversation. If nothing else, it was easier for opposing views to talk to each other and blame 'B' rather than each other."

"Henry's newspaper hasn't printed any because they stopped coming." Something just occurred to Hitty and she let out a gasp. "They stopped after Anna left the island! I always had a hunch that she was the author of those letters."

Maria paused to consider that. "Mayhap, but they did not seem as grim as Anna could be."

Before Maria could start enthusing on her comet tracking progress—for once she started on it, she could be difficult to stop—Hitty blurted out, "Maria, I think Benjamin Foulger . . . I think that soon he is going to ask to marry me."

"Who is he? Oh, hold on. Is he the Foulger who stands at the edge of the wharf and announces the world is coming to an end?"

"Nay! That's another Benjamin Foulger entirely, and I'm offended that thee would think I'd consider marrying a man with an affliction of the mind."

"Is he the Foulger who locked himself in his house until he discovered how to create a candle from spermaceti oil?"

"Nay, Maria. That's Walter Foulger." She frowned at her. "I'm talking of the law clerk from Boston. I *have* spoken of him to thee, Maria." She did not listen.

"Thee said that he was handling thy grandmother's estate, not that thee was in love with him. What makes thee think he is going to propose marriage?"

"He said so. When he left for Boston, he told me that he wanted to have a serious conversation about our future when he next returned. ''Tis high time,' he said."

"When does he plan to return?"

"Another month or so, he said."

Maria leaned back in her chair. "What about Isaac?"

"What about him?"

"I thought thee loved him."

Hitty sighed. "I did." *I do*. "But I am also nearing thirty years old, and I have to face facts. Thee has told me for years that Isaac Barnard is married to his work. Just like Anna Gardner is married to her causes. Thee has said so, many times." Maria was not particularly intuitive about people, but now and then, she could be surprisingly clairvoyant. "Besides, if thee remembers, I think Isaac is courting Lovinia Bunker."

"That Lovinia?" Maria pointed to the Hussey house down below on Centre Street.

She hadn't remembered. She never did.

"Well, he's in for a surprise, as she is engaged to my second cousin, Captain Miles Mitchell."

"Engaged to Miles? He's away at sea, I thought."

"Aye, but that doesn't interfere with her flirting with other men. I see it all, up here. Shameful." Maria tsk-tsked and picked up a dusty chronometer. "Why not be like me? I wish to determine my own path. I have no aspiration to marry. I am quite content with my life."

Hitty looked around Maria's small observatory. It was covered with books and papers and sextants and telescopes. And cats! Three were sleeping in the corner. But there were no children, no husband, and very few friends. This life worked well for Maria. It allowed her plenty of time to pursue the interests she loved. But it was not the life Hitty wanted. Somehow this moment untangled her confusion, just as she had hoped it might.

"If Benjamin does ask, I do believe I will say yes. He is a dynamic, compelling man, and he seems devoted to me." The thought still shocked Hitty, dazed and dazzled her. Benjamin was "right" for her, she told herself, a much smarter choice than Isaac would ever be.

"If thee thinks Benjamin Foulger will give thee what thee wants, then I am all for it. I must say Isaac is a fool, though."

Isaac wasn't a fool. He was many things—socially awkward, reluctant to express feelings, alone yet not lonely—but he was no fool.

The continued success of the *Illumine* astonished Henry. He had hired two young salesmen who solicited advertisements, and it helped balance out the monthly debits and credits. He was fortunate to have the cushion of the inheritance to set up the newspaper, for without it, he would have been in steep debt. But he knew this fragile balance couldn't last much longer. He would need to replace equipment soon and hire more workers. Zebadiah said he would quit if Henry expanded to any more pages—which was becoming inevitable—until he was promised an apprentice. That pacified the ornery typesetter, for the time being.

It was a deep-down satisfaction, finding work that one loved. Mary Coffin Starbuck had described her husband Nathaniel as a man made for the sea. Henry understood that, though he was a man made for the written word.

And then there was the role he played to benefit the island. Being a benefactor had started out as a way to outfox his grandmother, but he had grown passionate about making the island a better place for all to live. It was not easy to do, for the people of Nantucket were strong-minded, convinced they were right even if wrong.

Mayhap that was why the practical benefits Henry brought to the island were so doubly satisfying. The cobbles on Main Street were an example of something that brought good to all Nantucketers. It delighted him to see the difference those cobbles made. No more mud puddles, no more sandy gullies. He wondered of the cost to cobble more streets once the second portion of the inheritance was triggered.

He let out a sigh. The clock was ticking loudly on that issue. At least Hitty's future might be lining up with Grandmother Lillian's plan. He was far from making any progress toward finding a soul mate, but his soul was satisfied with his life. Pretty much.

Mary Coffin Starbuck

15 April 1701

Yesterday I spent hours at Dinah's, visiting with John Richardson and his companions (Susanna Freeborn, a Friend from Rhode Island, James Baker, a Friend from Virginia, and Captain Peleg Slocum, also a Quaker, whose sloop had carried them to the island).

They explained some of the positions of Quakerism to me, that it was the living Christ in every person who offered the key to salvation, aided by the Scriptures, and that in consequence, a Friend would never take up arms against another human being.

Susanna Freeborn did not say much, but she did add that all are equal in the sight of God, man or woman, free or slave. She said that many of those who rise to speak with a message are women, for they have much spiritual insight to offer. That pleased me deeply.

I had to tear myself away from these fascinating visitors and was late to open the store, and my oh my! I had some ruffled and upset customers to contend with! They were lined up outside, waiting for me, none too happy. I apologized profusely, but inside, I had to bite my lip to keep from laughing at the sight. Never would I have thought to see Christopher Swain, Stephen Hussey and wife Martha, standing behind (behind!) three tall and expressionless Wampanoags, who held in their arms large bags of goose feathers to trade. It struck me as funny, and I could not wait to tell my Nathaniel about it this evening. He got a chuckle out of it as well.

17 April 1701

Early this morning, John Richardson stopped by our house to meet Nathaniel. John had been intrigued that our house was referred to as Parliament House, because so many town meetings are held here, so I suggested he come for a visit. I did not expect such an early visitor, but I was pleased he came.

We had a lively conversation, John and I, and Nathaniel listened thoughtfully, as is his way. John looked around our large room, and indeed it is quite grand compared to most Nantucket houses.

He turned in a circle and then faced Nathaniel and me. "Might we hold some meetings here? To share the love of God?"

I looked first to my husband before I responded, and he gave me a slight nod with eyebrows lifted. "We are agreeable to that," I told John, for I doubted many would come.

21

It was hot outside, the air uncommonly still for Sixth Month. The deep heavy days of summer had set in. Hitty had brought lunch to Benjamin at his office above the hat store, but he met her knock at the door with a puzzled look. "What is it?" he said, not opening the door more than a few inches.

"'Tis so hot today. I thought thee might like a picnic lunch." She held up the basket in her arms. It had seemed like a good idea earlier this morning, to surprise him with lunch, but her confidence evaporated by the distracted look on his face. Nay, he looked irritated. Impatient. "Thee is busy," she said quickly, feeling the fool. "Another time." She shouldn't have come. Some people did not appreciate spontaneity. Benjamin, apparently, was one of those. She should have known, yet there was so much she had still to learn about him.

But all at once, his mood shifted. "Hold on, Hitty. It sounds delightful." He flashed a rueful smile, slid out the door, and closed it behind him, then started down the steps. They were halfway down when a crash came from upstairs.

Hitty stopped. "What was that?"

Benjamin glanced behind her, up at the door. "I must have left a book too far on the edge of my desk."

That's not what it sounded like to Hitty. "I can wait. If thee wants to check, I'll wait."

"Nay, nay. Let's make haste. I'm famished."

As they walked, he was very chatty, as if trying to smooth over the uncomfortable way he had greeted her, and she started to feel more relaxed. He seemed glad she had come, pleased she had surprised him, after all. She made too much of small things. It was a terrible habit, taking everything so personally.

They went to a bench near the wharf that Hitty knew to be Jeremiah's favorite spot. It was under a shade tree, providing some shelter while catching fresh wind that came in from the harbor. In the background was the lulling sound of the incessant waves. Hitty unpacked the basket Cook had prepared and handed Benjamin an apple.

He polished it on his sleeve. "It's nice, being here."

He smiled, his eyes lingering on her lips in a way that made her uneasy. "So island living suits thee?" she asked.

"Quite well. I like it here."

"But it must seem . . . somewhat dull . . . compared to life in Boston." She was doing a poor job of hinting, but she wondered about his world away from Nantucket. Where did he live? What did he do with his spare time?

"It's not. I like to see the same people every day. Actually, the same person each day." He winked at her, and she lowered her head to hide her smile.

She changed the subject. "Benjamin, thee does not speak much of thy growing up years." Not at all, in fact. She wanted to know more about him. She wanted to know *everything* about him. He was guarded, so reserved.

"There's not much to tell."

"Oh, but there is!" she said, handing him a ham biscuit. "Every life has a story. Thy parents, for example. Where are they now?"

Hitty noticed how his face suddenly clouded, how the sparkle in his eyes dulled. He looked out at a dory, bobbing in the water. "I never knew my father. He passed before I was born. Then my mother died when I was not much older than Marie-Claire."

Oh, but she understood that pain! She longed to talk more of it, but from the closed expression on his face, he did not want to expand on it. "So, then, where did thee go to school?"

He seemed very intent on polishing the apple to a shiny red. "Just the usual."

"Boarding school? Which one? The Quaker Boarding School in Providence?"

He glanced at her, lifting his eyebrows. "Thee knows of it?"

"Of course! Many Nantucket boys are sent there. Their mothers hope to dissuade them from running off to sea. Grandmother Lillian insisted Henry attend, but he returned home after a fortnight. Overcome with homesickness." She clapped her hands together. "So, then, after that. Where did thee attend college?"

He lifted a shoulder in a slight shrug, his eyes scanning the harbor. "Where would anyone go who wanted to learn the law?"

"Harvard College! Did thy path ever cross with Henry's?"

"Nay, nay. We are some years apart."

How many? She hoped he might volunteer the information. She had no idea how old Benjamin actually was. His looks were such that it was hard to pinpoint. Somewhere between thirty and forty, she guessed. Shouldn't she know? Assuming they were romantically involved, shouldn't Hitty know such things?

Benjamin took a bite from the apple, then another and another, before he threw the core into the water and watched a seagull scoop it up and make off with it. "Hitty, today is not the kind of day to talk about the past," he said in a decisive tone.

"It isn't? Why not?" she asked.

"Well, for one thing, it's too hot out today. And for another . . . the future is far more interesting."

"Oh, really?" Oh, *really!* Hitty could tell by the tone of his voice and the sudden light in his blue eyes that this was *it*. She sucked in a sharp breath. Her stomach flipped and twisted in somersaults. For one terrible moment she thought she might be sick. She'd been waiting for this moment all her life, but now that it was here, she didn't know what to do with it.

Benjamin took her hand in his, and for some strange reason, Hitty thought of Isaac's hands—long, tapered fingers—and how different they were from these hands. Benjamin's fingers were thick and strong, more like her grandfather's woodworking hands than those she would have thought belonged to a law clerk.

He gazed at her and smiled, his blue eyes tender and warm. She wanted to look away, but she just couldn't quite make herself. She felt that undeniable tug of attraction for him. He was extraordinarily handsome.

His face broke into a boyish grin, as if he could tell what she was thinking. She liked that smile best, for she thought it was a glimpse of the boy he once was. "Hitty, I would like us to marry." He reached up and ran his fingers lightly, lightly along her lips, and she felt breathless of a sudden. Perhaps she did love him after all. "Soon. Let's marry soon. Why wait any longer?"

But I wanted to be asked. It would have been nice to be asked. Clearly, he didn't expect her to turn him down, but then, why would she? Benjamin Foulger was as near perfect as a man could be. She doubted even Grandmother Lillian could find fault.

Hitty looked at Benjamin and smiled, feeling happy and shy and nervous. She thought he might kiss her, and waited for it, though they were in a public place and she knew him to be ever so mindful of social mores. She dropped her eyes, wondering if he might even tell her that he loved her. A gust of wind blew through the shade tree, gently ruffling the lace on her fichu. She took note of it all, trying to seal every piece of this important event in her memory. *Remember this, Hitty. Remember how this day feels, how the leaves dance when the wind swirls.*

And still, no kiss came, no declaration of devotion. When she finally risked a look at him, she discovered he hadn't been gazing tenderly at her at all, but staring at someone, off in the distance. "Benjamin?"

His head turned quickly, the way a cat did when it saw a mouse. He looked at her like he'd forgotten she was there. Distracted, he said, "I'll speak to Henry about a notice to publish our intentions in the *Illumine*." He rose to his feet, and held out a hand to help her up. "Shall we go, my dear?"

There didn't seem to be anything else to say after that, although Hitty was left thinking, *Should thee not tell me I am loved? I want to be loved.*

Hitty and Benjamin's wedding announcement was placed in that week's edition of the *Illumine*. Jeremiah was irritated with Henry for publishing it so soon and told him so. "Benjamin came to the office and paid for an advertisement, Jeremiah. Why would I refuse space to the man who wants to marry my sister?"

"Because I need time to digest the news."

"Well, thee had better get used to it. The wedding is but two weeks away."

"That's another bothersome thing. What's the rush?"

"It's the way Friends do things."

"Not in my day. The world is spinning out of control. Things are going too fast."

Brief engagement periods had always been common for the Society of Friends, which Jeremiah knew. Though Henry did not disagree with his grandfather's assessment of the world's condition, he knew that the real reason Jeremiah was so tetchy was that he didn't want things to change. Neither did Henry.

Mary Coffin Starbuck

19 April 1701

Most days are so ordinary, so predictable. And then comes a day that changes life forevermore. This was that kind of day.

I did not expect many to come tonight to Parliament House for the meeting with the Quaker missionary. It had rained all day, and the paths were thick mud. Toward sunset, the sun broke through the clouds and the air was sweet and warm. Nathaniel opened windows to allow for more ventilation.

One arrived, then two more, then a cartful. As the crowd increased, it became apparent that there was not room enough for everyone! We squeezed together inside, and many more remained outside, trying to get in. So my clever husband took the windows out of their casings so those who were outside were able to gather round the open windows. No one was excluded.

John Richardson welcomed all, and then instructed everyone to "wait on the Lord" in silence. And so they did. Quite astonishing when one thinks of how many people were crammed, shoulder to shoulder, in and around my house.

An awkward moment arose when John Richardson grabbed one of my cane chairs to stand on and I stopped him. Dinah whispered that I should let him use it for he is our illustrious guest. But if he stood on that beautiful cane chair, he would break it! I would not let my sons use a chair to stand on, so why would I do anything differently with a guest, illustrious or otherwise?

John did not seem as ruffled by my reproach as Dinah. He carried on, chairless, and spoke about the need to be "born again," like Nicodemus. It seemed as if he was directing his full attention to me. I listened intently, my spirit stirring deeply within me.

For as long as I can recall, thinking way back to my girlhood in Salisbury, I have been both repelled by and attracted to Quakerism. Repelled by what has seemed like odd beliefs, by the strong reaction others have had to them, and then by living on the same island as combative Stephen Hussey (he could convince anyone to avoid being a Quaker simply because he is one).

And yet, I have also been attracted to it for how genuine it seems, how close to the heart of Christ, how devoted the Quaker missionaries.

But what about baptism? I think infant baptism is foolishness, but adult baptism—why, I myself sought to be fully immersed as a young woman.

And then there are the other sacraments. Communion, for one. 'Tis no small thing to dismiss sacred traditions. When Peter Foulger baptized me, it was a holy moment.

I listened to John with these conflicting thoughts swirling in my head. At times I resisted what he had to say, other times I felt Truth in them. John grew weary and requested the meeting come to an end. No one would leave! They wanted more. I wanted more.

'Tis very late and I can no longer keep my eyes open. I must get some sleep. I will write more on the morrow.

24 April 1701

All week, I have been eager to find a quiet moment and pick up my quill to finish this story. John Richardson sailed away from Nantucket today, to share the Truth with other seekers. I am determined to put ink to this experience, while it is still fresh on my mind. I doubt, though, that I will ever forget.

During the meeting at Parliament House, as John preached, something broke within me, something hard that had grown brittle, and tears started flowing. I rose and held out my hand, palm raised. I looked around the room at the faces that were dear to me. I knew this direct approach to the Almighty was what we needed on this island, to allow God to guide us, without layer upon layer of needless traditions. The essentials of Christ Jesus, that was all we needed. I sensed the Spirit moving me, filling me with these words: "All that ever we have been building, and all that ever we have done is all pulled down this day, and this is the overwhelming truth."

I am a changed person, forevermore.

22

Three days before her wedding, Hitty made a beeline into the bakery on lower Main Street and nearly bumped right into Isaac Barnard, whom she hadn't seen in months and months. "Isaac!" she said, a little breathless. "How is Bitsy? I haven't seen her in quite some time."

A tender look lightened his face. "Good day, Mehitabel. Bitsy is fine, quite fine. Growing quickly." He glanced away. "She misses the Cent School . . . and you. She misses you." His voice softened and a faraway yearning flitted through his eyes, though mayhap Hitty just wanted to believe it was there. With a quick jerk, he lifted the package in his hand. "She loves these sugar buns."

So did Hitty. Lately, she'd been craving them, stopping by daily for one. Sometimes two.

"I read recently about . . . your marriage." Isaac's voice was tender, solicitous, but his expression was unreadable.

"Not yet," she said, a little too quickly. "I mean, it hasn't happened yet." Isaac was the first to look away. Hitty looked away too, feeling almost queasy. What did she expect? That Isaac would beg her to change her mind? Declare his love?

He did nothing.

If she still had doubts, this moment ought to convince her. He'd had plenty of chances. Isaac never cared for her the way she cared for him. He did not change.

But that was what she admired about him too. If he'd inherited the kind of wealth she and Henry had, she doubted it would change him in any way. He would be the same person. Would Benjamin change? If all went well, Henry would meet someone soon, fall in love, and marry, so that the second part of the inheritance would be released. At that point, as Hitty's husband, Benjamin would be fabulously wealthy. Would he change? She wasn't sure.

"I hope . . . thee will be happy with the law clerk, Mehitabel."

She swallowed around the lump in her throat that felt strangely like tears. "Benjamin Foulger could not be a more ideal match." *Why in the world did I say that?* As if she was convincing herself.

Isaac took off his spectacles and wiped them with his shirt. His eyes, Hitty noted, were glassy.

"Does thee not feel well?" she asked.

"Allergies," he said, putting his spectacles back on.

And here she thought she had known everything about him. He tipped his hat goodbye to her, and crossed the street. She watched him go, and felt a strange, slow tearing down her chest, a rip of regret, of sadness, of misspent happiness.

What am I doing? Hitty asked herself. She had an urge to run after Isaac, tell him she didn't want to be with Benjamin Foulger, that she only wanted him! She'd only ever wanted Isaac.

But she had Henry to consider, and his newspaper, and all the good he was doing, and the horrible inheritance with all those dreadful strings attached to it.

Time was running out, just like her grandmother had known it would.

With his granddaughter's wedding but two days away, the Grand House was brimming with women, and Jeremiah couldn't stand it. Every inch had been taken over: a fussy seamstress was finishing Hitty's silk wedding dress in the parlor, bossy servants had been brought in to help Cook prepare for a wedding dinner, and the rest of the house was being scrubbed from top to bottom.

Jeremiah spent these days as far from the Grand House as he could get. Mostly, he sat on his favorite bench, watching the goings-on of the harbor. This was where he always seemed to end up, like a dog to its bone. These last few weeks, he'd felt the sea calling his name again, trying to lure him to her. He thought he'd ended his love affair with her, once and for all, but she was not so willing to be put off.

Today, though, he had good reason to spend the day down by the water. He pulled out his scrimshaw pipe and tamped down some fresh tobacco from a pouch he kept in his pocket. He lit it and took in a deep breath, then coughed and coughed, a deep rattling sound. That awful cough! It never left him.

Someone started pounding his back. He looked up to see Isaac Barnard smacking his back like his hand was a mallet. "That's enough!" Jeremiah coughed a few more times. "Thanks, but that's plenty." That cute little girl of his, the one who bit the lawyer, peered curiously at him. "Well, look at y'. Y've gone and grown up."

The girl grinned, showing off missing front teeth. What was her name? Jeremiah couldn't remember. Her father handed her a bag of stale bread, so she ran down to the water's edge to throw some crumbs out for the birds. "'Tis so hot today," Isaac said. "I told Bitsy we could come down to the water and cool off."

Jeremiah had the same notion. "Pretty hot here, though." He moved over to make room on the bench for Isaac.

Isaac sat down next to Jeremiah. He said nothing to Jeremiah, nor did Jeremiah say anything to him. He'd always thought Isaac to be a man of long, deep thoughts. A little like Henry. Good-hearted. A little slow to act, but Jeremiah had faith that they would end up in the right place. They just needed a little push sometimes. He glanced at Isaac. "I lost m' darlin' wife when m' boy wasn't much older than yer girl. Takes a long time to get over something like that."

Isaac gave a nod. "It does."

"I was always . . . a little sorry I didn't give love a second chance."

Isaac had his gaze fixed on his daughter. She was throwing bits of bread crumbs to two squawking seagulls.

"She doesn't look much like y'. I guess she takes after her mother."

"She does." Isaac crossed one leg over the other, and Jeremiah noticed how threadbare the hem of his pants was. "Is Mehitabel much like her mother?"

"Hitty? Nay, nay. Jane was the wispy willowy sort, in danger of being blown over by a stiff breeze. Hitty, she's more like her aunt Daphne, blessed with womanly curves."

"I don't mind curves," Isaac said softly.

"Oh, Hitty complains about it, but I wouldn't change a thing about m' granddaughter."

"Nor would I."

Jeremiah snapped his head up to look at this man, whom most everyone overlooked for his quiet, unassuming ways. Few paid any mind to the fact that Isaac Barnard was the one responsible for making the island more hospitable to sailors by reducing danger around the shoals, and providing shelter for those who did shipwreck. Henry might have provided the funds, but Isaac was the driver. The man cared deeply for others' welfare, strangers or neighbors.

Lo and behold, this good and fine man had a soft spot for Hitty. From the sorrowful look on Isaac's face, a discovery dawned on Jeremiah. This man loved Hitty. *Well, I'll be blowed.* He couldn't speak for a long moment. There were no words.

Hold on, hold on. Indeed there *were* words for this situation. *If there's no wind, then row.*

The heat wave was so oppressive during Seventh Month, a rainless month, that Henry got into the habit of getting to the office before dawn. It was impossible to work past the noon hour, for the loft turned into a bake oven. He was on his way back to the Grand House when he saw Isaac Barnard and Bitsy making their way slowly up Main Street. Walking oh so slowly, because Bitsy was jumping from one cobblestone to another. She was never still, that one.

"I just spoke to your grandfather," Isaac said, waiting for Henry to catch up to them. He pointed a finger toward the wharf. "He's down by the water, sitting on a bench under a tree."

Henry smiled. "Trying to stay cool, I'd imagine." And stay out of the hive of wedding activity at the house. He kept that thought to himself.

"He's waiting for someone to arrive." Isaac's eyes kept glancing over Henry's shoulder to look at two shopkeepers, standing outside the bakery stores to get a little breeze in the shade.

"Something on thy mind?" He knew Isaac that well by now.

Isaac turned to Henry. "I just spoke with those two. They told me they don't bother with fire buckets any longer. The fire department can handle it all, they say."

"Is that so wrong?" Cisterns were below Main Street now, a ready water supply. "We've made such progress." Isaac seemed uncertain, but then, Henry thought, he was prone to worry.

"Aye, there has been progress, but with the flammability of whale oil down near the wharf, these shops would be like dry tinder in a fire. No fire department could handle that. Everyone still needs to look out for their own property, and for each other. They won't, though."

"Why not?"

Isaac pointed to each store and ticked them off with his hand. "Segregationist. Integrationist. Segregationist. Segregationist. Integrationist." He dropped his hand. "The issue has cut a groove so deep that neighbors refuse to help each other." He crossed his arms against his chest and lifted his chin. "Look at that."

Henry looked to see what he meant. The two shopkeepers, who had been chatting in the shade, spun around to face the wall as another shopkeeper walked past them. They refused to acknowledge him. What really irked Henry was that all three were Friends. Different factions, but all Quakers.

"Something has happened to Nantucket. Something has been lost." Isaac tapped the toe of his boot onto the road. "Like these cobbles. There's no denying that they've helped the stability of the road, but islanders used to pitch in to help fill in the holes on the street. I recall Saturday mornings as a boy, working alongside my father, pushing a wheelbarrow of sand up the road from the beach."

Henry shrugged. "'Tis no longer needed."

"With each improvement comes independence. Pride, mayhap." Isaac shifted slightly to look at the storekeepers, who had turned back around to pick up their conversation where they'd left off. "All the money in the world can't stop a raging fire if neighbors don't come to each others' aid to help put it out."

Isaac excused himself and started after Bitsy, slowly at first, then he picked up his pace to catch up to the running girl. Henry was left with an unsettled feeling. In the next moment, the feeling disappeared, replaced by another one. For up from the wharf came Marie-Claire Chase! Accompanied by none other than his grandfather Jeremiah.

Marie-Claire, she took Henry's breath away.

Having Marie-Claire arrive in time for the wedding was a wonderful surprise for Hitty, arranged entirely by Jeremiah. He had sent word to her to come right away, via a fisherman friend, and enclosed an envelope filled with fare. No wedding gift could've been more welcomed, Hitty told Jeremiah, tears coursing down her cheeks.

"Fie!" he said gruffly. "'Twas nothing," but he was pleased by her fuss.

The two women talked long into the night, catching up on the last few years. They had exchanged letters, but there was nothing better than a face-to-face visit. Marie-Claire had been working as a secretary for another lawyer in Boston. "Why not for Benjamin?" Hitty asked. "I've wanted to know for the longest while."

She had known of Marie-Claire's change of employment, but not the reason for it, and Benjamin was evasive.

"'Tis not a big secret," Marie-Claire said. "Benjamin no longer had need for my services. But it's only temporary, he said. As soon as the second portion of thy inheritance is set into motion, he has promised I can return to Nantucket and pick right up where I left off."

"After tomorrow, the timing of that will be left to Henry."

Marie-Claire smoothed out her skirt, looked down at her hands. "But I thought Anna Gardner was not on island. I have heard of her many speaking engagements throughout New England. She is certainly well thought of."

"She's an impressive woman. Destined for great things, I think. But I am quite confident she will not be marrying my brother. To quote my friend Maria Mitchell, 'Anna is married to her causes.'"

Marie-Claire's head stayed tucked down, but Hitty thought she caught an upturn at the edges of her mouth. "A few months ago, I heard her speak at a forum on abolitionism at Harvard College." She lifted her head. "She was eloquent."

"No doubt." Hitty gasped. "Oh! I must remember to tell Henry that Benjamin went to Harvard College."

Marie-Claire blinked twice, then again. "Benjamin told you he attended Harvard College?"

"Indeed. As well as Quaker Boarding School in Providence. Henry went there too, but only for a fortnight. He hated it and threatened to run away. Father relented. It made Grandmother Lillian furious, as she had provided the funds for Henry's schooling and insisted he attend."

As Hitty was talking, Marie-Claire walked to the window and stared outside.

"Is the weather changing?" Oh, Hitty hoped so. This heat wave. The humidity! Her hair was a riot of curls, a mop, a mess. When she did not answer, Hitty repeated the question. "Marie-Claire?"

Marie-Claire jerked, startled. "I didn't realize . . . I hadn't known . . . well, sometimes I wonder how much I really know about Benjamin."

Hitty felt the same way!

Mary Coffin Starbuck

11 July 1701

My son Nathaniel brought news to me of a letter written by John Richardson, filled with reflections on his time with us. He likened me to Deborah the Judge and called me a "great woman." Then he commented less favorably on my dear husband.

"Nathaniel Starbuck," John wrote, "was not a man of mean parts but his wife Mary so far exceeded him in soundness of judgment, clearness of understanding, and an elegant way of expressing herself . . . that it tended to lessen the qualifications of her husband."

Why must I be compared to my husband, or he to me? John Richardson, of all people, believes in the value of individuals, each one unique, each one made in the image of God. Comparisons are odious.

I suppose it saddens me that my Nathaniel is often underestimated, simply because he is a quiet man. He has been a fine and faithful husband to me and a wonderfully doting father to our children. While we share different characteristics, we support and respect each other. He has never once tried to "snuff my fire," as my first teacher had warned me. And I have never belittled or mocked him because he cannot read.

Long ago, my Granny Joan taught me a valuable lesson about marriage. It was a summer day, and I was only a maid of sixteen. We were sitting under the live oak tree that we both loved.

Granny Joan and I were much alike. She spoke up on civic matters while her husband, my grandfather, did not. She said that she had learned to express an opinion by including her husband in it. "My husband and I have thought on this issue, and here is what we think." She said that it made all the difference to others and how they listened to her, and it gave much respect to her phlegmatic husband. I have followed her example throughout my marriage and found the same results.

Marriage is full of difficulties. Why make it any harder than it needs to be?

23

The wedding ceremony of Hitty and Benjamin would occur at the end of First Day Meeting, without fuss or fanfare. Some fuss, though. Hitty had planned and perfected her wedding hundreds of times in her mind, ever since she was a lass, and knew just what she wanted. Despite his frugal nature, Benjamin readily agreed to all she hoped for—a new silk dress, a dinner reception for friends and family—and told her to have the bills sent to him. His only request was that her new clothing be useful for other occasions.

She wore a dress made of a lush taupe color, and the silk rustled beneath her shaking hands through the long morning. Marie-Claire reached over at one point and took one of Hitty's hands in hers, just to keep it from trembling. Hitty was a nervous wreck. All trembly and shaky, as if she'd been sipping on Grandmother Lillian's apple brandy.

So much silence! So much waiting! Hitty was eager for it to be over with. Her stomach twisted and turned, growled and grumbled, and she felt a little dizzy. By contrast, seated across the aisle with the men, Benjamin seemed quite calm, utterly at peace. It gave her needed confidence, a man without doubts.

Did other brides feel full of doubts? She wished Daphne were here to ask. She couldn't ask Maria or Marie-Claire, for they'd had no experience with marriage.

And then suddenly the waiting was over. An elder asked Hitty and Benjamin to step forward and stand next to each other in front of the elders' bench. Another long silence ensued.

For one brief moment, Hitty wished she were somewhere else.

Just as the elder cleared his throat and started the proclamation that would join Hitty and Benjamin in marriage, Jeremiah rose to his feet, clearing his throat in a way that made everyone take notice of him. "In all good conscience," he said in an overly loud voice, "I cannot allow this marriage to take place."

"What?" Hitty whirled around to face her grandfather. "Why not?"

Marie-Claire jumped up from the women's side. "I am in agreement with Jeremiah Macy! They should not marry!"

Benjamin's head rocked back a little, as if he'd just been slapped. "Sister! Sit down and be quiet!" He stared at her, fierce and unsmiling.

"Why not?" Hitty said, her head turning from Marie-Claire to Benjamin. "Why not!"

Marie-Claire's gaze was fixed on Benjamin. "Brother, this isn't right."

Benjamin scowled at her. "Sit down!"

"What isn't right?" Hitty said, thoroughly confused. No one said another word. The room was eerily quiet, everyone leaning forward in their seats to see who would speak next. Hitty was the only one who moved, her silk dress rustling in the silence, turning from Jeremiah to Marie-Claire to Benjamin.

And then Isaac Barnard, who'd been sitting in the back row of the meetinghouse—whom Hitty did not know was even here—rose to his feet. All eyes turned to him, especially Hitty's. "Nor can I allow this wedding to occur."

"Why not?" Hitty said. Without hesitation, she left Benjamin's side and marched down the aisle. "Isaac Barnard, tell me why this wedding should not take place."

Isaac's shoulders stiffened, and he snatched off his hat.

"Isaac, 'tis thy last chance to speak up!" She put her hands on her hips like a schoolteacher. "Hear me! 'Tis thy last chance."

Isaac stood tall. Taller than Hitty had ever seen him stand. In a loud, confident voice, he said, "Because I love you, Mehitabel. And I think . . . I believe . . . that is, I hope you might love me too." He stared at Hitty and she stared back at him. All in the meetinghouse waited for something to happen.

Then a slow smile began on Isaac's face, starting with his eyes, the smile she loved best. Her heart answered for her.

"I do believe thee is right," Hitty said.

Early the next morning, Henry went to seek out Benjamin Foulger in his office, to console him after being so thoroughly, completely, horribly humiliated yesterday in Meeting. Chin to his chest, Benjamin had silently walked out of the meetinghouse yesterday, all eyes following him, and hadn't been seen since. While Henry was privately pleased that Isaac stepped up to claim Hitty—at last!—he had no lack of empathy for Benjamin, not after Anna had broken things off with him in such a sudden way.

As Henry walked along Main Street, he had the strangest feeling that he was being watched. He stopped and turned in a circle. The hour was early, the streets were quiet. He shook off that odd feeling just as Walter Mitchell, the cashier to the Pacific Bank, called out to him from the steps of the bank.

"Henry," Walter said, waving him to a stop. Henry met him at the bottom of the bank steps. "Henry, I had to put a hold on the drafts thee wanted sent out for the *Illumine* this month."

"Why?"

Walter leaned closer to Henry and lowered his voice. "Thy account. 'Tis overdrawn."

"There must be some mistake." Henry frowned. Normally, Benjamin transferred an allowance into the bank each month—just enough for Henry to cover bills. Mayhap with the wedding, he'd forgotten. "I'll take care of it today."

Walter smiled. "As soon as the funds are there, the drafts will go out." He patted Henry on the shoulder. "Thee is doing fine work with that newspaper. Keep it up. I was pleased to see another 'B' letter in last week's edition." He leaned closer to whisper, "My wife and I, we think the author of the 'B' letters is Absalom Boston."

"I've had the same wondering, Walter." Absalom Boston, a black man, had been a whaling captain. Retired now, he ran a lodge and was highly thought of. He was involved in Nantucket politics.

"Come now." Walter's bushy eyebrows lifted in a question. "Does thee truly not know?"

"I do not. Truly I don't. I have no idea."

William Geary's hat store had just opened for the day, so Henry waved to William and took the stairs to the upstairs office two at a time. The door to Benjamin's office was locked.

"William, when thee sees Benjamin, let him know I'm looking for him."

"Doubt he'll be in today, after being jilted at the altar by your sister. I heard all about it." He shook his head. "Not sure what your sister was thinking—to choose Isaac Barnard, who doesn't have two nickels to rub together, over an ambitious fella like Benjamin Foulger." He let out a snort. "Bet you're not going to feature *that* story in the *Illumine*."

Henry frowned. "Speaking of, I must get to work. Please give Benjamin my message. I do need to see him today."

By day's end, Henry felt more than a little worried that Benjamin hadn't stopped in. He checked at William Geary's hat store again, but the door to the upstairs remained locked tight and William said Benjamin hadn't been in.

As Henry left the hat store and walked onto the cobbled street, he had the strangest sense again that someone was watching him. He stopped and turned in a circle, looking carefully over the clusters of townspeople on the street. He shook off that odd notion and hurried toward the Grand House, hoping Walter Mitchell was not peering out the window at the Pacific Bank. He did not know what to tell him to do with the overdrafts, not until he met with Benjamin.

As soon as he went into the Grand House, he sought out Marie-Claire. "Has thee any idea where Benjamin is?"

She looked as distressed as he felt. "Nay. Not a word. Thee hasn't seen him?"

Henry's worry heightened a notch, but he didn't want to

cause alarm. "He must have been distraught. By yesterday, I mean."

An odd look came over Marie-Claire, as if she was fighting back tears. "Henry, there's something—"

Before she could finish her thought, Hitty and Isaac burst through the front door, with Bitsy between them. Whatever was troubling Marie-Claire was set aside. There was not another quiet moment to the evening, not with Bitsy in the house.

Early the next morning, Henry woke before dawn and hurried down the stairs. It would be another hot day, and he wanted to get as much done as he could before the soupy humidity set in.

Marie-Claire met him in the foyer. She looked tired, and he wondered how long she'd been waiting for him. "Please don't go, Henry. Not yet. I must speak to thee. 'Tis important."

"All right. Let's sit down."

She followed him into the parlor and shut the door. He sat in Grandmother Lillian's stiff armchair, but she would not sit. Instead, she stood by the marble mantel and gripped her hands.

"Henry, during Hitty's wedding to Benjamin, I stood up to object."

"That's right. Thee did, and Jeremiah did." There was such a stir after Isaac's bold declaration of affection that he hadn't given much thought to anything else.

"Benjamin turned to me and said, 'Sister, sit down!'"

"I remember now."

"He did not use the term 'Sister' as the Friends do."

Henry's eyebrows shot up and his heart started to pound.

"Benjamin, he is my older brother." Marie-Claire pressed

one hand over her mouth, as if trying to push back her confession. Then she shook her head, as if to say, *It is out now*. She turned away from Henry's searching gaze. "He is my half brother. We have the same mother. Had. We had the same mother."

Henry stared at Marie-Claire with his mouth hanging open. "Well, I'll be blowed. He must be much older."

"Aye, he is. When my mother died, there was no one else in our family. My father, he had deserted us long before. For all practical purposes, I was orphaned. It was just the two of us, Benjamin and I."

He rose to face her, standing a rod apart. "Why did thee never say so? It wouldn't have mattered."

"Benjamin felt it might have mattered, that thee would be slow to trust him. It was important to him that thee trusted him completely, especially so after Oliver Combs became impaired." She kept her head down. "Henry, I owe a great deal to my brother. He kept me out of an orphanage and put himself through law school by working three jobs. Sometimes more. He has worked very hard to make something of himself. For me, as well. So hard that Oliver Combs noticed how diligent he was and offered a position to him, despite that Benjamin had not the credentials that so many other law clerks did."

"Then why . . . ?" This was hard for Henry to grasp. "I'm not sure I understand why thee would object to Benjamin marrying Hitty."

Marie-Claire didn't answer him at first but walked to the window, holding her elbows against her middle. With her back to him, she said, "Benjamin does not love her. She deserves to be loved. The way Isaac Barnard loves her."

Oh. Oh, oh, oh. Henry sat down in the chair again. A sick

feeling started in the pit of his stomach. He hated to ask, but he needed confirmation. "So, then . . . he was marrying her for her money." It wasn't really a question.

Marie-Claire nodded. "The terms of the will. He knew she had to marry soon."

Well, that information changed Henry's sympathy for Benjamin.

"Henry, I'll make arrangements to leave straightaway. Today, if possible."

Too fast. Too fast. Henry needed to think this all through, understand what it meant. "Don't leave. Not yet. For Hitty's sake, stay. And don't tell her what thee has told me. She . . . likes to believe the best in others." Hitty was so happy right now. She deserved this time. "Hold off for now."

"Thee has no reason to trust me. Benjamin and I, we have been living a lie. I should have spoken up sooner."

Henry rose and walked over to her. "Thee stood up in Meeting to stop the wedding, Marie-Claire. I would say thee is a person who can be trusted." It was Benjamin whom Henry no longer trusted. His stomach roiled as he thought of those outstanding bills, waiting in the Pacific Bank for funds. Funds that might not be coming. "Where might Benjamin be? Thee must have some idea."

"He left Meeting without a word to me, only an angry look. I have wondered if he might have gone to Boston to see to other clients." She bit her lower lip, then said, "Henry, please try and understand. We grew up so very poor. Benjamin is ambitious. Very, very ambitious."

Aye. That's what worried him.

July was a beast of a month. Even as a boy, Jeremiah disliked July. He could never sleep well in the pervasive humidity, when it felt the very air stuck to a man's skin. Around ten o'clock at night, he decided to walk down to the harbor and feel the sea breeze.

As he walked along Main Street, he pulled out his pipe and filled it with tobacco. Breathing had become increasingly labored for him. He couldn't seem to get a full breath to fill his lungs, and when he tried, he would be overcome by a coughing fit. Hitty complained it was his pipe smoking, that he should stop for a while and see if it helped. Fie! The doctor told him that if he didn't quit the pipe, he'd be dead within a year. Double fie! Naught but poppycock.

He knew what cast him down. He missed the sea. She would not leave him be. All he could think of lately was returning to her.

When Ren and Daphne returned, and that should be soon, he thought he might try talking his son into heading out for one more whaling voyage. Just one, before the *Endeavour* was permanently retired.

She was an old hulk to begin with. He wondered how she was faring for Ren on this trip. He wasn't worried. His son could manage any repairs the old ship needed. Ren was a fine captain, better than any Jeremiah had served under. Someday he might even tell his son that very thing.

The thought of planning another voyage cheered him, as did the feel of a breeze on his face, albeit a warm one. At long last, after weeks of no rain, mayhap the weather was turning. He hoped so.

His thoughts drifted to Henry. He wondered if he could talk the boy into joining him and Ren on a voyage, but then dismissed the notion. Henry was convinced Nantucket was losing its grasp on the whaling industry. The sandbar that impeded the harbor was only growing larger, and ships had to anchor farther out in the Sound, depending on costly lighters and stevedores to transport goods. Last week's newspaper reported that more syndicates had moved their ships over to New Bedford or Sag Harbor.

Syndicates. Cowards, all! Greedy parasites, lacking the grit to get on a ship themselves but happy to feather their nest by risking others' lives. His father refused to rely on investors to back a ship, as did Ren. They believed a captain would not, could not make wise decisions when he had investors to please.

Jeremiah pulled a handkerchief from his pocket to wipe his brow. Nearly eleven at night and he was still sweating. He left the wharf and made his way up Main Street, admiring the cobbles Henry had commissioned. At least his grandson had been able to do some good with Lillian's money.

Along the business district, he noticed the door ajar to William Geary's hat store. Forgotten by the lazy night watchman, no doubt. Ever since he'd discovered someone had been getting into his Easy Street cooperage, he was sure the night watchmen slacked off. Who was there to see that they did their job? It was nothing more than shouting out the hour, checking locked doors, and sending naughty lads home past curfew. What a cushy job that was.

He crossed the street to close the door to the hat store but stopped when he heard voices, two men arguing inside. He tilted his good ear against the crack of the door. Jeremiah heard one growl, "I want out. This has gone too far."

Any hair that remained on the back of Jeremiah's neck

stood up; he recognized that voice. It belonged to Benjamin Foulger.

"Avast, avast," the other man said, in a placating tone. "Nothing has changed. It's still as easy as skimming the slicks. Henry's never even realized what's gone missing, has he? They don't pay any attention, now do they? Just like I'd said."

"Thee never said anything about the second portion," Benjamin said. "Until now."

Then there was silence.

"Wait just a minute." The placating voice grew ugly. "So *that's* why you tried to marry her. You've gone greedy and found a way to take it all for yourself. Don't forget that *I'm* the one who found *you*, Benjamin. If it weren't for me, you'd still be Oliver's errand boy. Instead, you're a wealthy man."

Jeremiah's heart started to pound. He took the pipe out of his mouth and slipped through the door, quietly making his way to the rear. "Well, I'll be blowed. I shoulda knowd! All along, I shoulda knowed. I felt it in m' bones. Somethin' weren't right. I knew some dark soul was sneakin' in m' cooperage. I shoulda knowed that devil to be none other than Tristram Macy." And with that, a coughing fit overcame Jeremiah, doubling him over so that he grabbed the stovepipe for balance and accidentally shifted it.

Mary Coffin Starbuck

5 November 1701

Nathaniel is convinced he spotted a comet's tail in the sky last night, using his spyglass. There is a common belief among the seamen that when a comet is seen, something unusual is soon to happen.

I wonder what it might be?

24

Hitty woke slowly, feeling confused. She stared into the darkness. Something was wrong. She sniffed the air and smelled a whiff of smoke. Was the fire not out in the downstairs fireplace?

Suddenly she heard footsteps pounding down the hall. Henry burst into her room. "Hitty, wake up! There's a fire in town. I'm going to help. Get dressed. Wake Marie-Claire and Jeremiah. Be prepared to leave the house if the wind shifts west. The fire is moving fast." He turned and left her room as abruptly as he came.

Hitty bolted upright and practically leapt out of bed. She fumbled with her nightdress and slipped out of it, then pulled on yesterday's dress. She heard shouting out the window, and when she pulled back her curtain, she could see the eerie yellow light in the night sky, coming from town. She gasped. This was no small fire. Even as she watched, she could see the smoke grow thicker, absorbing the light. "Oh Lord, keep people safe. Keep Henry safe." She stared in the direction of town, blinking back tears, the simple, heartfelt prayer running in a silent loop through her mind.

She heard a frantic knocking at the front door and rushed downstairs, thinking Henry had come back again. She opened the door to Isaac, with Bitsy beside him. He pushed her forward into Hitty's arms. "Take care of her. I'm going down to help."

"Isaac!"

Midway down the porch steps, he pivoted to turn to Hitty. "Be safe! Come back to us!"

He stilled, just for a few seconds, then bolted back up the stairs and grabbed Hitty's shoulders. "Will you marry me?"

She thought her heart might have stopped.

"Mehitabel?"

"YES!"

His face broke into a smile, then he cupped Hitty's face and kissed her, right on the lips, gave Bitsy a peck on the top of her head, and away he hurried, disappearing into the darkness.

Hitty stood there, stunned. What was happening to the world? *Isaac Barnard just asked to marry me!*

Bitsy looked up at Hitty. "Hitty, I'm scared."

Hitty hugged Bitsy close against her. She was eight years old now, growing tall, yet right now she looked like a very little girl. "Worry not. Thee is safe, Bitsy."

"What about Papa?"

"God is watching over thy papa." And Henry. And the fire wardens.

They went to Marie-Claire's room, knocking gently, then more forcefully. "Get up, Marie-Claire. Get up now." She tried her best not to scare her but couldn't keep the urgent note from her voice.

Marie-Claire rolled over and stared at Hitty as she opened the door. "What's happened?"

"There's a fire in town. Bitsy is here with me." She went to the window and pulled back the curtain. Marie-Claire's window had an even better view of town. Hitty could see only smoke, dense and black. Then the wind changed direction and blew the smoke away, and Hitty could see that the fire had already doubled in size. Alarm bells rang through the air, warning people, calling men to come help douse the fire.

Marie-Claire jumped out of bed and went to the window. "Henry? Jeremiah?"

"Henry has gone to town. I'll help thee dress, then we must go to Jeremiah. Henry says we must be ready to leave the house."

Even in the darkness Hitty could see Marie-Claire's expression change swiftly. She didn't bother to dress. She grabbed a blanket, wrapped it around her shoulders, and hurried out of her room to knock on Jeremiah's door.

"Wake up! Wake up! Jeremiah!" She opened the door, Hitty and Bitsy following.

Marie-Claire and Hitty looked at each other, both thinking the same thought. Jeremiah's bed was still made up. It was untouched.

All through the night and into the next day, from the second floor windows of the Grand House, Hitty would stop to watch the fire's movement. She released the servants, insisting they return home to care for their families, hoping she was not sending them straight into danger. Now and then, bursts of explosions filled the air, and she wondered if the fire was spreading down near the wharf, past the warehouses filled with flammable whale oil. A verse in the book of Proverbs came to mind, something about that which was never satisfied. "Fire," wrote King Solomon, "never says, 'Enough!'"

Would this fire ever stop? When would it burn itself out?

It took until the afternoon before Hitty could see the end was finally in sight. Black clouds still hung in the air, soot rained down from the sky, but when she looked toward town, she no longer saw angry smoke billowing up. Thank God, she thought. Thank God.

A few hours later, Henry and Isaac came through the front door, exhaustion covering their faces, reeking of smoke, clothes covered with soot and ash.

Hitty welcomed them, barely able to keep herself from throwing her arms around them. "I'm so glad thee are both safe and sound." She looked at Isaac. "Bitsy finally fell asleep, upstairs in my bed. Shall I get her? She's asked for thee all day."

"I'll wash up first, then I'll wake her." He put his hand on Hitty's shoulder and gave her a weary smile. "Thank you for looking after her."

"Jeremiah," Marie-Claire cut in. "Thee has seen him?"

"Isn't he here?" Henry said, confused. "He was home last evening. I'm sure of it."

"When we went to his room, his bed was untouched." Marie-Claire looked from Henry to Isaac, then back to Henry. "Did thee not see him among the firefighters?"

"Nay," Henry said, "'twas all confusion and chaos."

"Then, where could he be?" Hitty asked, her voice filled with concern.

"I don't know. Mayhap helping the fishermen move their dories away from the waterfront. The wharf was the last to go."

"Straight Wharf . . . it is . . . 'tis gone?"

Henry shared a defeated look with Isaac. He let out a deep sigh, as if mustering his last bit of energy. "Three of four wharves are gone. Nearly one third of the town has been wiped out. The Atheneum. The Episcopal church. Hundreds of homes."

"Have there been any deaths?"

"It's too soon to tell." Before Hitty could ask another question, Henry stopped her with a raised hand. "I know what is running through thy minds, but 'tis not time to worry. Jeremiah could be anywhere."

He was right. It was too soon to worry. And it was characteristic of Jeremiah to stay close to the water, to help the seamen. "Come, then, sit down in the parlor and rest," Hitty said.

"We must clean up, first." Henry tried to give Hitty a smile. "Grandmother Lillian would be outraged to have soot on her parlor chairs."

"Fie on that thought!" Hitty said, meaning it. "Thee has earned a sit down." They did not need any more persuasion. Henry went into the parlor and sank into the nearest chair, Isaac following behind. Hitty and Marie-Claire sat across from them.

"We heard explosions," Marie-Claire said. "We thought it might be the whale oil factories."

"It could have been," Isaac said, "but it might have been dynamite. The fire wardens tried to protect buildings by . . . stopping the fire in its tracks."

Hitty's mouth fell open. "By blowing buildings up?"

"The fire spread in all directions," Isaac explained. "The upward flow of heat created its own wind currents. The firestorm swept through narrow streets, and sparks flew through the air. Houses that seemed safe suddenly had roofs on fire." He leaned forward in his chair, eyes focused on Hitty. "Maria Mitchell stopped the firemen from destroying the Methodist church."

"The Methodist church? Then . . . the fire went down Centre Street?" The Cent School! Her family's little cottage! It was her childhood home.

"Very nearly. Maria convinced the firemen that the winds would soon move in another direction and her prediction was correct. But the observatory her father built on top of the Pacific Bank . . . it was burned."

Hitty's hand clenched and unclenched. She wished she could go to Maria, to comfort her. How many hours had she spent in that little cupola, observing the night sky? Maria and her father, that little garret brought them such joy.

"It's mind-boggling, the loss. Seven whale oil processing factories, a dozen warehouses, hundreds of houses." Henry rubbed his face with his hands. "I wonder if the island can rebound."

"Nantucketers are resilient," Hitty said. "Surely they'll rally together as they've done before."

"I don't know, Hitty. This is different." Henry shook his head. "No one knows whom to trust."

"How could that be? They're old friends. Everyone knows each other."

"Old friends? Hitty, there are more than ten thousand people on this island. Down near the fire, right now, are . . . looters, pilferers. It's each man for himself. The sheriff can't manage it. They're stealing whatever can be found in the cinders."

Hitty felt punched in the stomach. "Looters? Stealing from those who have lost everything?" How could that be? How could anyone allow himself to be so morally bankrupt?

Henry shrugged. "Is it any different from scavenging the beach for treasures after a shipwreck? 'Tis the way of the island."

"It is different," Hitty said. "Entirely different. Those who died in a shipwreck no longer have need of their belongings. The people of Nantucket Town . . . they are still living."

"I heard a selectman say that over eight hundred people are homeless," Henry said.

"Eight hundred and two," Isaac said, rubbing his temples. "My house was burned to the ground."

Hitty gasped. "Sister Hannah? She is safe?" She had given no thought to her.

Isaac nodded. "Before I brought Bitsy to thee, I took her to Sister Alice's, just across the street."

"So many homeless," Marie-Claire said, rubbing her forehead. She stopped and looked up. "This house! It can hold families. We could help." As Hitty stared at her, Marie-Claire got a look on her face as if she suddenly realized she was offering hospitality that wasn't hers to share. She rushed to add, "If thee might be willing, that is."

But that wasn't what Hitty was thinking. She turned to Isaac. "What about food?"

Isaac let out a deep sigh. "The dry goods stores, groceries. Gone, all."

"If homes are gone and markets are gone," Hitty said, "how will people eat?"

Henry frowned. "Another problem. The selectman said there isn't enough food on the island to last a week."

"This house, it has a full pantry," Marie-Claire said, looking to Hitty for approval. "If thee is willing, we can feed people. We could make big pots of soup and bake loaves of bread, and make a meal each day for those who are hungry."

"Of course," Hitty said, wishing she had thought of it. So often, she could only see the problem, not the solution. "Of course we're willing!"

"'Tis a fine idea," Henry said, his eyes fixed on Marie-Claire. "Let me wash up and change clothes, and get something to eat. Then I'll go back to town and send some folks up this way. I'll find Jeremiah and send him home too."

"We'll go with thee," Marie-Claire offered.

Henry shook his head. "Absolutely not. Not today. 'Tis a terrible sight to behold."

"'Tis Sodom and Gomorrah," Isaac said, and Hitty shuddered.

"Mayhap 'tis a good thing that Benjamin had left island." Marie-Claire started toward the door but spun around to face Henry. "He did leave, did he not?"

"Yesterday morning," Henry said, "I went to his office above William Geary's hat shop. The door . . . 'twas locked. William said he had not seen him." He touched her shoulder in a comforting pat. "No doubt he is safe and sound in Boston."

"Is thee going to the *Illumine*'s office?"

When Henry didn't answer Marie-Claire's question, Hitty looked up. She saw her brother fight to hold back tears.

"The newspaper's office," Isaac filled in. "'Tis gone. Burnt to the ground."

Henry cleared his throat and rubbed his face with both hands. "My new printing press . . . 'tis melted down to slag."

Four separate families arrived at the house, saying that Henry had sent them for temporary shelter, and Hitty welcomed them all in. It was difficult to know which need to care for first—baths, fresh clothing, sleep, or food. Hitty and Marie-Claire were up and down the stairs, toting bath water, carrying down singed, smoky clothing.

At one point, Hitty was coming down the stairs as Marie-Claire went up. "'Tis so much better to be doing something than to sit and anxiously wait for news of Jeremiah."

"And Benjamin," Marie-Claire said softly, skimming past her.

Shame covered Hitty. From the moment Isaac had spoken out in the meetinghouse to say he loved her, she'd been so absorbed with her own happiness that she had scarcely considered Benjamin. And when she did think of him, it was with only with a sweeping relief that she had not married him.

Henry was stunned. He had stopped by the Mitchell residence to thank Maria for her brave act to save the Methodist church from getting dynamited, when her father quietly confided that he had not insured the Atheneum. It had been burned to the ground.

"Thee did not . . . insure it? Thee is president of the trustees!"

"The cost," Walter Mitchell said, ashen-faced. "'Twas prohibitive."

"Does thee know what this means?"

"Aye," Walter said in a low voice. "Aye, I do. I have made a grave error."

There was nothing more to be said. Henry left without waiting to talk to Maria. The Atheneum, the most important building on the island, how could it ever be rebuilt?

Numbly, he walked down Main Street's cobblestones, the only thing that survived the fire. On each side were blackened, burned-out remains of brick buildings. Or, if made of wood, empty cellars filled with smoldering ashes. It already had a name: the Burnt District.

Henry turned at the sound of someone calling to him. Isaac was walking toward him, a somber look on his face.

He handed a charred pipe to Henry. "Do you recognize it?"

It was a scrimshaw pipe, one Henry knew well. "Aye, it belongs to Jeremiah."

"Henry," Isaac said softly, "the fire wardens just found two bodies in William Geary's hat store. This was near one of them, found in the rubble."

Henry had to sit down, right on the cobbled street. Sobs laddered in his chest. He tucked his head over his knees and wept. Without a word, Isaac sat down next to him and put an arm around his shoulders.

Mary Coffin Starbuck

15 October 1702

Eleazer Foulger came into the store today. He and I are great friends, and I always enjoy his visits. In so many ways, he reminds me of his father. Today, though, he seemed anxious, waiting nervously until the store emptied out.

"Mary, I must get into the treasure," he said. "My eldest son has been accepted at Harvard Divinity School." He looked away. "I have no way of paying for it," he lowered his eyes, as if in shame, "until I remembered our treasure."

Years and years ago, before I was married to Nathaniel, Eleazer and I would scrounge the beach after storms to see what the ocean might have turned up for us. Usually, discoveries were modest. Shipwrecks brought all kinds of odds and ends, flotsam and jetsam. We made use of it all, every bottle, every tool, every rope, pieces of wood. It was the island way—whoever found it, claimed it.

Our scrounging was always great fun, though we never left the beach without saying a thank-you to the Almighty for whatever we had discovered, for we never forgot we were benefiting from someone else's misfortune.

Until one day, when we found a treasure box filled with Spanish pieces of eight—a fortune! At least to our young way of thinking. We made a pact: we would not tell others about it, and we would only use it to help others.

"Eleazer, that is what we wanted to use the treasure for! I am delighted."

"But you haven't used it, have you?"

"Aye! One time. To ransom a fugitive slave."

Twice, actually. A few leftover pieces went to save Elsa Coleman. I kept that information to myself.

Eleazer turned and walked around the store, pausing at the small window. He spun around. "Is seminary a good enough reason?"

"Indeed!"

"'Tis not saving a man's life."

"Even better. 'Tis saving men's souls."

He pondered that for a while, staring out the window. I could tell it was troubling him to get into the treasure, and I understood why. Its presence has been a reassurance for us during lean times. Its very existence gives me great comfort. Once or twice, during a poor summer harvest, I have wondered if this might be the year I need a few Spanish pieces to help make ends meet. But I have never needed to.

I took his hand in mine, for I could tell he felt some shame at needing to dig it up. "An education is a fine and noble thing. 'Tis exactly the kind of thing we had hoped for when we made our promise to each other." I squeezed his hands to reassure him. "I will help thee dig!"

And so I did. We had an adventure together, Eleazer and I. Nathaniel had gone to the Cape for supplies, so the timing was perfect to steal away early one morning without need to provide an excuse. We met on the cart path, surrounded by swirling fog, and for once the gray weather added worth to the drama.

The woods were not quite as hard to walk through at this time of the year. But nearly. Narrow paths wove between overgrown vines and scrubby bushes. Despite the cold snap, much of the wet, boggy ground remained soft and muddy, sucking at our feet with each step.

My special tree stood proudly guarding our treasure, and Eleazer marked off six paces from the largest branch—which is now even larger. Years ago, it marked off the canopy of the tree, as we took care not to disturb its roots. Six paces measured only half the branch now! It took some steadfast digging, as we have not had rain the last few weeks and the ground was hard, but that did not deter Eleazer. When the shovel hit a metal sound, we both looked up at each other. Then we burst out with a laugh! There it was, just as we had left it. The sun had burned off the fog by the time Eleazer worked the box up and out. He brushed it off, treating it ever so carefully, and jimmied it open. Inside were the Spanish pieces of eight, a bit more tarnished than I recalled. I had brought linen sacks to put the coins in, for I worried of the elements affecting the coins. Eleazer took out what he needed for Harvard's tuition and started to close the lid.

"Wait!" I took a small note from my pocket, stating the date and the reason the coins were taken. "I want our children and grandchildren to know how we spent the money, and how we want it to be used."

On the way home, our step was lighter. The years had peeled away; we were young and without cares. How good it feels to do good!

25

There were a number of reasons Henry wanted to sail to Boston, just three days after the Great Fire and one day after he buried his grandfather Jeremiah's remains.

A fire warden told him that the fire had begun in William Geary's hat shop, starting in the stovepipe. Two volunteer fire companies arrived to put it out, but as they argued as to who should do it, the fire spread quickly out of control. They did not realize anyone was inside the store, he said.

Henry needed to tell Oliver Combs, in person, something that he hadn't yet told Marie-Claire, nor Hitty. He couldn't tell them, not yet, and he hoped they would not hear of two bodies in the store, only of Jeremiah's. He feared Benjamin was a fatality of the fire, the other body found in William Geary's hat shop, though he still held out hope that the law clerk was alive and well, in his Boston office, recovering from the shock of his wedding gone awry. That's what Marie-Claire and Hitty had assumed, and he let them continue to think that. He needed to find out the truth.

Henry had found a fisherman who was sailing his schooner at high tide to the mainland, to bring back needed lumber for rebuilding, and talked him into letting him come aboard. He sent word to Hitty, through a boy on the wharf who was willing to deliver a message for a loaf of bread, that he would be off island for a few days and not to worry.

Leaning against the small boat's railing as it left the harbor, Henry felt sickened by the charred wasteland of Nantucket. All that was left of the town was stark, blackened bones. He pivoted around, no longer able to look at it, and tried to cheer himself up by thinking of the second half of the inheritance. He had a plan to liquidate it all, as soon as possible, to provide the means for Nantucket to rebuild. It just now occurred to him that at least those first projects he'd commissioned—the cobblestones, the lightships, the Humane Houses— were untouched by the fire, and he let out a sigh of relief. But this fire had created so much need on the island. He needed cash and currency to make a difference, to help, and he had none.

Rebuilding the Atheneum was first on his mind. There was something about that library that represented the heart of Nantucket—the books, the gathering place for lively public discussions. If the Atheneum could be rebuilt as soon as possible, he reasoned, the entire island would benefit from the wind of optimism.

Mayhap the severity of the fire would convince Oliver Combs of the need to adjust the conditions set forth in the will for the second portion of the inheritance. Hitty and Isaac wanted to marry, despite the fact that he was not a Friend in good standing. Not even a Friend. But Isaac was willing to be a convinced Quaker, he told Henry, for it mattered not to him where he worshiped, only that he worshiped, and his ancestry could be traced back to the first families. Might that suffice?

And then there was Henry's own obligation to marry. Thoughts of Marie-Claire crowded his mind and warmed his heart. He had never thought he could feel this way about another woman, not after Anna. But his mind, his heart, they were changing. He did not hold Marie-Claire responsible for omitting that she was a sibling to Benjamin, for he understood the reasons. And she did come forth with the truth. That said much about her character to Henry. About her loyalty.

As soon as he arrived at the port of Boston, he took a hack to Oliver Combs's office, hoping, hoping, hoping that Benjamin might be there, toiling away as he often imagined him to be. Alas, the office was dark, the door locked.

Next, he went to Oliver Combs's residence on Beacon Hill, not far away. Henry was told to wait in the library by Oliver's nurse, an unsmiling woman, who went to fetch him. The library was a beautiful room, paneled in dark wood, with a round arched fireplace, flanked by a black marble mantel. Henry stared at the cold fireplace as he waited. Would he ever look at a fire again without thinking of that awful night?

Henry turned when he heard the squeak of wheels coming toward the library. He tried, without success, to mask his shock at the sight of the elderly man. Oliver Combs had once been a large, imposing man, with a bold handshake. He had shriveled, markedly aged, his skin had a gray pallor to it. He sat in a wheeled chair, his lap covered by a blanket even in this summer heat. Henry reached out to shake his hand, but quickly retracted it when he saw that Oliver was unable to lift his limp hand. "Oliver, I'm sorry I haven't been to see thee."

The elderly man spoke with great effort, and Henry had

to strain to understand him. “I haven’t been up to receiving visitors.” Oliver dismissed the attendant, who left the room only after she slid a glance Henry’s way—a warning. First things first. “Oliver, has thee received word from Benjamin?”

Oliver shook his head.

“Thee has heard of the Great Fire?”

Oliver nodded. “It’s in all the papers.”

“The island . . . ’tis in great chaos. I need to have a conversation with Benjamin, but I haven’t seen him on island. I went first to thy office, hoping he was there, but it was locked tight. Would thee trust me with a key?”

Oliver blinked in confusion. “A key?”

“Aye. A key to thy office. So I might get in.” How much should Henry tell him? As little as possible, but he did need to get into that law office and search for any sign that Benjamin had been there recently. “I have no idea where Benjamin resides. I thought I might find the location of his residence in the office.” It was not a lie. It was simply not the whole truth.

Oliver surprised him by lifting his left hand and pointing to the desk. “Top drawer.”

Henry jumped up and fished through the drawer for a key. “I thank thee. I will return with it in the morning.”

Oliver nodded. He had a look on his face as if he wanted to say something, but it would take too much effort.

Henry lifted the key in a wave. “I’ll be back, Oliver.”

He hailed a horse and hack and went directly to the law office. He’d been there once or twice before, accompanying his grandmother. He remembered spending his time gazing out the window that had a view of Boston Harbor. Inside a narrow building, up a stairwell to the second floor, he found the door to Oliver Combs’s law office. The key turned the lock, and he walked into a dark room, for it was past nine o'clock. He lit a lantern and looked around the desk for evidence of recent activity. It was extremely neat, everything in its place, as he would have expected of Benjamin. But most telling—hauntingly so—was a thin layer of dust that coated the desk. Henry sighed. Everything was pointing to the one discovery he was loath to believe: Benjamin Foulger was indeed the other body in the hat shop. No other Nantucketer had gone missing, only Jeremiah and Benjamin.

He opened each desk drawer, hunting for Benjamin's address. Mayhap . . . mayhap there was still some hope. Mayhap the law clerk was at home, licking his wounds, though even to Henry's ears, it did not sound like Benjamin. One drawer was locked. He hesitated, just for a moment, but he was in too deep not to turn over every possible stone to find Benjamin. He jimmied it open to find a thick folder of legal documents, all carefully labeled with his grandmother's name. He settled into the desk chair and moved the lantern light to read through the documents.

An hour passed, then another. This folder held the paperwork for the first portion of the inheritance, and everything looked in order, neat and tidy, then he read through a second time. He turned the page of one document to the end, and that was when something hooked him, and his mind started to spin. The last page of each document had an amendment that he hadn't noticed. Hitty's signature was on each one, transferring title of the asset over to Benjamin Foulger and Tristram Macy.

Henry wasn't sure if he could breathe, if he could feel. His body felt thick and numb, his heart turned to stone. He turned pages over, faster and faster. Very few assets had been liquidated, as Henry had been told they were. Nearly each one had its title transferred, funneled to Benjamin and Tristram. How? How could this be?

He went back to the beginning to look at the date when Hitty first signed over an asset. 1841. Right after Henry started the *Illumine* and was wholly preoccupied. And he couldn't remember the exact date, but he thought Oliver's stroke occurred around the same time.

Henry went to the window to open it for fresh air. As he lifted the sash with arms upraised, the lantern on the desk blew out and the room went dark. He fumbled to find the lantern, and then something hit his head, hard, so hard he saw stars, and fell to the ground. By the time he stumbled to his feet, found a match, lit the lantern, and looked around the room, he realized the door was ajar. He peered down the dark hallway. Empty. Rubbing the bump on his head, he returned to the office, noticed something small and shiny on the floor, picked it up, and sat down at the desk.

The folder was gone.

Hitty couldn't wait for Henry to get home. She had news! Good news, and that would be a welcomed relief after the sorrows of the last week. Not one day after Henry sent word that he had sailed to Boston, she received a letter from Daphne. The *Endeavour* was making its way back to Nantucket at last. The voyage had not been a greasy one and the hold was not quite full, Daphne had written, but it was good enough, with many exciting adventures to tell.

There was so much to catch them up on, starting with

Jeremiah's death. The fire. Her engagement to Isaac. She needed them home.

Hitty and Marie-Claire went to greet Henry at the only wharf that still remained after the fire. Henry hadn't explained why he'd gone to Boston, but Hitty hoped it was to convince Oliver Combs that Isaac could be considered a Friend in good standing, even if he was a convinced Quaker.

As the dory drew close, she saw Henry's face and let out a gasp. "Henry! Thee looks awful!"

Henry jumped onto the dock with a laugh, touching his bruised forehead with a fingertip. "'Tis a good thing my head is so hard."

Hitty peered at his face. Dark purple circles shadowed his eyes, his forehead was swollen. "What has happened to thee?"

"Quite a bit. I have glad tidings and I have"—he rubbed the lump above his brow—"some that is less so."

"Tell us," Hitty said. "Tell us everything. Don't wait until we reach home." She lifted a gloved hand in the air. "Wait. First, I will give thee glad tidings. Father and Daphne, they are soon to return." She smiled. "Now, thee may tell us thy news."

"Mayhap it should wait." Henry's eyes, Hitty noticed, fixed on Marie-Claire with a question. She, too, gazed at him with a solemn and quizzical look.

"We have a long walk ahead," Hitty said, and indeed it was long, as much of the burned-out parts of town were impassable.

Marie-Claire waited, unmoving. "Did thee see Benjamin?"

He took in a deep breath. "He's part of the news that I have to tell thee."

"Please, Henry," Hitty said. "Good news first."

"Sister, as far as Oliver Combs is concerned, thee is free to marry Isaac."

Hitty stopped abruptly. Then she let out a shriek. "Henry, that's wonderful!" She couldn't believe it. Simply couldn't believe it! "So thee did meet with Oliver. He is well, I hope?"

"I did. He is . . . improving. He is a determined man. More so than ever." He smiled at her, but not with his eyes.

"So then, what is the bad news?"

His smile started to slip and she saw him struggle to get it back. "Our inheritance, Hitty . . . 'tis gone. All. Part one *and* part two." He tipped his head, lifting a finger in the air. "Avast. Not all. The Grand House, the title is still in our names. And the Centre Street cottage. And Jeremiah's Easy Street cooperage." He sighed and shook his head. "Nay, I forgot that was burned to the ground."

Hitty thought he was making fun. "Stop, Henry. Jest not about such things."

"I do not, Sister."

She stared at him, as her head tried to sort his meaning. "But what has happened to the inheritance?"

Henry sighed and started again to walk toward the Grand House. He unfolded the sequence of events, of finding the folder in the locked desk drawer, of discovering the titles of assets had been transferred to Benjamin Foulger and to Tristram Macy.

Tristram Macy. Dazed, Hitty remained silent, so silent, as understanding broke over her, a terrible pain. "I did this!" she said. "I signed those papers without reading them. I *couldn't* read them! They were so complicated, Henry. Filled with huge words that I couldn't understand." She covered her face. "I did this. I did it to us."

"Nay, Hitty," Marie-Claire said firmly. "Benjamin, he did this. Thee trusted him, and he took advantage of thy trust."

"He did not act alone." Then Henry explained that he believed it was Tristram Macy who hit him on the head and stole the folder.

Hitty felt her chest start to burn.

Marie-Claire stopped. "Mayhap . . . could it have been Benjamin?"

Henry dug into his pocket and pulled out a cuff link with the initials *TM* on it. "I found this on the floor of Benjamin's office. I think it came off when Tristram hit me."

Hitty tried to come to grips with what had happened. "Tristram *came* to the office? He hit thee and stole the documents?" She told herself not to cry. She would *not* cry, but the tears, they came anyway.

"There's more," Henry said. "Though by now, thee might have already heard the news. Before I left, Isaac told me there were two bodies found in the rubble of the hat store."

"We heard," Hitty said. "Everyone's heard."

"Has the fire warden identified the other body?"

"Not that I know of," she said. "Why? Has thee tidings to tell?"

"I fear it might be . . ." Henry hesitated, glancing first at Marie-Claire.

She finished his sentence for him. "Benjamin's."

Hitty gasped, watching Marie-Claire. Her complexion was drained of all color, her skin bloodless and white as snow.

"This can't be true," though Hitty knew it was, had even wondered when she'd heard a rumor that the fire wardens had found two bodies. "I can hardly believe it."

"Believe it," Henry said, more forcefully than he needed to.

Hitty put her arms around Marie-Claire, but she felt stiff and wooden, and so, sensing her distress, she released her. And yet, she also realized that this information was not a complete shock to Marie-Claire. As if she had already been told this news. "You knew this?"

"The fire warden sought me out yesterday," Marie-Claire said. "He said they'd found some evidence that led him to believe the other body might belong to Benjamin. Silver buttons from a coat, he said, that were known to be made by a smithy in Boston." Her eyes grew glassy. "I was hoping that Henry would return with news that might . . . prove him wrong."

"I'd like to ask thee some questions, Marie-Claire," Henry said, in a hard, accusing voice.

"Henry!" Hitty said. "Not now."

Her brother refused to be put off. "There are questions that need to be answered."

"Ask." Marie-Claire wiped the tears from under her eyes with her gloved fingertips and took a deep, shaky breath. "Ask me anything."

"Now?" Henry stepped back, putting some distance between them.

"Now."

Marie-Claire was tougher than Hitty would've thought, though this young woman was always surprising her. She stood before Henry straight as a mast, her face calm. Her brother, by contrast, could barely conceal his upset. His hands clenched into fists as he gazed hard at her.

"Was Benjamin acquainted with Tristram Macy before he first came to Nantucket? Was this whole thing . . . was it masterminded in advance?" His voice had started off in a reasonable pitch, but now it rose with anger. "Is that why thee moved into the Grand House? 'Twas all part of an elaborate scheme?"

"Nay!" Marie-Claire looked genuinely shocked by his accusation. "I'd never heard the name of Tristram Macy, not until I arrived in Nantucket and learned of him in Lillian Coffin's will." She squeezed her eyes shut, then opened them. "I think Benjamin came here with noble intentions. I truly do. In fact, I have no doubt that he did." She dropped her chin to her chest and spoke so softly that both Hitty and Henry had to lean in to hear her. "But then there was a change in him. A notable one."

"After Oliver Combs's stroke?"

She nodded. "Benjamin spent more and more time in Boston that first winter, and when he was here, he was increasingly . . . stressed, short-tempered. Vague about his plans."

"So Tristram Macy found him?" Henry said. "Put pressure on him? Is that what thee thinks?"

"I don't know. I don't. I just . . ." Marie-Claire stopped, collected her thoughts, then started again. "My brother saw all of thee living with such wealth, such ease. Even me, living at the house, with plenty of food, a warm fire, while he was working hard on everyone's behalf. I wonder . . . with Oliver's absence . . . he was left on his own. Mayhap he grew susceptible to temptation. To someone tempting him to do wrong." She dipped her head. "I am deeply ashamed."

Hitty walked away a few paces, then spun on her heels. "I am sorry for Benjamin. I truly am. But I am not sorry to lose that inheritance. It brought nothing but problems. 'Tis cursed, that fortune."

"'Tis not that simple, Hitty. Nantucket . . . it is in great need of money. I had hoped to help. Now, I can do nothing. Even my livelihood, my newspaper, 'tis gone."

"Mayhap this fire," Marie-Claire said, in a quiet, low voice, "mayhap 'tis acting as a refining tool, to remind everyone of what is truly important. Of what can't be taken away."

Henry stared for a long moment at Marie-Claire, so long that Hitty wondered what he was thinking.

They started walking again, slowly and thoughtfully and silently, digesting all that had been discussed. As they came to the gate of the Grand House, Hitty felt her spirits lift.

On the porch, Isaac was playing a game of checkers with Bitsy. Bright potted red geraniums flanked each porch step. It looked so welcoming. This house, she realized, had become a home after all, because it was filled with loved ones.

She turned to her brother. "Staying here, Henry," she said, "being part of the Nantucket that will emerge from the ashes. That is our true inheritance." That would be their legacy.

At First Day, just five days after the Great Fire, the old meetinghouse—which had survived the fire—was packed. Not a single pew remained unfilled. How sad, Hitty thought, how wasteful, that it took tragedy to cause people to seek God. He had never left them, but they had left him.

She glanced across the aisle to the men's side and shared a smile with Isaac. He had told Hitty that it mattered not to him where they worshiped, as long as they were together as a family. If that were true, she had told him, she would much rather he become a convinced Quaker than she become a reluctant Methodist. So he had come.

When Maria Mitchell wiggled down the pew, Hitty barely

held herself back from hugging her. She'd been worried about Maria. Only a few days after the fire, while Henry had been off island, another alarm had sounded, and Maria reacted so fearfully that she destroyed all her diaries and letters. The fire turned out to be nothing but a false alarm. What a shame!

"Maria," Hitty had asked her. "Why? Why would thee destroy thy work?"

Maria had looked at Hitty as if it was so obvious. "Had it been a real fire, my work might have been looted. It might have ended up in the wrong hands. The comet, Hitty . . . I am so close. *This* close." She pinched her fingers together. "I could not risk letting my calculations end up in someone else's hands."

"But how will thee locate the comet now, with all of thy work gone?"

Maria pointed to her head. "'Tis not gone. 'Tis all up here."

Ah! Another benefit of being brilliant.

That conversation put to rest her concerns that Maria's mind had been afflicted, but there were other gnawing worries. Hitty had heard talk of many—nay, most—residents who planned to leave the island for good. There was no reason to stay, they said. Their livelihood was gone, the town was a burned-out wasteland. The fire took it all.

As she sat in the silence and tried to let her mind settle, Hitty felt a knot of emotion suddenly well up in her throat. Aye, there was great loss, and sorrow too. But there was so much to be thankful for. She didn't know where to begin, her heart felt so full. In the silence, she heard a cough and then a nervous, restless stirring as Henry stood. Wait. *Henry?*

Hitty found herself sitting up straight and feeling a bit apprehensive. He was not known for speaking in Meeting. Ever.

Henry's tone was conversational as he started off. "This Great Fire is a tragedy, that is undeniable. But 'tis also a blessing. We pass through this world so distracted by material desires that we're blind and deaf to the Spirit of God that each one of us possesses. 'Tis no wonder we grow intolerant and judgmental, treating each other without sympathy and charity. God . . . he sees the pure Light within, not the silk clothing, the grand houses."

He paused for a moment, dropped his chin, and rubbed the bump on his forehead in an absentminded gesture. When he raised his head again, he wore a harder, more determined expression. "This fire has given us an opportunity to stop striving amongst ourselves—be it race or religion or social stratification—and to recognize the same spirit in each other that shines within ourselves. Nantucket has always been a place of second chances, of new beginnings. Did not the very first proprietors seek a second chance by coming here? They did, and they stayed, and they persevered, turning this island into a thriving community. Let us pray today that the light of God's Spirit will fill our hearts and inspire us to be known by our acts, and that our acts will reflect God's love for our neighbors. All of them."

Well done, Hitty thought as she watched Henry sit down. *Well done, Brother.* But would it make a difference?

Mary Coffin Starbuck

17 February 1705

There is a saying, "Friends move slowly." I would like to add, "And so do husbands."

Nathaniel insists he needs more time to reflect upon the validity of Quakerism, certainly before he agrees to donate land to build a meetinghouse.

We are growing in strength and numbers, so much so that our group has come to a decision to attach ourselves to the Quaker association on the mainland. Doing so created another reason for Nathaniel's hesitation, as he feels we are contradicting the very reason we moved to Nantucket Island in the first place.

"Times have changed," I told him. "We are not isolated any longer, and connecting to other Quaker bodies will help us grow stronger."

"And avoid church taxes."

I frowned at him. Not that old rag again! Nathaniel was suspicious that the rapid growth of our meeting had more to do with people wanting to avoid taxation. Ever since Nantucket was annexed to Massachusetts, each town had been required to impose a tax for the support of a church and minister of the Established Order.

At that point, I left him alone in the house. The room had darkened with late afternoon shadows. I couldn't wait for spring to come. The older I get, the more weary I grow of short, dark winter days.

I'd noticed a hawk circling the yard and wanted to

make sure my hens were safely in the henhouse. When I came back to the house, Nathaniel stood at the open door, an odd, sweet look on his weathered face. "You're watching over Nantucket in the same way, aren't you?"

"How so?"

"Keeping the hens safe from the hawk. That's what you're trying to do for the islanders. That's why you're so determined to build this meetinghouse. To strengthen the Quaker stronghold."

I laughed. "I suppose so! I believe this is the right path for us. For our children and their children."

His gaze swept over our land, and then over to the sea that he loved so very much, and settled back on me, whom he loved even more. "Then you shall have it. I will donate the land for the Friends' meetinghouse."

I walked toward him, holding out my hands to him, and he reached out to take them. "And thee, husband? Thee will join us?"

He smiled. "If I don't, I'll soon be the only non-Friend left on island."

Early the next morning, I waited until I knew Nathaniel's fishing boat had left its mooring and he was gone for the day. I put a sign on the store, stating that it would be closed until I returned from an errand. I found Nathaniel's shovel in the shed and went to the Founders' Burial Ground, where so many dear ones were now at rest—my mother, followed five years later by my father, then nine years later came my father-in-law, Edward. I walked along their gravesites, paying my respects, before I went to the oak tree. My oak tree.

I marked off six paces and found the spot. Then I started to dig. And dig. And dig. Oh my, I was hot and sweaty and dirty! If anyone had come by, they would've thought me dotty. There I was, a sixty-year-old woman, digging a big hole under a tree. If Eleazer were on island, I would have asked for his help, but he was on the mainland, off to hear his grandson deliver his first sermon to his congregation.

So I kept on digging. One hour, then two. And finally, my shovel hit the metal sound I was waiting for. Another hour passed as I worked and wiggled that box out of its hiding place. At last, up it came. I brushed it off with my apron, opened it, took out the linen sack that held the Spanish pieces of eight—half expecting it to be gone! But it was all there. I took out what was needed to pay the lumber receipt that my brother Peter brought from the mainland. (I ordered it prior to Nathaniel's agreement to donate land . . . for I did not think it would take so long for him to agree! And after discovering how reluctant he was to donate land, I dare not ask him to pay for the lumber too.) I left a note in the sack, stating the date and the reason I had used the treasure: "A bit of silver taken to purchase lumber for Nantucket's First Meeting House."

Satisfied, tired, and oh so happy, I closed the treasure up, patted it fondly—for who knew if I were to see it again? I am not so young as I once was—and set it care-

fully back down in the hole. The filling of the hole was much more expedient than the digging.

Later that year, the first Quaker Meeting House was built, constructed by many willing Nantucket hands. It was the first building on Nantucket Island that was erected for religious purposes.

My prayer is that it is not the last.

26

Early the next morning, Marie-Claire came downstairs and found Henry in the dining room, sipping his tea. “A hack will be here soon. I located a schooner bound for Boston. It leaves at high tide this morning.”

So soon? Henry’s mind went blank. She hadn’t said she was leaving. He didn’t know. He needed time to think things through.

She handed him a package, a medium-sized thin box, tied with a ribbon. “For thee,” she said.

He opened the box to find a sketch of the door that led to the *Illumine*’s office, with its sign—the sign made of walnut wood that Jeremiah had carved and given to Henry—hanging above the door.

His throat felt thick. He couldn’t speak. It was beautiful, preserving an important part of his life that was now gone. His eyes met Marie-Claire’s. “This is amazing.”

She scooped up the box. “It’s just a sketch from memory. But I hope it will remind thee of happier times. And a hope that the *Illumine* will continue. In time.”

He wasn't so sure. "I thank thee, Marie-Claire. I will treasure this."

"I'm glad," she said softly. Her expressive eyes seemed serious for a moment, as if there was something she wanted to tell him.

He rose and walked over to her. He wanted to say more, but he didn't dare, for he didn't know what he wanted to say, not yet. He needed time to think, to reflect, to ponder. He wasn't good at this.

Philemon came into the room. "The hack is here for Miss Marie-Claire."

She reached out a hand to Henry. "Goodbye, Henry. I will never forget thee."

He looked at her hand and took it in his, and when he lifted his eyes, he realized tears were streaming down her cheeks. A sharp wave of regret sliced through him. "I'll go along to the wharf, to see thee off."

"Nay, I'd rather thee stay here." When he started to object, she said, "Please. I've already said my goodbye to Hitty. I'd rather remember thee both here, at this Grand House."

Henry nodded, feeling a wistful, sweet yearning for her as he watched her walk down the quahog shell path to the waiting hack.

Hitty came up behind him, watching over his shoulder as Marie-Claire climbed into the hack. "Henry, did thee mean what thee said in Meeting?"

"Of course," he said. "What part?"

"About giving others a second chance?"

"I did."

"Brother," Hitty said softly, "thee hesitated over Anna

and regretted it. Will thee repeat that mistake? Will thee let a second chance at love go by?"

Henry turned his head slightly. "Thee makes everything so simple. This is not so easy."

"Mayhap it's simpler than thee wants to believe. Matters of the heart, anyway."

Could it be? Should it be? The door shut on the hack and the driver walked around to his side, taking the horse's reins.

God, he prayed, *what say thee?*

He listened, and heard nothing.

It had started as a gray summer morning, typical of the month, with low-lying clouds hinting of rain. But as the driver climbed up on the hack, a cloud broke open and a beam of sunlight shot through, straight down on them.

Something Henry had read in Great Mary's journal a long time ago popped into his mind: *God lifted clouds so that we may walk clearly.*

He lifted his eyes to that ray of light beaming down through the cloud. *Is that what thee says, Lord?*

The driver flicked his reins, and the horse was on its way. All of a sudden, something broke inside Henry. He started down the shell walkway, calling for the hack to stop. The driver didn't hear him, so Henry started to run, through the gate and down the sandy road so fast that he caught up with the hack.

"Marie-Claire! Don't go. Stay here. Stay with me!"

She leaned over the hack, eyes wide. "Henry! What is thee doing?"

The driver still hadn't heard his shouts to stop as Henry ran alongside, so he grabbed onto the ledge and jumped up. "I am keeping myself from making a terrible mistake. Marie-Claire, I love thee. I want thee to stay."

"But . . . there's still my brother between us. The terrible things he did."

"That's all behind us."

Finally, the hack driver realized Henry was hanging onto the ledge, and he pulled over, a curious look on his face. "Did y' lose something?"

"Very nearly," Henry said, his eyes on Marie-Claire. "But not again." He opened the hack door and climbed in, taking her in his arms. His heart was flooded with love, so full he could hardly speak. He didn't know what else to do but kiss her.

Henry made a decision. He was going to dig up Great Mary's buried treasure. The town of Nantucket needed it now more than ever. He had done this once before, when he was but a lad, and hoped he could locate it again.

Early one morning, after a heavy, soaking rain, he took a shovel from the garden shed and headed out to the Founders' Burial Ground. As he walked, he pondered how strange it was that the lingering smell of smoke from the fire was even stronger after rain. It was as if the rain released something the ground had been grasping. When he reached the cemetery, he went to the old oak tree and gave it a fond pat. He squeezed his eyes shut, trying to remember which branch marked the buried treasure. He opened his eyes with a sigh. He couldn't remember.

He sat down, pulled Great Mary's journal out of his satchel, glad he'd thought to bring it along, and leafed through it to find entries she'd written about the tree. It took some doing, but he narrowed down which branch was the one she meant, walked out a few paces, then started to dig. And to hope. He dug and dug and dug, grateful for the rain that had softened the loamy soil. He was just about to give up on that particular branch as the identifier when his shovel hit something that made a clinking sound. He froze, then dug again. There it was! He leaned over the hole and scooped the rest of the dirt out with his hands. The metal box took a long time to pull, but at last, with the sun high overhead, he was able to yank it up and out. How had Great Mary done this on her own? He knew she was wise, he did not know she was physically strong. Then again, he recalled, she had borne ten children. That would take great strength.

He opened it up, took out the linen sacks of Spanish pieces of eight silver—all that remained—and in its place left a note:

22, 8 mo. 1846

The last of this treasure was used for the future of Nantucket.

Henry Coffin Macy

Then he paused for a moment. Great Mary's journal sat on the ground next to the shovel. It was in very poor condition, due to the effects of time and Hitty's childhood scissor mishap. Without a library like the Atheneum to store it, there was no safe place to keep it. More important, he did not have any idea whom to pass it down to.

He dumped the Spanish pieces of eight out of the linen sack and into his satchel. Then he put the journal inside a sack, placed it inside the box, and scribbled an addition to his note:

Here lies the true treasure of Nantucket Island.

He tucked the note inside the box and closed it tight to bury it deep under the oak tree. For now, this was where it belonged.

Discussion Questions

1. One theme that runs through this story is about underestimating people. Anna Gardner underestimated Henry Macy. Henry underestimated Isaac Barnard. Benjamin Foulger underestimated Jeremiah Macy. And everyone underestimated Tristram Macy. When have you ever felt underestimated? And why? How did your situation unfold?

2. Anna Gardner felt Henry should use his editor role at the *Illumine* to agitate public opinion. Henry believed news should be objective, and abided by the equal time rule of journalism. What is your view on this issue?

3. Who do you think wrote the "B" letters that were published in the *Illumine*?

4. Consider Anna Gardner for a moment. She is a factual character (1816–1901), a passionate abolitionist and dedicated educator, who spent her life fighting against

slavery and for social justice. What was it that drew Anna and Henry together? And what kept them apart from each other?

5. Compare Anna Gardner to Marie-Claire Chase. They were very different characters, but both had a powerful impact on Henry. How did Marie-Claire contribute to Henry's life? When have you ever had someone like her in your life?

6. Marie-Claire's faith in God was more grounded and more sincere than any other character's, yet she was the youngest one in the novel. How does the example of her faith impact Henry and Hitty? Even Jeremiah? Does she remind you of anyone you've known?

7. Mary Coffin Starbuck saw the results of a community without faith at its core. She is credited for establishing the Society of Friends as the dominant religion on the island in the early 1700s. Yet over a century later, the Quaker influence on Nantucket, which had provided strength and structure and principles to the island during its substantive whaling period, was fading, considered irrelevant. "But God," Marie-Claire said, "is never irrelevant." What does that mean to you?

8. Benjamin Foulger was a complex character. If Marie-Claire's assessment was correct, he began his work on Nantucket as legal counsel to Henry and Hitty with noble intentions. Then, after Oliver Combs's stroke, he was left without accountability. There's an old say-

ing, "Even a saint is tempted by an open door." Do you think that's what happened to Benjamin Foulger? If so, where in the novel is the moment when Benjamin crosses the line of no return? Have you ever experienced or observed a similar downfall in a person? How did that story unfold?

9. Would you have preferred an ending to the story in which the second portion of the inheritance went to Henry and Hitty? Why did it not greatly disturb them to have the money go, legally, to Tristram Macy? What had they discovered about their grandmother's legacy?

10. Hitty Macy was not a character overflowing with wisdom, but her perspective on wealth, consistent throughout the story, was very wise. How would you describe Henry's perspective on the inheritance? What would you have done, if you were in their shoes and received an inheritance with some strangling conditions?

11. Nantucket Island became a character of its own in this novel. Henry, in particular, felt very protective of the island. So did Mary Coffin Starbuck. What place in your life has become separate and distinct in your imagination? And why? What's made it special to you?

12. Someday, plan a visit to Nantucket Island. While you're there, look for old Nantucket. Walk along Centre Street (nicknamed Petticoat Row) and think of the characters in this novel. Look up at the stately Methodist church and imagine Maria Mitchell on the steps, shouting to

the fire wardens on July 14, 1846, as the Great Fire raged. Walk along Main Street's cobbles. Search out Mary Coffin Starbuck's Parliament House (10 Pine Street) and think of that night when Nathaniel took the windows out of their casing so that people standing outside could hear the sermon given by Quaker missionary John Richardson. Walk around Nantucket's oldest house and think about Jethro Coffin and Mary Gardner's love story that put an end to hard feelings from the half-share debate. Head out to the Founders' Burial Ground and see if you can find the old oak tree. Mayhap, Mary's treasure is still there.

Author's Note

Much of this novel is based on true events that occurred during 1837–1846, a decade of Nantucket's history that was rich with drama and strife. There were so many directions I could have traveled, focusing on fascinating true characters (social reformer Lucinda Coffin Mott, former slave Frederick Douglass, sea captain Absalom Boston, editor Samuel Jenks). I chose the central, multilayered issue and multilayered events—integrationists versus segregationists, abolitionists versus preservationists—and wove a story around them.

The controversy over public school integration in Nantucket went from a simmer to a boil during that decade, coming to a conclusion in 1847. The state of Massachusetts had legalized integration, so the island of Nantucket was not in compliance with the state . . . until threatened by a lawsuit. A father, Absalom Boston, filed suit against the Town of Nantucket because his daughter Phoebe was denied entrance to high school. At last, Nantucket backed down and the system was integrated. As Mary Coffin Starbuck noted in her journal, "Pennies and pence are dear to us."

The Anti-Slavery Conventions, planned by Anna Gardner and held at the Atheneum, were full of impact. I studied different reports of the conventions and tried to make them come to life.

There was a newspaper started in 1840, the *Islander*, with a young, prolific editor, that elbowed its way right into the hottest topics of the day.

And then there's the Great Fire of Nantucket. What a story that was. It's thought that the fire ushered in the end of whaling on Nantucket. Before the fire, the island had over ten thousand residents. Not long after the fire, only three thousand remained. And then came the California Gold Rush that lured many of Nantucket's young men away.

I tried to keep to the actual dates of events, to allow it to be "scaffolding" for the novel. Most of the dates are factual, but there were a few unimportant ones I had to bend, just for the sake of a good story. I'm sure I made blunders, despite my best efforts, and am a little worried about Nantucket historians taking me to task. Hopefully, readers can overlook the blunders and tweaks to enjoy the story of Nantucket's wonderful past. What a unique place that island was, and still is. It holds a special part of my heart.

What's True and What's False in *The Light Before Day*?

Is there buried treasure on Nantucket?
Maybe. There's a legend that John Swain, one of the first proprietors of Nantucket, heard a French privateer had landed on the island and so, out of fear, he buried his money somewhere in the Polpis woods. Swain did such a good job of hiding his stash, wrote Nathaniel Philbrick in *Away Off Shore*, that he and several subsequent generations of Swains have been unable to find it.

Did Henry and Hitty Macy provide the funds to cobble the iconic Main Street in 1841?
False. It was actually cobbled in 1837, and definitely *not* funded by just one or two individuals. But here's a piece of trivia—it's unknown where the cobbles came from. Some scholars think they came from the ballast of English ships. Others assume them to have been imported from rivers and streams in Europe.

What about those "B" letters in the newspaper that used Scripture to address controversial topics relating to abolitionism?
True. They appeared in 1841 in the *Islander* newspaper. No one ever knew who wrote them.

Did Maria Mitchell actually burn her diaries and letters after a false alarm of fire in 1846?
True. After the chaos that ensued from the Great Fire, she feared her private papers would be looted. *Such* a loss. One year after the fire, Maria made a sighting of a comet that earned her worldwide attention and the gold medal from the king of Denmark for being "the first discoverer of a telescopic comet."

Did Anna Gardner plan the first Anti-Slavery Convention held on Nantucket?
True. She was only twenty-five years old when she planned the convention in which fugitive slave Frederick Douglass spoke publicly to a white audience for the first time. The accomplishments of Anna Gardner are true—she taught at the African School, she worked very hard to allow Eunice Ross to enroll in the public high school, she planned Anti-Slavery Conventions, and she was the secretary for the Anti-Slavery Society. The one detail that was not factual, besides her romance with Henry Macy, was that she did not leave the island until later in her life. She never married.

About the story of Jethro Coffin and Mary Gardner, akin to Romeo and Juliet (without the dramatic end)—did their love story truly end the half-share feud on the island?

True. It seemed to have a healing effect on the settlers. Peter Coffin supplied lumber from his mills to build son Jethro Coffin's house. It's now the oldest house still standing on Nantucket.

Did lightship crew members really make baskets because they were bored?
True. Lightships were floating offshore lighthouses, and the crew members turned to basket making to keep their hands busy during long watches. The baskets are oval-shaped and made by tightly weaving flexible oak staves. They're extremely valuable today. Abram Quary (1768–1854) was one of the last two Wampanoag Indians on Nantucket. Like his mother, Sarah, he was an expert basket maker, and some of Abram's baskets still survive. He lived on a bluff in Shimmo that continues to carry his name: Abram's Point.

Did Great Mary leave a personal journal?
False. But . . . she did leave an accounting book from her store. The Nantucket Historical Association has one of Mary Coffin Starbuck's ledgers, protected deep in its vault. Reading this old sheepskin-covered book with its faded ink is slow going, but it opens a window to the daily life of early Nantucket. And to Mary's daily life!

The Great Fire . . . did it really start in William Geary's hat store?
True. It started in the stovepipe in the rear of the store around eleven o'clock at night on July 14, 1846. The month of July had been rainless, hot, and windy. The fire quickly spread out of control and burned out one-third of Nantucket. It was a fulcrum point for the island, hastening its decline as the world's wealthiest port.

Resources

These books provided invaluable background information that was helpful to try to imagine and re-create what life was like for Mary Coffin Starbuck in the seventeenth century as well as Hitty and Henry Macy in the nineteenth century. Any blunders belong to me.

Barbour, Hugh, and J. William Frost. *The Quakers*. New York: Greenwood Press, 1988.

Brady, Marilyn Dell. "Early Quaker Families 1650–1800." *Friends Journal*, June 1, 2009. https://www.friendsjournal.org/2009060/.

Cook, Peter. *You Wouldn't Want to Sail on a 19th-Century Whaling Ship!* Danbury, CT: Franklin Watts, 2004.

Drake, Thomas E. *Quakers and Slavery in America*. New Haven: Yale University Press, 1950.

Forman, Henry Chandlee. *Early Nantucket and Its Whale Houses*. Nantucket: Mill Hill Press, 1966.

Furtado, Peter. *Quakers*. Great Britain: Shire Publications, 2013.

Jenness, Amy. *On This Day in Nantucket History*. Charleston, SC: The History Press, 2014.

Johnson, Robert. "Black-White Relations on Nantucket," *Historic Nantucket*, Spring 2002.

Karttunen, Frances Ruley. *Law and Disorder in Old Nantucket*. North Charleston, SC: Booksurge Press, 2000.

———. *Nantucket Places & People 1: Main Street to the North Shore*. North Charleston, SC: Booksurge Press, 2009.

———. *Nantucket Places & People 2: South of Main Street*. North Charleston, SC: Booksurge Press, 2009.

———. *Nantucket Places & People 4: Underground*. North Charleston, SC: CreateSpace, 2010.

Leach, Robert J., and Peter Gow. *Quaker Nantucket: The Religious Community Behind the Whaling Empire*. Nantucket, MA: Mill Hill Press, 1997.

Marietta, Jack D. *The Reformation of American Quakerism, 1748–1783*. Philadelphia: University of Pennsylvania Press, 1984.

Moulton, Phillips P., ed. *Journal and Major Essays of John Woolman*. New York: Oxford University Press, 1971.

Philbrick, Nathaniel. *Away Off Shore: Nantucket Island and Its People, 1602–1890*. New York: Penguin Books, 1994.

———. *In the Heart of the Sea: The Tragedy of the Whaleship Essex*. New York: Penguin Books, 2000.

Philbrick, Thomas, ed. *Remarkable Observations: The Whaling Journal of Peleg Folger, 1751–54*. Nantucket: Mill Hill Press, 2006.

Whipple, A. B. C. *Vintage Nantucket*. New York: Dodd, Mead, 1978.

Acknowledgments

A thank-you to my first readers, Lindsey Ciraulo and Tad Fisher, who spent Thanksgiving weekend reading the messy first draft of *The Light Before Day*. They gave me all kinds of helpful suggestions to improve the story.

To Karen McNab and many others on Nantucket Island, thank you for your help in researching information about the Quakers of Nantucket so that I could create credible historical fiction.

My appreciation goes, as always, to Revell Books, a publishing house that is dear to my heart. To Andrea Doering and Barb Barnes, an extraordinary editing team. Truly extraordinary! And to the marketing team—Michele Misiak, Karen Steele, Hannah Brinks—you never grow weary in finding new ways to support my books. You're the best! To Cheryl Van Andel, who put such attention to detail to make the Nantucket Legacy covers as realistic as possible to appear eighteenth-century Quaker-ish, on Nantucket Island prior to the invention of photographs. Thank you, Cheryl, for caring so much!

A special nod to my mother, Barbara Benedict Woods, who happily shared her Nantucket Lightship basket to be included in the cover photo.

To my readers, so faithful and encouraging, I wish I could personally thank each one of you. You mean so much to me, more than you might think. One of the best parts of this writing gig is the connection I've made with so many of you.

And to the Almighty, who holds all things together in his loving hands—*all things!*—I give my deepest gratitude.

Suzanne Woods Fisher is an award-winning, bestselling author of more than two dozen novels, including *Anna's Crossing*, *The Newcomer*, and *The Return* in the Amish Beginnings series, The Bishop's Family series, and The Inn at Eagle Hill series, as well as nonfiction books about the Amish, including *Amish Peace* and *The Heart of the Amish*. She lives in California. Learn more at www.suzannewoodsfisher.com and follow Suzanne on Twitter @suzannewfisher.

Coming Soon from

Suzanne Woods Fisher

Mending Fences